PLAYING DIRTY

THE LAURA SERIES, BOOK 2

JAMES GREY

Lots of (dirty!) hugs Jeanette!

Jenny

CONTENTS

CHAPTER 1

*C*ome ON, Laura! Who cares about clothes? This is an emergency! Get going!

In front of me stood an open door. The cool shackle around my bare ankle was gone. Yet I felt paralyzed by doubt.

After what felt like minutes, the message to move got through to my body. Like a rookie gymnast on a beam, I placed one bare foot in front of the other, terrified that this whole thing was going to end badly.

And it had to, didn't it? Disregarding my nakedness for a moment — and that was more easily said than done — this invitation sounded too good to be true. A trap. What could be more natural for those sick sadists Tommy and Claire?

But I had to try. Resist the urge to flee back to what I knew, even if that had been a prison cell with bouts of stinging torture thrown in. If I didn't walk now, they would have defeated me already. And like *hell* was I going to let that happen. Especially after they'd just rubbed my face in their blatant ecstasy.

I made my unsteady, cautious way towards the lift foyer. The elevator stood unguarded, its button waiting to be pushed.

My mind was beginning to switch into planning mode. Was I really going to run out of this building without a stitch of clothing on? No, seriously…I needed *something* to cover myself. A stray curtain; an apron from a janitor's closet — anything!

I knew it was nuts to think about finding something to wear at a time like this. Somebody might change his mind at any moment. *GET OUT OF THE BUILDING!*

But still…if I could just find some scrap of material…

The foyer was open at the far end. I took a few steps and peeked into the space beyond it. But all I found was a mirror image of the office floor I'd been looking out on for the past few days. It was in a similar state of abandonment. One glance told me there wasn't any kind of creative fashion solution on offer in that expanse.

I scurried along the inside wall to what looked like washrooms. First I tried the men's. Then the women's. Both bare. A couple of the stalls still had rolls of toilet paper, but that was about it. Nothing that could be used to spare my blushes. My heart sank.

You gonna sit here and fashion a dress out of toilet roll, or get the fuck out of the building, Laura?

I backed out of the women's. I wanted to feel all the urgency I should feel, but how could I do that when it brought the nightmare of running naked across New York City closer?

They were laughing at me now. I was convinced they had some device set up to watch me out here. I could almost hear them cackling.

Fine. No point delaying things, whatever those things might be.

I summoned up all my resolve and went back to the elevator. I reached out and pressed the down arrow. As my finger touched the chrome disc, I fought a powerful urge to rush back to my cell. My heart thudded as I waited. I heard the elevator's mechanism settling behind the doors. Instinctively, I took a step back as I sensed them about to open.

But it was empty inside. And, as far as I could tell, ready to take me to any floor I chose. I caught sight of my naked self in the mirror around the side — that mirror in which Tommy's reflection had loomed when I arrived here, a crumpled heap on the floor.

At least I'd had my coat back then.

Horror film scenes flashed through my brain as I stood on the threshold. 'Don't get into the elevator!!!' was just the kind of line you screamed at some panicked, sweat-streaked heroine from your seat in the movie theater, wasn't it? But what did I have to lose? I *might* have been stepping into a dead end where some psychopath prowled — but I knew for sure I was stepping out of one. With the information I had available to me, the rational move was to take the elevator ride.

I walked in, my head down to escape the taunting mirror. Then I turned and surveyed the panel of buttons.

We were on the nineteenth floor. It looked like this wasn't the highest in the building, but who cared what was up? I was only interested in the street level…wait, hold on a second! We'd come down some stairs from the sidewalk when I'd been brought here, hadn't we? A minor back entrance, perhaps for lightweight deliveries or the like.

This was just what I wanted for my escape too, wasn't

it? Who was to say that other parts of this building weren't in regular use by regular people? That if I pressed the wrong button, I wouldn't emerge onto a plush concourse where receptionists and workers alike would turn to stare at me? Though I doubted even Tommy could be so brazen as to allow that to happen — surely he had some awareness that my being seen would mean *him* getting caught?

So I pressed the lowest button, labeled '-1'. If I really *did* emerge into that tiny tradesman's lobby, then maybe my release didn't have to be so mortifying. Maybe I could hide just outside the door and flag the attention of a passer-by. Preferably a female one. A man might take his sweet time helping me out, if at all. But a woman would understand how important it was to lend me her coat, just until I got home.

She would ask questions, though. Didn't Tommy *know* that?

And how was this homecoming going to work, anyway? I didn't have my keys. I didn't have my phone either, so I couldn't call the kids for a spare set. Would I have to resort to breaking windows?

The elevator was now well into its descent.

As the numbers counted down into single figures, I broke into a cold sweat. *Fuck!* It was like the time I'd gotten into that roller-coaster at Disneyland, and then, just as we crawled those last inches to the top of the plunge, realized I didn't want to be there after all. Too late! Could I override the buttons; cancel my order; go back up?

What floor had I come from again? In my panicked state, that detail had escaped me already. Pick a random number and emerge in full view of a boardroom? No thanks! I looked up at the ceiling of the lift, wondering if I could shrink, crawl up into a corner and hide like a spider.

But this was a one-way ticket. And I'd almost arrived.

I felt the lift touch down. The doors slid open.

And there he was again, the bastard.

Right across from me, arms folded and leaning in the bay of a fire escape door. He'd evidently found his jeans again. He'd also sourced a shirt since his recent television appearance, but it was unbuttoned. I could see a good portion of his body art behind his loose-hanging sleeves.

And yeah, he looked as smug as they come.

Rage bubbled up like roasting lava. Sarcastic lines itched to spew out of my mouth. And that was before I even noticed a shock of blonde to my right: Claire had made it down here too.

I forced myself to take a deep breath and remain silent. If I genuinely still had a chance to get out, I didn't want to blow it.

I knew I'd come to the right little subterranean lobby. The sound of the elevator doors opening reverberated around a cold, functional echo chamber. There was no daylight on offer, but this time the neon lights were on. A yard or two to my left, without a doubt, was the heavy door through which I'd been steered against my will on the night I was taken.

Also, right next to it, a bulbous green plastic button marked 'OPEN'.

If the offer to leave this place was for real, I was free to go over and push that button. No need to say a word. Don't poke the bear.

I hesitated. The big tyrant and his sidekick seemed to be the only ones hanging around down here. If I was going to get help, I would have to do so on the street beyond that door. Naked.

"So, you're really going to leave us?"

At these words from Tommy, which were enough to make me clench my fists, Claire came across and nestled up against him. I couldn't look her in the eye. It was hard enough trying to shake the outline of her messed-up hair from the corner of my vision. I knew *why* it was messed up — and she knew I knew.

What twisted game were they playing now? Just as they'd done on screen a little earlier, they were conducting themselves in a way designed to make me jealous. And it was working, too. But the way he'd said his last line had been more than that. A coo, dripping with temptation…it was almost as though they were suggesting I'd really miss out on something if I left.

I didn't say a word.

But I didn't move, either.

"It's a *very* quiet street out there, you know, Laura," continued Tommy as something like a glint appeared in his eye. "Not sure how many passers-by you'd encounter. You might have to run up to the main road if you want to get away fast."

He let that unpleasant image sink in before continuing.

"I suppose you could wait around in the doorway, but it's not such a warm day today, you know. It'll be chilly on that freshly shaved pussy of yours. *Really* chilly."

Christ, I'd forgotten that. Who was going to believe I'd been kept prisoner if I came running up to them, begging for help, in my current state of grooming? Prisoners have unkempt bushes; exhibitionist nymphos are waxed smooth as an egg. I'd be taken for the latter, wouldn't I? People would turn their backs.

My jaw tightened and a long string of curse words ran through my head.

"Still, it's up to you, Laura," he said. "I've got plenty to entertain me here…"

Claire, as if she'd been trained like a puppy, looked beseechingly up at him as he said these words. He didn't touch her — but he didn't need to. I could smell her desire for another round of *that*. I could see that she was going to get it, too. Whether I ran out or not.

They knew how to toy with a woman alright. The mocking depictions of how silly I was going to feel when I got through that door. Coupled with their clear allusions to the sexy playtime that would continue unabated on this side of it. Plus the screaming, taunting unknown: would I be a part of those games if I stayed?

It was malicious, that was what it was. It stirred up a loathing I never knew I could summon.

And it made up my mind for me. Just as they intended it to, I guess.

In that fight-or-flight moment mere yards away from freedom, my swelling hatred forbade me to choose flight. Not in this state. Not on *their* terms. Instinct had kicked in: I would fight.

As my thoughts sharpened in this vivid moment, a clear conviction overcame me. That victory in the war would begin with giving him this battle. I would escape one day, but not under his ignominious conditions. I didn't see why I should humiliate myself for this bully. This teasing, stirring bully.

He would take my choice to remain as surrender, of course. Only *I* would know it wasn't as simple as that.

My eyes narrowed as they settled on some vacant space on the wall behind my tormentors. Yet my mind was dangerously focused.

Play the lust card, Laura. Play it for all you're worth. Let them think that's *the reason you won't leave today.*

I dropped my gaze to the floor, letting my lips part as if my mouth had gone slack in a moment of desire-fueled weakness. Then I looked up at him, hoping I could hide the hot little pools of anger still festering within them.

"I…I think…maybe it could be fun to stay?" I whispered.

"Clever girl," he said with a perfunctory nod that suggested my capitulation had been inevitable. "So then, why don't you head back on upstairs to your cage, where you belong? Claire will escort you."

My throat tightened and I fought back one last impulse to leap across the space, slap that green button and disappear from this madhouse.

"Okay," I murmured, stepping back inside the elevator. The Frenchwoman joined me, hitting the '19' button as my mind raced. What had I just done? Blown my only chance?

I thanked my lucky stars she wasn't the type to make small talk. I could be alone with my thoughts as we climbed back towards the top of the building. And it wasn't a moment too soon to shout down those doubts. To remind myself that I'd made the right call. That this had *not* been the moment to go all-in.

Tommy had already said that my employers at Kerstein weren't expecting me for a while — whatever 'a while' meant. I had to assume he had those communications under control on an ongoing basis. And I'd seen the messages that went out to my family. So the long-game approach wasn't going to hurt anybody — except very possibly myself. Nobody would be getting concerned about me for a few weeks at least. I had time on my side.

Time enough to play him like a fiddle.

CHAPTER 2

*B*ack in my 'office', and shackled up once again, I had to work hard not to let any smiles betray my plan. I knew that showing any smugness could be extremely dangerous. I couldn't let anybody sniff a rat. I had to assume that I was being watched at all times. They would only see the despair and longing they expected to see.

But inside my head, I was almost dancing. There, my thoughts could roam free — and what thoughts they were! After a couple of days of confusion and jumble, the lawyer in me was thrilled that everything had crystallized as I stood on that elevator threshold. I knew what I was doing once again — and that was freedom enough for now.

It was all so simple, really. Tommy was a criminal. Tommy was a psychopathic egomaniac too. And Tommy was also...insanely sexy. What did this mean for me? Well, first of all, he needed to be brought to justice. Second of all, he was vulnerable to any behavior that affirmed his bloated sense of self-worth. And third...I could have a lot of fun whilst manipulating him and gathering evidence.

Looking at Claire, I saw a brainwashed girl struck dumb by the man's extraordinary alpha vibe and rugged looks. I guessed she was enjoying her life, and there was something to be said for that. But if she had been kidnapped like me, and subsequently 'marked', that was *not* okay. How many other women had Tommy done that to, and how many more were on his hit list? He needed to be in a courtroom, and then behind bars.

If I was going to see that happen, then obviously I could not allow myself to fall into the same trap Claire had. I couldn't let him get into my head. There had been several moments already when he'd done exactly that, of course. And I had no doubt that *he* thought I was well on my way to the kind of robotic worship he'd inspired in her.

But I wasn't a clueless, twenty-something kid like Claire. I was a smart, self-aware woman in my forties. Tommy had picked too intelligent a target in me — and showing him that was going to be a lot of fun. Because although I would play his game for a while, I would win in the end.

If I could achieve the kind of trust Claire had, I felt sure it would be easy to slip out of this sticky web. For one thing, she was allowed to wear clothes, at least some of the time. Surely I would be afforded the same privilege if I could convince him that I too was a slave to his every whim and would never dream of leaving? I'd already begun the process by declining to leave that elevator. Once he completely believed he had me on his side, I was convinced he would drop his guard.

I didn't think it would be all that difficult. I was dealing with an ego the size of Mount Rushmore, after all. And thanks to working with Andre, I already had some experience in how men like that worked. There were subtle ways to turn things to your advantage.

And, in this case, there were plenty of not-so-subtle ways too. I looked forward to those. Yeah, I wanted to fuck him — and fuck him I would. I deserved to! After everything he'd put me through, and then watching those scenes with Claire...he could damn well give it to me. He'd already left me gagging — quite literally — more than once. He'd knowingly and cynically worked me into a state of lustful jealousy. So I was going to get laid in whatever creative, lascivious, kinky ways he had to offer. I was, in a funny sort of way, invested in this place now. And hey, I was single again! That teenager who fooled her way around Thailand deserved a chance to come out and play again after the divorce, didn't she?

There was just that one gigantic caveat to my plot: *don't let any of those emotions get real.* If envy came knocking at my door once again, I had to consciously use it as motivation. As rocket fuel to seduce him into giving me an even bigger orgasm than he gave *her.* And if pain came my way, then it would be a reminder to keep my plan on track. A plan that would see him put away in some particularly unpleasant penitentiary.

I could imagine myself as counsel for the prosecution — how about that for a carrot? I hadn't done criminal cases as such, but technically I was qualified and entitled to. Okay, I think a judge might have something to say about my personal involvement in the case — a witness role would be the only appropriate one. But as a vision to keep the bigger picture on track, the image of Tommy in the dock and me rising to give an impassive, impeccably-researched closing statement worked well.

As I sat on my threadbare mattress and mulled it all over, I realized I was looking forward to this challenge. I hung my head and buried my face in my hands. Where they wouldn't see the grin on my face.

Despite the new attitude, I was desperate for a few key improvements to my living conditions. The sooner I could get away from cameras and observation, particularly whilst deprived of my clothing, the better. The thought of succumbing to wild moments of lust with my captor was one matter, but I could do without the Big Brother stuff. A knife and fork would eliminate those crushing doggy-style mealtimes. And it would be *terrific* if I could use the toilet in private too.

I was convinced Claire was afforded all these privileges, maybe more. My first step, then, had to be learning more about how she'd done it. If I could take care of those basic comforts, everything I had in mind would be a lot more pleasant to execute.

I watched her closely when she brought me my dinner that evening. As usual, she volunteered nothing. Which figured, considering she'd evidently lost the ability to think for herself some time ago.

I had to tread carefully with Claire. If I suddenly began to quiz the woman on how to please Tommy, it would make my strategy a little too obvious. I had to work on the assumption that every conversation in here was audible to somebody, so I would need to be subtle. Arouse no suspicion that I was faking anything. Especially now, so soon after the scene down in that subterranean lobby, where I'd stood so close to freedom. The correct emotion for the moment was quiet despair mixed with horny curiosity.

So I kept my thoughts to myself and murmured my thanks as she placed a burger and fries (food I could eat with my hands again!) on the floor. I watched her as she made her way back across the office towards the elevators. I had to admit, I'd never seen a woman so perfectly made for white lingerie. Delicate, petite, blonde: bold colors were for women with more of a physical presence. Clad in bright white, Claire was all set for life up on a cloud in the sexy part of heaven.

Sure, her underwear was relatively modest. It had a few frills around the edges, but it was hardly provocative. Yet that only accentuated the whiteness, which I guess was the point.

When I'd finished my food, Tommy turned up for a chat. To nobody's surprise, he seemed pleased with his day's work.

"So, it looks like we really are making some progress with you," he mused as he wandered towards the window and took in the panorama. The day was fading and lights were beginning to flicker on all across town.

I stiffened, on high alert. I was more concerned about appearing unnaturally eager than I was about some sort of violence occurring. For today, at least, I couldn't lay it on too thick. A large part of me was still fuming about how they'd made a fool of me earlier — no acting required in that respect. But I didn't want any more chokings or savage blows, so I watched my tone.

Innocently, then: "Is that because I didn't leave?"

"Of course. You're starting to think the right way."

I considered this for a moment.

"Okay...but I'm wondering if that door would really have opened anyway. Surely you know there would be police everywhere if I'd landed up on the street? How else could I explain my state? People would want answers."

Tommy didn't miss a beat.

"*Aye*, the door was unlocked, Laura. That's the truth. Allowing you to go would have meant nothing if it wasn't for real. But I knew you wouldn't take the offer. One hundred percent."

"What made you so sure?"

He took a deep breath. I could see he was watching my reflection in the mirror.

"Apart from the fact that deep down you're too curious to leave? You're too ashamed of your body, Laura. You wouldn't run out of a burning building if you were naked. It's one of the things you need to work on here."

I looked down at the floor. He was right and we both knew it. Still, who was *he* to decide what I needed to 'work on'? There remained a tiny part of me waiting to wake up from this nightmare, or for him to declare the whole thing an elaborate practical joke. The latter seemed almost plausible in civilized moments like this one — yet arrogance like this was so far-fetched that it had to be true. You'd never script it.

"Maybe," I mumbled. "So what happens now?"

"For a start," he said, turning around to face me, "you need to be reminded of your basics. What have you forgotten?"

Shit! I was supposed to kneel.

It had genuinely slipped my mind.

I pushed my dinner tray out of the way and scrambled onto my knees. But it was too late, wasn't it? Who knew what torture was coming now? This was a repeat offense, after all.

"Much better," he said evenly. "I'll let it pass this time. You look so much better like that than sitting behind a laptop at a conference table, you know that?"

Well, that depended on your point of view, I supposed. But I held the thought, too busy breathing a sigh of relief that he was going to skip the cruel and unusual punishment.

"Speaking of which," he continued. "I suppose you might be interested to hear news of how the negotiation is progressing?"

A stubborn voice inside me said I didn't give a shit. One way or another 'the negotiation' had gotten me into this fix by introducing me to Tommy. But if I wanted to get him to open up, I couldn't say no to any information he was trying to offer me. That would be a bad start.

And anyway, I *was* curious. What had been going on in that boardroom a few blocks across the sky?

"Sure," I conceded.

"It's done," he declared, jerking his head in the direction of the Kerstein building as an evil grin began to spread across his face.

"*Done?* But...I'm...I'm not..."

"That's right, you weren't there," he crowed. "Actually, neither was your chum Andre, in the end. So Danscombe and I got exactly what we wanted."

I was reeling now. *No Andre?*

"But how...it's only been a couple of days, hasn't it?"

Had I lost track of time?

"Sure, but what do you think Kerstein did when they received notification from a 'specialist doctor' that you'd had a breakdown and were going to be unreachable for several weeks? They weren't going to wait. They brought Karl to the table in your place."

"*Karl?* He's got no experience of—"

"Exactly," laughed Tommy. "And Alan was *pissed* about having to do that. He really got into Andre for making you snap. People heard what he said to you before you left the building. Andre is off all projects pending a disciplinary hearing."

Despite my chains, a little part of me jumped for joy at those words.

I had many more questions to ask. How did my capture tie up with the way things played out? Would it have happened anyway? Was there *anything* Tommy didn't know about and couldn't manipulate?

But for now, it was enough to know that there was nothing urgent waiting for me back at the office.

CHAPTER 3

I'd always thought Andre was utterly invincible. The sparks between us had become an almost daily circus at Kerstein, but we'd both understood that our respective talents outweighed the drama and conflict. The show always went on.

If what Tommy said was true — and I would need a little more time to get a feel on that — then Andre had a limit after all. Alan could tolerate his theatrics, but if they actually hounded the only legal mind capable of handling such a deal from the building, then a line had to be drawn. The fact that so many people had heard the raised voices and seen the state in which I'd left that meeting room meant Alan couldn't sweep Andre's role in the matter under the carpet. At some point, an example had to be set.

Basically, me storming out and going for Prosecco on a Monday morning had given Andre his comeuppance. If I disregarded everything that had happened since then, that made me feel a little bit of a heroine. I wasn't the only Kerstein employee he liked to attack, after all.

As for the deal being signed and sealed in Danscombe's favor...I could have told anybody that would happen with Karl in my seat. He was a good guy, but hopelessly out of his depth at that level. Tommy hadn't said who took Andre's place, but anybody else at Kerstein was a mouse in comparison. With his alpha counterpart out of the picture, *of course* Tommy could drive a steamroller over Kerstein.

Oh well, it was what it was. Maybe, if I hadn't been dragged out of my own home by a pair of crooks, I'd have gotten up the next morning and resumed the fight at work like nothing had happened. But right now, I really didn't care. Say what you like about kidnapping, but it certainly helps put your priorities in perspective.

As for that desire that had been swelling within me, it simmered down after my little trip in the elevator and my subsequent 'discussion' with Tommy, which had been all business and no sex. Apart from that, I had too much buzzing through my mind again. How was I going to progress my plan at the next opportunity? I put another sleepless night to good use by rehearsing any number of scenes and conversations in my head.

But the longing came back to the fore when the sun began to stream in through the big, broad windows the following morning.

I was just trying to maneuver myself into its rays, and trying to recall the last time I'd gone three days without coffee, when that screen flicked on once more. The movement attracted my attention instantly.

I was looking at the same plush bedroom where Tommy and Claire had had their fun the day before. My stomach twanged into an instantaneous knot.

This time, the camera panned. I was treated to a view of

more than just the bed — and realized how truly luxurious a suite this was. Away to one side were the sofa and chairs I'd previously seen in the background, their fall palette easy on the eye. Understated lamps dotted the scene, perched on bookshelves, coffee tables and a polished writing bureau, probably antique. A crystal decanter and a set of glasses sat atop a stout sideboard at the far end of the room. The bed was plump with rich linen and fat pillows. Not a thing looked out of place, as if the scene was straightened out every single day. If this room was in a hotel, it would be the king suite.

But I knew now that it had to be in this very building. I'd seen Claire go from this screen to my prison in just a couple of minutes. Was this where Tommy *really* lived?

The next time the camera panned onto the lounge area, my captor was center stage on the couch. Behind him, of course, stood Claire. In her snowflake underwear. And Tommy? It looked like much the same outfit he'd worn on the first day I met him, when he strode into the Kerstein office. All business. The uniform of a deal-winner.

As the camera panned away from them, a ripple of anger steamed through me.

They were going to goad me again, weren't they?

I steeled myself.

The next time the pair came back into focus, Tommy's cock was out of his pants and nestled in Claire's willing palm. She was only moving her hand slowly, but that just made the mockery seem worse. Especially as his eyes were closed, lost in pleasure. And now the camera stopped spinning.

We were into car crash territory now. Could I look away? Would that be a good strategy anyway? I had to start showing I was interested. But right now, it looked like doing so would involve a ton of frustration.

Then, after a minute or two of this torture, Claire spoke softly in Tommy's ear. I couldn't hear any of it, but she was looking directly at the camera as she did so. At *me*. Tommy's eyes opened, focused on the camera, and that twitch I'd seen at the edge of his mouth before appeared once again.

He nodded.

Claire let go of her grip, stood up straight and floated out of the room.

My heart leaped.

Was this going where I *thought* it was going?

A few moments later, the French angel appeared at my door. Tommy, with just the top of his cock peeking out of his trousers now, watched me wordlessly through the monitor. I was wriggling already.

"Come, Laura. *Monsieur* Tommy wants you to join us."

I held my breath as she unchained me, then took me by the very same hand that had just embraced Tommy's manhood. Her skin was dry to the touch, but there was a warmth there too. She led me to the elevators.

Join us. Did that just mean playing look-but-don't-touch at closer and more agonizing quarters? Or was this a real invitation?

If it was the latter, then it sounded like I would have to share him with Claire. Hmm. Well, I could manage that, if that was how it had to be. She wasn't...unattractive. I could think of worse adventures. And it would be way better than envying her, wouldn't it?

Inside the elevator, Claire pressed button 23. Now that I was being hyper-attentive, I could see that the numbers went no higher than that. I was about to move up in the world! I trembled at the thought of this glimpse into the bigger picture as much as at the thought of what might be about to happen.

We emerged into an identical lift foyer. It didn't lead to an open-plan area, however: each end of it featured a sliding glass door leading onto a carpeted hallway beyond. We turned right and headed for one of those doors.

Claire opened up with another touch of her finger — it looked like everything worked by fingerprint ID around here — and we stepped onto the same soft carpeting I knew from 'my' room downstairs. The corridor was featureless apart from a few indoor palm plants and some nondescript wall paintings. Standard office fare, really. Doors on either side led into what looked like empty — if not necessarily abandoned — meeting rooms. Up ahead, at the far end of the hallway, was a large pine door with a swooping brass handle. Claire took me by the hand once again and opened this up.

Her perfume smelt more pronounced as we entered a small antechamber. More provocative, too. She paused for a moment, looking over her shoulder to catch my eye. I could feel her switching into some other gear — one I hadn't seen yet — as she flashed me a genuine smile. I didn't know all the layers of emotion behind it, but whatever they were, she was feeling them for real. And there was no doubting the most prominent of these: *I'm about to let my lust out to play.*

"Come, Laura," she whispered, pulling me around the corner and into the same suite I'd seen on the monitor. Tommy hadn't moved.

I barely had time to take in my surroundings. Clearly the camera had been on the same side as the vast windows, panning between the bed to its left and the living area to its right. I guessed the bathroom led off the antechamber somehow. But I had more pressing concerns at this moment as Tommy motioned me to kneel in front of him.

Claire, who seemed to need no instructions at all, kneeled down next to me. Really close. Her right shoulder brushed my left, but so lightly that it didn't feel quite like a touch. More like a mixture of sexually charged air and the tiniest hairs on our skins intermingling.

She took a deep breath through her nose, straightened up her back and opened her shoulder blades as if to say *I'm yours*. A hint of drunken eyes and a smile of anticipation came across her face. I tried my best not only to copy all of this, but also to remember it for future use.

I caught sight of my nipples as I settled into position. *Rock hard*. I'm not sure I'd ever seen them so ready. Well, good. Tommy would know I wasn't faking any arousal here.

My heart thudded as the potency of the situation hit me. And a thrill descended as I understood that I was now getting a real share of the action. I'd ridden out the teasing. Now, here I was, kneeling beside the woman I could only assume was his favored Goddess.

The only part that didn't make sense was why he would even *want* me here. Claire was probably fifteen years my junior and could still have passed for a high school cheerleader. She had a French accent, too. How could I belong in such exalted company? There had to be an ulterior motive, and I was going to figure it out.

Imagine you're nineteen again, Laura. Your body is firm, tight and tasty.

The thought calmed me. This was not the moment for questioning myself or anyone else. This was the part I got to *enjoy*. I'd earned it.

"Well, Laura," began Tommy. "I want you to show me what you can do with your mouth. Nice and slow — we're in no hurry today."

As Claire shifted slightly to one side to give me room, I looked up and gave him a shy nod. I kept a little smile there too. No way was I going to beam at my captor *per se*, but I could certainly grin about the fun I was going to have. That's what I told myself, anyway.

Tommy's buttons were already loose, and the trousers weren't a tight cut anyway. All I really had to do was pull the package completely out of his underwear. I was glad to see that he was already hard and pulsing. To his credit, he was also shaved completely smooth. Nothing stood in my way.

Resisting the urge to cram his length into my mouth right away, I took my time as instructed. It was a little difficult to reach his balls, which were still hiding in his underwear, but that was okay because I had several inches of shaft to keep me occupied. I started with gentle kisses at the very base, softly pecking my way around it, letting my nose suck up his cedarwood scent straight from the skin. The cleanliness, the polish and the aroma: now those *definitely* weren't anything 19-year-old Laura had known. Tommy may have been a rogue, but you couldn't point fingers at his grooming.

I settled into my work, leaning forward on my knees with one hand steadying myself on the sofa cushion and one holding his hard cock exactly where I wanted it. After kissing him all the way to the top — where I was pleased to feel a droplet on my tongue — I began to taste him more openly. I felt myself weaken with pleasure as I licked his shaft voraciously whilst his immensity nestled in my palm.

It was at just that moment that I felt a touch slithering around my right hip from behind, then down towards my crotch. *Oh!* I groaned as Claire's fingers dipped into my pussy for a hit of moisture, then very slowly withdrew. Things were clearly ramping up here, so I moved my mouth back to Tommy's tip and plunged him right into my mouth.

That was exactly the second Claire expertly landed two fingers on my clit.

Oh, she knew her way around alright! An animal growl I'd never heard before sounded deep in my throat. I almost came there and then.

I don't know how many minutes passed like this: Tommy stiffening deliciously in my mouth whilst Claire settled into rubbing two moistened fingers in a firm-but-friendly stripe across my clit. All I know is that I stumbled into a jolting orgasm that came almost without warning, and I had no choice but to stop and catch my breath.

I buried my face into his shaft, panting and wondering if this was some kind of breach of protocol. Was I going to be in trouble for stopping?

But if Tommy was displeased, he didn't show it. In fact, I swear I heard something like a satisfied *mmm* from up above. Though I knew he himself hadn't yet come.

I could feel Claire moving to join me, no longer concerned with keeping the body contact light. I lifted my head just in time to see her coming towards where I'd been working. I could see her swirling a supply of saliva in her mouth. The grin on her face was now an openly wicked one. She jerked her head gently towards his cock. *Oh, my, were we going to...?*

Poised at the base of his penis, she raised her eyebrows at me twice in quick succession. I took the hint and got my tongue ready for further action. I moved in close and Tommy groaned. Then we were on our way, each of us traveling slowly up his endless shaft on our respective sides.

I could feel Claire's hot breath in my mouth as we reached the top — and it only got further out of hand as we repeated the trick. Soon we were all but kissing, only with Tommy's tip pulsating between our lips. Then we were taking turns: one sucking him while the other swooped in at the base to pleasure him there.

Tommy began to squirm so hard that it was like being on a raft in a storm. I knew it couldn't last much longer.

"Enough, girls," he said abruptly, pushing our bobbing heads off his crotch with not inconsiderable force. "Laura, I want you to take off Claire's panties. Fast!"

The Frenchwoman sprang to her feet. I managed to adjust to the quick change in mood, hooking my fingers into the white fabric that was now at my eye level. I pulled them down as quickly as I could without tripping her up as her dainty feet stepped out of each hole.

Then everything seemed to move into overdrive. Claire swiftly and silently moved around to the back of the sofa, placing her forearms over the front of it. An awful, *awful* smile spread across her face as she looked me straight in the eye.

Tommy joined her in a flash, rudely shoving me out of the way as he leaped up and went around behind Claire.

"Stay right there, Laura," he barked.

My lips parted as if to protest, but I checked myself. Still coming down from my orgasm, but with at least another one in me, I didn't know *what* to feel right now. I remained kneeling on the floor in front of the couch, completely lost.

Now both of them were looking me straight in the eye.

They barely blinked as his body sank into hers. They were trying to wind me up again! It was written all over their faces.

Or was it just a way of making me hornier for the second round? For *my* turn! Claire and I had shared nicely so far today. Surely it had to continue that way?

Her little body began to shake like a rag doll's as he accelerated his thrusting towards full power. Her hitherto straight, tidy hair lost all sense of decorum and gathered around her face in those messy yellow streaks I knew so well from her previous performance. I could see her knuckles turning white as she clutched the fabric, fighting to hold herself steady against the onslaught.

And still the two of them watched me with unrelenting gazes.

Fuck!

"Are you ready, Laura?"

I brightened like a summer dawn at Tommy's words.

"Of course..." I whispered, wondering if I should get up or wait until instructed.

"Good," he said through gritted teeth, slowing down his pounding just a little.

He straightened, then grabbed Claire around the torso like a pouncing wrestler. Then he wrenched her up from where she'd been and *threw* her to one side with sickening force. Shocked, I heard a thud from somewhere behind the sofa as she hit the carpet.

Before I could even think of what to do or say, Tommy was towering over me. *Shit!* If he did *that* to *her*…

"Turn to the left!"

Stunned into submission, I spun ninety degrees to the

side. To find Tommy's glistening cock poised above my face.

He began to work it himself. I could see it would swell no further without exploding.

"Part your lips and look up at me."

And I braced myself.

CHAPTER 4

*I*t spattered hot and heavy, successive squirts pumping onto my top lip, nose and forehead. Shocked and speechless, I gasped.

I had played out a host of scenes in my mind so far, but *this* had never crossed it. Like Tommy's semen, the surprises were coming thick and fast.

A mountain of feelings clashed and clanged within me. Debasement, subordination, outrage, titillation, shame, privilege. Not knowing what to think, I couldn't have moved even if I had wanted to. As some of the dense liquid slithered down my forehead towards my eyes, I instinctively closed them. A little of what had landed on my lip dropped across the cavern of my mouth and hit my chin. Still more slopped down onto my kneeling thighs.

Even Tommy seemed to be having a moment. I could hear him releasing long, contented exhalations above me. It screamed of his satisfied hubris. It was insufferable. The conceit. The arrogance. At some point, it stopped being sexy...right?

I began to think about wiping my face.

My God! What about Claire? Was she okay? I couldn't keep up with my emotions on her either. When she was getting fucked by Tommy thirty seconds ago, and looking at me the way she had, I'd probably have been happy to throw her into a mincing machine. Now, having seen what he did to her after that, I felt nothing but concern. That poor, brainwashed, beaten-up victim!

Sensing that my eyelashes could now deal with any remaining semen, I opened my eyes and blinked a few times. And there she was, just behind Tommy's legs, crawling towards me like a cat. Claire was up and moving again, apparently none the worse for wear. As Tommy pulled up his pants with one hand and moved back to the sofa, I sensed she had a plan.

Closer and closer she crawled. I stayed rooted to the spot, wondering if my heart could take yet another dose of the unexpected.

She looked across at Tommy, enquiring with her eyes. I followed her gaze. He gave her a regal nod. I examined his vulnerable, post-orgasmic eyes for a moment, then turned my attention back to her.

She came right up to my face...and began to lick.

Jesus, could this get any weirder?

Her agile tongue made light work of the biggest puddles that had pooled on my face. It felt strangely promising as it slithered across my chin, ticklish as it worked around my nose, and soothing on my cheekbones. Wisely, she left the area around my eyes alone.

I could hear Tommy murmuring his approval some-where in the distance.

Well, I was glad *he* was happy.

Claire looked pleased with herself too.

Me? I was seething, mostly. But whether that was because of the latest turn of events or the fact that I didn't see where that second orgasm was coming from, I couldn't honestly tell you.

"Take her back down, Claire," said Tommy, hooking his hands behind his curly head of hair and stretching. "And you can let her off the shackle."

He was talking like I wasn't there. And he knew exactly what he was doing. But hey, no problem. I wasn't in the mood for engaging with Tommy right now either.

Claire, on the other hand, was a different story. For the first time, even if it had only been for a moment now and then, I'd felt like we were in this together. When you've shared such intensity — and perhaps even felt the same wrath — the first thing you want to do is compare notes. I couldn't help peppering her with questions now as she led me back to my floor. After all, maybe the hallways and elevators were the only places where you could speak without eavesdroppers.

"My God, are you okay?" I asked as we stepped out of the door leading to the suite apartment.

"Sure," she said, throwing me a look best described as a mix of perplexion at my question and a grin.

I had to press further. I sensed that she would be at her most honest now, right after sex. Still wearing only her inappropriately virginal white bra, she too looked more vulnerable than I'd yet seen her.

"Oh, good...it's just that it looked so *bad*. Maybe just because it was so sudden, I don't know..."

"It only hurt for a moment," she said, as if that made everything okay. Something about this girl definitely wasn't right. Even now, asking her questions to which you could get a useful answer was far from easy.

"But look, you have a bruise!"

She glanced at her upper right arm, which had evidently borne the brunt of the fall.

"Ah, *oui*," she conceded, inspecting the damage with some interest. "I have a bruise…"

And then, as we stepped into the elevator, she seemed to get a little dreamy.

It was dawning on me that this woman had enjoyed *everything* that had happened to her back there.

"But what if…has it ever been…you know, worse than that? More than a bruise?"

Claire shrugged, as if she didn't really bother with remembering things that happened to her. "Maybe…"

I sighed inwardly. I was beginning to think she wasn't unwilling to open up, but rather incapable of it. Yet there was a human that could stir in there: I'd seen it in the way she looked at me when Tommy penetrated her. And she wasn't so much of a robot that she couldn't come hard. There had to be a way to get on her wavelength, but it was going to take some practice.

Apropos orgasms, another question occurred to me:

"Did you actually come back there?"

"*Non.* But this is not relevant. And I can do this any time, anyway."

Wow, so much still to ask! And we were about to get back to my cell, where the walls certainly did have ears.

"Any time…you mean, with Tommy? Or by yourself?"

"With Tommy, a lot. Maybe even now, when I go back up. But by myself is also permitted. Or even with the others on my floor."

Others?

What 'others'? Men? Women? Prisoners? Kidnappers?

Wait a second! Did she say she might get some more from Tommy when she went back up? Bitch!

By now she had opened my door and was showing me into my quarters. I was desperate to know more, but a voice in my head was telling me not to seem too keen, too prying, too investigative. Not if I was now being observed once again. Just one question then. A perfectly natural one.

"Wait, before you go...how do you get to go up and down as you like, and have all this freedom, and I get locked up?"

She seemed to weigh up her answer more than most.

"That is for Tommy to explain, not for me." She paused. "But...I can see that you suck cock very nicely. This is good..."

"Hmm...right...thanks!" I cleared my throat. "Your fingers are very talented too..."

With a hint of a smile, she nodded and closed the door. Leaving me, as instructed, without that shackle on my ankle.

I hardly had the capacity to celebrate this small concession to freedom. I guessed it wasn't even ten in the morning yet, but I felt mentally spent. Still, I was able to appreciate the tiny mercy that was being able to use the toilet without needing to spread my legs. *Modesty has become a nonsensically relative notion in here*, I thought to myself as I sat down and did my thing.

Nonetheless, there had to be some meaning to my being unchained. Tommy had apparently made this call just after I'd acceded to his emptying his load on my face. Had I done something *right* back there? I certainly didn't think I'd done anything wrong, but when they'd suddenly changed tack and turned me into a desperate, cheap-seats observer, had that been a response to something? Or had they set it up that way from the start?

I was leaning towards the latter theory. They — well, Tommy and his blithe shadow — had let me feel like I belonged for a few moments, but then they had snatched it away to create intense feelings of envy. Perhaps they'd wanted to see if I would snap? But if that move and my subsequent dousing with my kidnapper's seed had been a test of my robotic servitude à la Claire, then surely I'd passed it? Hence my being allowed to move freely around the room now.

As an explanation, I quite liked it. Particularly the fact that I had stuck to my guns and *not* allowed that childish jealousy to get in the way of showing *him* what he needed to see. The growing 'devotion' that would ultimately be his downfall.

I went to the sink and considered washing my face. Spunk and spit is a yucky combination when it all dries off. Claire's tongue had dealt with the thick, dripping blobs, but it was no substitute for soap and water. She'd forgotten my thigh too, come to think of it — and sure enough, a crust was forming there now. *Hmm.* How many more tests would I have to pass to get a shower around here?

A sixth sense told me to check out the screen behind me before turning on the tap. Thank God I did, because there was a message:

Don't touch your face.

Of course. I suppressed a grunt. Keeping my expression neutral was the real challenge, not the washing interdiction itself. So I turned back to the sink and dipped my head away from any prying gaze for a moment as I washed my hands. And *only* my hands.

I curled up on my skinny mattress with a sigh. What was I supposed to *do* with myself after all that? It was still early in the day — I wasn't going to fall asleep despite the fitful nights I'd been having. Especially with my mind buzzing on new stimulation and information. I'd been to another floor of the building and visited the king's suite, which made being back here feel all the more like cabin fever. I'd pushed Claire for a couple of tiny nuggets but ended up with another hundred questions on the tip of my tongue. I'd experienced a certain sex act with which I wasn't completely unacquainted...not if you counted my riotous months on the road in Asia, half a lifetime ago. Back then I'd been...well, I'd been a multiple offender...and I'd *loved* it. Today, though, it had all been so unexpected, tied up with the bundle of complications you get when you're trying to outwit a maniac.

But I certainly hadn't disliked it. No, I couldn't say that.

The unfinished business of the second crest was nagging at me. *Great, just great!* What was I supposed to do about that in here, with who-knew-who watching my every move?

But then I thought:

You know what, Laura? FUCK it! Who cares? There's nothing they haven't seen anyway.

And I knew that unless Tommy threatened to come down and choke me or punch me or worse, I was going to see it through. I was into stubborn, pig-headed territory with regard to my own satisfaction now. And right away I felt proud to have pushed through that barrier.

The only concession to modesty I made as I got onto my back was to turn my body around so that I was facing away from the main screen, which I felt sure doubled as the primary spying portal. It was hardly going to make a lot of difference, but there was at least a chance nobody would be peering right into my vagina as I did what I was about to do.

Also, it meant I wouldn't be able to see any random messages appearing on the screen. This felt like a situation where it was better not to know.

Pleased to be doing this of my own accord, I splayed my knees and pushed my toes gently up against the skirting. Then I began to tweak that left nipple of mine.

But I only did this for a moment. It was a gentle ease-in that I didn't need right now. My clit was still buzzing from Claire's attentions, of course. It felt like a lightning strike as I touched it once again, so soon after. Just as well, because I was disgracefully out of practice. The only time I'd tried something like this of late, I'd been ambushed by hoodlums before I even got going. But I gave myself a mental slap for having let the divorce suck the fun out of me for all those months before the attack.

I busied myself with thoughts of Thailand. Because no, I wasn't going to give Tommy the satisfaction of getting off to anything that went on up on the 23rd floor. Sure, there was no shortage of tinder there, but it was important on any number of levels that I didn't allow him to own my thoughts. Otherwise, I'd end up an automaton like Claire. So back in time I went.

So was *that* the dirtiest thing I'd done out there? Or was there something else, something even sluttier and hotter and more depraved? Hmm, well there was *that* time when

I...oh, but wait, how about *that*? How many had it been, exactly? Oh, *Christ*, I'd been such a dirty girl away from home.

I didn't even need to replay those faraway scenes. Just making the list in my head — the fact that I *had* such an appalling, shocking, deeply pornographic list — took me over the edge for the second time that morning.

And I don't think I was exactly shy about it, either.

I took my time to float back down to earth. It wasn't like I had anywhere to be, was it? I shut my eyes for a few minutes and let my breathing return to normal.

Only when I was bored of looking at the wall, and starting to get paranoid about the office outside my door suddenly filling up with respectable workers, did I sit up and turn myself towards my familiar view.

The first thing to catch my eye was the screen. The message was as unequivocal as all the others had been:

Congratulations, Laura. That was good to see.

My heart surged. And that was down to relief as much as anything else. It was the first time I'd seen anything on that monitor that wasn't ominous and threatening.

And boy, it was great to hear that I'd done something right for a change!

CHAPTER 5

The rest of the day and night passed without incident. Claire, who had showered and dressed since I'd seen her last, brought me lunch and dinner but didn't seem to have time to talk. There was a quickness to her step as she disappeared around the corner to the elevator. The screen didn't stir once.

I was losing track of time already — I must have been here a week by now, surely? Could it be Saturday? Starting to care less about who saw me and what they thought, I went to the window and tried to discern something from the traffic levels on the couple of big streets I could make out. But how could you really say? This was, after all, the city that never sleeps. Even Sundays were a logjam.

Not that it really mattered. Whatever day of the week it was, I was going to go crazy soon without anything to read, watch or do. Even the odd sex adventure didn't go far towards filling a day, did it? Not when all the other hours were spent staring at the wall. And the nights dragged too, partly because I had nothing resembling a comfortable bed and partly because I was doing almost nothing to tire out either my mind or my body.

Just how much patience was I going to need to get Tommy where I wanted him? Not that I had any choice in the matter now, unless another opportunity to walk out of the door came my way. I suspected I'd had my chance on that, however. It was unlikely to have escaped his attention that I'd already lost some of my inhibitions with regard to 'being seen'.

Claire had a purposeful look about her when she brought me my breakfast the next morning. I ignored the unappetizing prospect of granola without a spoon and threw her the question that had now scooted to the top of my list.

"Do you think I could be allowed a magazine or something? I feel like my brain is dying in here! Maybe...Tommy wouldn't mind if you brought me one?"

"I understand," she said with what sounded like a degree of sincerity. "But don't worry, you will have something else to look at from today. You are moving up to the twentieth floor after breakfast."

I perked up at the unexpected news. Any change was a good change as far as I was concerned.

"Oh, thank God! I mean...that's a good thing, right?"

"Sure," she replied. "Tommy said you have done enough time here. And now you will have some changes."

"Like...?"

"You will find out directly after you eat. I will be bringing you something to wear, also."

"Really?" My heart thudded. This was *good*. "Well, I'll be eating fast then!"

That was easier said than done. While some meals were

no problem without cutlery, this was one of the undignified ones. But I slurped and crunched all of it up with the bowl in my hands, giving my tongue a good workout. Maybe that was the whole idea with this style of dining — keeping the mouth agile. *Hmm.*

Claire returned bearing a small fabric bag with a pair of drawstrings. As always, she closed the door carefully behind her. I stood up, ready for new clothes and a new room. But above all, I was ready for progress!

"*Alors,*" she began, starting to pluck things out of the bag and hand them to me. "Before I take you up, you need to put these on."

It didn't take her long to empty the bag. Because calling this assortment 'clothing' was a severe overstatement. You might even call it a tease. I eyed the bra, panties and stockings with thinly-disguised disdain.

"Is this...everything?"

"For now, yes. Wait, before you put it on, I need to inspect you quickly."

And with that, she dropped to her haunches, clearly intent on having another good look between my legs.

I found myself widening my stance. Why did I obey her so blindly? Was it because she never actually said 'do this' but rather 'you *need* to do this' — as if she was only carrying out instructions from someone else? Yeah, that was probably it. Smart girl.

She ran her dainty fingers all the way around the edge of my pussy, pulling the lips gently towards the opposite side as she did so. Thoughts of what those fingers had done to me the day before rushed back into my head and made me tremble. Then she made me blush as she pulled my butt cheeks apart to get a clear view of how things were shaping up in there. Claire was nothing if not thorough.

"*Bon*," she said, emerging from somewhere beneath my crotch and standing up again. "Still smooth. It will be enough to shave you again tomorrow."

"Okay," I said, trying to recover from the unexpected distraction. "So should I put these things on now?"

"Yes, you can go ahead."

Despite my disappointment at the extent of my new wardrobe, slipping those navy blue panties over my legs and into place was a blessed relief. Finally, *finally*! Sure, if my busy pussy had been broadcast over the internet for the past week, there wasn't much point covering up now. But it still felt good to have a shield down there, even if only to feel a little less vulnerable in front of Claire.

The bra, on the other hand, turned out to be no more than a decoration. It was one of those brazen things that basically just held up your boobs underneath, but left them *completely* exposed. And actually pushed them out like fruit to be plucked. Not one for everyday use, then — unless you lived in some kind of fetish club.

Still, their blue matched the panties, just like the thigh-highs, which I now slipped on and pulled up tight. This was *nice* — you just couldn't beat the feeling of stockinged feet on carpet. And the cold toes I'd occasionally suffered since being thrown in here might just be a thing of the past now. Especially with the weather getting...*No! surely you're going to be out of here before spring turns to summer?*

I could feel my reactions were turbocharged right now. Because minimal though the 'clothing' was, having something on my body felt like a sensory attack.

"Good, now we can go upstairs."

I didn't dare to look back or bid my room farewell as she led me out and through the abandoned open plan. I couldn't get my hopes up. It might not take very much for me to end up back in here again, more than likely naked once more. I would have to keep on proceeding with mighty caution.

Well, it was either that or overpower Claire in the elevator, go all the way down and run out of the building. I had underwear and could cover my breasts with my hands; it wouldn't be so bad. And I was a couple of weight categories above Claire, that was for sure. As long as she wasn't trained in some form of martial art, I felt like I could take her.

Unchained as I was, there was nothing to stop me from doing it — except the fact that I knew these people thought of everything. They probably had some thug stationed down below for exactly this purpose. And then I'd be in for some searing pain. This time, it felt like I *did* have something to lose.

Clever, these people.

So I stepped into the elevator behind Claire, meek as a mouse. I wasn't going to get out of here by taking the most obvious opportunity. Biding my time and earning trust was still the only plan worthy of the name. By not trying anything despite what might be seen as a clear opportunity, I knew I would be earning another large tick in that 'trust' box.

My escort pressed the button for the twentieth floor and we made the short journey skyward. I caught myself holding my breath as the doors slid open.

We stepped into a carbon copy of the lobby area below,

then turned right towards what looked like a suspiciously familiar open space. Was it literally going to be the same cell, directly above the one I'd just left? If so, could I hope for a few more comforts?

But instead, we took a hard left into a brief chute leading between solid walls. Clearly this floor had more to offer when it came to interior fittings and divisions. What lay around the corner? Claire had been right about one thing: this was better than flicking through some waiting-room magazine.

We emerged into a much broader passage lined with glass-fronted rooms on either side. With a solid wall at the far end, the effect was almost like stepping into a small courtyard. Then a movement caught my eye.

In the nearest room to the right stood a tall woman with long, black curls and light brown skin. She wore exactly the same get-up as I did, only her ensemble was pink. While she seemed to watch me with friendly interest, my brain almost went into shut-down mode. In the blink of an eye, I had it confirmed: I was *not* alone.

And there was another woman in the room beyond hers! And another at the back on the left! This was nothing short of a small jail! How many more were there? God, how was Tommy getting away with crime on such a scale?

I couldn't hold back from shaking my head at the scene unfolding before me. We were dealing with something much, *much* bigger than I had imagined here. I felt a new rebelliousness swell up inside me as the extent of his sick game revealed itself, but I choked it down for now. I was going to need some time to re-calibrate. *Don't do anything stupid.*

Claire was already halfway down the space splitting the rows of cells. She was beckoning me to follow her. Still in a stupor, I obeyed. She showed me into the second room on the left. And I could see right away that it really *was* an upgrade.

The first thing my prisoner's eye spotted, over in the far corner, was exactly the next thing I'd have chosen after clothes: a blanket. It was folded up neatly at the foot of what looked like a real mattress, which was in turn covered with a fitted sheet. And my spirits rose further at the sight of a pillow. I felt like I was moving into a five-star hotel. My first thought was to crawl under that blanket right away and get some quality sleep. It would be the first time in about a week. Just the sight of it made me want to yawn.

As had been the case in my cell downstairs, there was a sink in the back-left corner. But it was huge in comparison to the little mouse-tub I'd had before — and better yet, there was a new toothbrush and fresh toothpaste perched on the edge. It also had a small, round mirror installed on the solid wall above it. The *only* solid wall, actually: I was beginning to register that the divisions between each room were also transparent. I had windows for walls on three sides.

Hmm, so everyone could see what everyone else was doing. But were there still other watchers beyond the neighbors? Was there a giant, spying screen up here too? I scanned all four sides of the room and was relieved to find there was no monitor installed.

The only other features were a simple wooden chair and a full-length, free-standing mirror, both parked in the corner to the right of the entrance.

"You still can't leave the room on your own," said Claire.

"Only authorized fingerprints can unlock the door. And you may not communicate directly with any of the others."

I wasn't sure what I should say to that. 'Okay' was the first thing that came to mind. But it *wasn't* really okay, was it?

"Oh," was all I could think of. And then I came up with a more constructive question. "What about using the bathroom, then? I don't see a toilet in here…"

I held my breath again, half-expecting her to say she was going to bring me a bucket. But I really hoped that there was a more civilized solution up here in the lofty heights of the twentieth floor.

"Ah, I will show you the toilet room. You can use it now, and then you will have to use it only at the times when you have an escort."

She led me back out into the central aisle, where I could feel the eyes of the other women all lasering into me. Now that I'd caught my breath, I could see it wasn't as many as it had at first appeared, confused as I had been by the clear dividing walls. There were just three rooms on either side, so it was actually quite compact as prison wings go. I could only glance fleetingly at the rest of the inmates right now — blonde, red underwear; brunette, turquoise underwear — but I guessed there would be time enough up ahead.

I hadn't noticed the three doors away to my left as we'd come in. Now, as I followed Claire back up towards the top of the wide cell corridor, they were right in front of me.

She opened the one on the left to reveal a dresser table and mirror running all the way along the opposite wall. The room was wide enough to accommodate five chairs, all neatly tucked in beneath the dresser, which was littered with all the accouterments a beautician might need. In another corner stood the kind of sink for washing hair that you would see at a hair salon, complete with that special chair in which you had no choice but to let go and be pampered.

"Hair and makeup," she declared. "I will also take care of your grooming here from now on. You must be ready to come here any time when it is necessary, or when there is a request from upstairs."

I couldn't help snorting at this.

"Well, I don't exactly have anything lined up for the foreseeable future. So I think you can assume I'll be available."

"*Bon*," she said, inevitably missing the sarcastic note in my voice. "Now for the shower room."

This was an open-plan affair divided into two parts by a raised step running across the room in front of me. Beyond that line, which I guessed demarcated the wet area, the walls began to curve in from either side like a kidney bean. This allowed for exactly six showerheads to be arranged in a crescent formation, all facing outwards. The effect was that of a small indoor arena.

It didn't look like shower privacy was going to be a thing here. And why on earth should that surprise me? All the same, it would feel wonderful to get myself clean. I could still feel a distinct flakiness on my face from my adventures the day before.

I thought about asking Claire if I could wash right away, but stopped short. Asking for things only left you frustrated around here. I'd learned that it was better to try and be Zen about whatever issue you had. Showers, like everything else, would happen when they happened.

I did take up Claire's offer of using the basic toilet room

beside the showers, however. I was allowed to close the door while she waited outside: another moment of mercy that was over all too quickly.

Then she led me back to my new room, closed the self-locking door behind her, and disappeared.

CHAPTER 6

*W*ell, if I wasn't going to get a shower then I *was* going to get some sleep.

I might still have been digesting my breakfast, but there was just no stopping me at the sight of that mattress, pillow and blanket. Even better, I discovered there was a light switch next to the door and flicked it off. There was still brightness filtering in from the hallway and my neighbors, but it did create a hint of dark. After all, there was no natural daylight complicating matters in this cell block of ours.

But losing my skyline view was the least of my worries as I sank onto something actually designed for sleeping for the first time since, well, those two delinquents yanked me off my bed at home. I banished that particular thought. There would be plenty of time for thinking thoughts later — my many hours of excruciating boredom had taught me that much.

And there would be plenty of time to take a closer look at my fellow prisoners too. To plot and scheme and worry and — I felt ashamed to think it, but I couldn't help myself — do wild things with Tommy.

For now, though, I just nestled down on my side, enjoying the soft crinkle of the pillow as my head settled in. I pulled the cover all the way up to my temples: I had hidden myself from the world's gaze at last!

And that was the best sleeping pill of all.

You know when you wake up in a strange place and have zero idea where you are for the first few seconds? After a deep, dreamless, uninterrupted sleep, it was just like that now. At first, cruelly, I thought I was back home in my bedroom. But then what were all those lights coming at me through glass walls? Was I at the office?

Then it slowly came back to my addled brain. I was still a prisoner… but what was this unfamiliar place? Ah yes, I'd been moved upstairs! *The twentieth floor.* They had soft mattresses, blankets and pillows up here. Each one of them was a very good reason why it was taking so long for me to come to my senses.

As I stretched under the blanket, feeling the rub of nylon on nylon, I was reminded that I wasn't completely naked anymore. It felt strange to wake up that way — and I liked it. Then, as I rolled onto my back, an aggressive push beneath my breasts reminded me of the bra I'd been required to wear. The bra I would *have to keep on* until instructed otherwise. It wasn't hard to slip back into my role after the long sleep, was it?

Instinctively, I took a quick peek outside the blanket to try and figure out what time it was. Daytime sleep throws you off course even when you're able to look out of a window. Here, with nothing but neon lights showing the way, it could have been noon, midnight, or anything in between. And I hadn't noticed any clocks in this strange new world. I knew I wasn't going to like this part of my latest living arrangement. It was unnatural to be lost in that way — especially if you were still addicted to the structured day an office job gives you.

Yet again I understood how many smart, calculated layers there were to this whole capture deal. A feel for time, after all, gives you an illusion of control. He who removes the clocks strips away another shred of your will. Tommy was going to use this trick as another way to chip away at mine. I tucked my head back under the blanket and gritted my teeth.

But I couldn't stay in bed forever. I knew the moment had come to poke my head out and take a closer look at the lay of the land. My hope was that the other women would have found something better to do than stare at the new arrival by now, and I could scope out the joint in peace.

Now that I really focused on taking in my surroundings, I realized I only had one neighbor on my side of the corridor. The cell to my right was unoccupied and prepared in the same way mine had been — all the way down to the blanket folded at the foot of the mattress. And I knew it was set up for the next poor woman Tommy would snare. I regarded it with cold disapproval for a moment, then turned away to the other side.

I was met by an intense pair of blue-tinged eyes. She had evidently been freshening up at her mirror but must have noticed my movement and was now looking at me through the transparent partition. I nodded cautiously at the deeply tanned woman. There was no reason to be bitchy, right? We were all victims here.

She was a sporty-looking girl alright. A healthy kind of stocky, carrying a hint of power in her calves and thighs. Those compact brown legs had been shooting goals at some point in her life, no doubt about it. They complemented a butt that certainly wasn't petite but whose firmness I could feel from the next room. Her hips had just a whiff of 'child-bearing' about them and her breasts were so tight and full that her turquoise push-up bra looked surplus to requirements. Her dark brown hair was cropped short, leaving her bronzed shoulders open to view, but it had a volume to it that screamed vitality. And she couldn't have been a day past 27.

She gave me a friendly, inquisitive look. Though she didn't exactly break into a grin, I noticed a dimple forming at the edge of her mouth and it made me warm to her. I got the feeling my glowing neighbor was the kind of girl who'd always be popular, and whom you couldn't begrudge it.

Talking to her, however, wasn't going to be an option. I'd been told that in no uncertain terms already. And anyway, these walls were clearly quite soundproof. I sat up, looked from side to side, then back at her. I threw up my hands, shrugged and shook my head. She got what I was trying to communicate. With an understanding nod, she put her index finger to her lips. *Shh.*

Now I looked across the corridor. Of the three cells on the other side, only two were occupied: the one directly ahead of me and the one away to the right, in which I had spotted the curly-haired woman upon our arrival. But it was the theatrics in the room in front of me that caught my eye now: its occupant was upside-down.

My first thought was that Tommy had hung her up like that, as some twisted kind of torture. I shivered at the image. But then the slim figure lowered its legs gently away from the wall against which they had been propped. I could see that she was supporting her own weight after all. And now, abs straining furiously, she was folding her feet over her head as she dropped into an even more impossible position. This was nothing other than an advanced yoga routine.

I watched in fascination. After the better part of a decade spent telling myself 'I really should get around to doing yoga' but always letting my work press the plan onto an indefinite delay cycle, it was beyond ironic to be confronted with it here. What a good idea! If I'd known even a few simple moves, it might have been a way of staying sane in my cell downstairs. And if it gave you a body like that...well...

Because this woman, who had clearly reached an advanced level, was the classic statuesque beauty. She had long blonde hair not dissimilar to Claire's, but she was a foot taller if not more. She was into the realms of *serious* height for a woman. Yet her frame, subtly filled out with toned, tight muscles, didn't appear to have drifted into dangerously skinny territory. I watched her contorting and stretching into a variety of challenging poses. Lost in her meditative routine, she simply wasn't noticing me.

The only thing that looked a little unusual was the bra, which must have been uncomfortable in certain postures. Stockings would be an odd choice for a yoga session too, I supposed. The fact that she'd kept her ruby-red kit on was a clear reminder that you weren't supposed to touch it, come what may. More irony: after spending the better part of a week forced to be naked, I could finally see a situation where stripping down made sense. Only now it was forbidden.

I wondered about the lanky *yogini*'s age. From the other side of the hallway, I guessed she was a few years younger than my neighbor. 22, maybe? Then again, maybe her outrageous flexibility was playing with my perceptions.

I shifted my gaze diagonally across the hallway, where the dark-haired woman with the curls was sitting on the bottom corner of her bed and looking towards the showers. I could see her in profile: sharp, sleek features and full lips. Her vibrant curls, black as a raven's feathers, rolled out halfway down her back. Her skin was a shade lighter than that of my tanned neighbor, but it looked like she hadn't needed any sun loungers to get there. I guessed she was Latina. The pink of her bra was striking.

I watched her lean back on the mattress, supporting herself with the palms of her hands. In that position, her plumped-up breasts seemed to reach for the ceiling. She seemed lost in some kind of pleasant reverie.

So, now I knew whom I had for company. But as I glanced at each of my three fellow inmates in turn, one thing puzzled me: none of them looked remotely unhappy with their lot.

It turned out I'd slept through most of the day. When Claire brought me my next meal, she assured me it was dinner.

"I didn't wake you when I brought lunch," she explained. "You need to rest whenever you can now that you are here. There will be times when you need a lot of energy."

She laid my tray down on the floor and put her hands on her hips.

"You will also have to be ready for sexual duty at any time, yes? And you have to be perfectly presented. So we will take you out of your room every morning for showers and every evening for hair, makeup and grooming. Eat now, and then we will do this."

I nodded without a word, suddenly aware that I was ravenous and that everything else could wait. Risotto was on the menu tonight — but there was still no sign of cutlery on my tray. I sighed: eating like a human being obviously wasn't included in this upgrade. I considered my options, including lifting the bowl to my face rather than setting it on the floor and getting down low. But a quick glance around revealed that the others had already been delivered the same meal and were already enthusiastically tucking in on all fours. *Best not to stand out, Laura.* And surreal though it was to be a part of this abasement, knowing I wasn't alone made all my self-consciousness slip away.

A few minutes after I was done eating, I managed to at least make eye contact with the pair across the hallway and give them a casual, neutral nod of greeting. Then Claire returned with a towel. She told me to wash my face at my big new basin — and I was only too happy to get rid of the mix of dried semen and sticky risotto that adorned my features. Then she led me to the dressing room at the top of the hallway. I was surprised to find another woman there.

"Hi, I'm Sandra," she said, putting out her hand.

The respectful, everyday introduction threw me.

"Oh, right!" I said, glancing at Claire as if for assurance, then looking back at the friendly woman's face. "I...I...it's nice to meet you."

"Please, have a seat over here so we can wash your hair," she said.

"Er, thanks!" I said, struggling to place this lady's confident, casual manner in my strange new world. She didn't have anything of the kidnapper vibe about her whatsoever. Nor could I imagine that she was a prisoner either: she wore blue jeans and a perfectly respectable black blouse. On top of that, she was nothing special to look at and didn't appear to be under anybody's spell.

But my, she knew how to give a girl a makeover! After more than one violent struggle, various sexual antics and about a week sleeping on the floor, a good wash and blow dry was exactly what my tangled mop needed. Sandra straightened it out and gave it a trim, too. Finally, she pulled my hair into a ponytail. In recent years I'd let it hang loose down to my shoulders, just bringing it along for the ride through each full-throttle day — and I couldn't help liking what I saw in the mirror now. She'd curled my eyelashes and hit me with some dark yet delicate traces of makeup too. If I forgot the bitter reasons why I was here in the first place for a moment, I had to admit there was a knockout woman looking back at me.

Apart from the fact that I hadn't been asked for my preferences even once — Sandra consulted Claire on what was to be done with me — it really was like a normal salon visit. And Sandra seemed for all the world like a professional who could come and go from this place.

But Claire stayed in the room the whole time, so I didn't dare ask Sandra any probing questions. Apart from the pair of them occasionally conferring, there wasn't much chat going on. It didn't feel awkward, because Sandra hummed away as she worked and was one of those presences who could make people feel comfortable without needing to say anything.

I must have spent at least an hour and a half getting spruced up. As far as I knew, though, I had all the time in the world. So I let myself enjoy this new pleasure. Then, when I followed Claire back to my cell looking hotter than I ever knew I could, and I felt the eyes of that stunning trio following me, I couldn't help feeling I belonged.

CHAPTER 7

*I*f my hair and makeup appointment had smacked of normality, morning showers snapped me right back out of it.

The drill began with Tommy appearing at the top of the hallway; a moment the other girls appeared to have been anticipating. As soon as he came into sight, wearing a crisp blue shirt with cufflinks that shone like lighthouses, I noticed a flurry of movement in the other three cells: all three women had sunk to their knees, hands clasped behind their backs.

I'd always thought the rule only applied when Tommy entered your room...but what the heck did I know? I was one story further up, and maybe that meant the obedience expected went onto another level too. I quickly copied their example. Having a crowd I could follow felt like bliss compared to the guesswork I'd gotten used to down below.

Claire, who had been lurking behind him until we all got into position, then proceeded to open all of our doors. Then Tommy stepped forward and addressed us:

"I want all of you out here in the hallway before showers today. Come and assemble in front of me."

The others got up and stepped out of their rooms without a hint of hesitation. Still quite happy to take my cues from my more experienced fellow kidnappees, I hung back a little, watching their movements closely. I couldn't help but notice that there wasn't a hint of rebellion about them as they fanned out a respectful distance in front of Tommy and knelt once again. As I joined the end of the row and sank down, my mind raced. There were four of us and two of *them*. Granted, one was a Highland warrior...but such passivity when you had double the numbers and weren't actually being restrained? What enchantment had he put these women under? He couldn't turn *every* captured woman into an indoctrinated automaton like Claire, could he?

My blood ran cold as the thought crossed my mind that he'd been putting something in the food to take the fight out of these women. If *that* was the case, and he was doing the same thing to me too, then my plans to outwit him might very well be doomed to fail.

For now, though, I felt my thinking was as clear as it had been at any point since arriving here. I was *choosing* to go along with this cocky beast of prey. Just for the moment. *Only* for the moment.

"You will all have noticed the new arrival in your midst," he said. "Her name is Laura. Speaking amongst yourselves is forbidden, as all of you know by now, but I like you to know each other's names. Laura, your fellow slaves are Lisa in turquoise, Sabrina in pink and Tammy in red."

Slaves. He'd said it out loud, the smug bastard. It stung, that word.

But he wasn't wrong, was he? If we weren't slaves, then why weren't we leaping up and telling him to go fuck himself? Did we all think somebody else was going to do it? Or was I the only one thinking of revolt at all?

"Thank you," I whispered, glancing directly at him for the first time today and hoping it was the right move.

"Good," he said, apparently pleased with my response. "Now stand up, all of you, and strip for your showers as usual. Laura, do as the others do."

We all clambered to our feet. I watched the other women all reach behind their backs and unclip their bras. Each then lay hers down on the floor at her feet. I did the same, feeling the weight of my breasts for the first time since the previous morning. It was an oddly liberating sensation.

We repeated this procedure first for our stockings, then for our panties. After laying down this last item of underwear, each of us stood naked in front of Tommy, a small pile of wispy clothing set before us. The vibe I was getting was a kind of amplified group submission. Not even the extraordinarily tall Tammy, standing right next to me, exuded the slightest hint of self-determination.

Tommy took his time to enjoy us with his eyes. He walked a full circle around our quartet, taking in every angle. I noticed the other women kept their hands behind them when he was up ahead, and in front of them when he passed behind, ensuring that he always benefited from a clear view. I made sure to do the same.

He looked quite resplendent this morning. He must surely have been on his way to his parallel life in the outside world. His hair still appeared wet from what must have been a recent shower, and although he didn't come ultra-close at any point on his inspection, I could smell that he'd applied a fresh dose of some irresistible scent. He looked a million bucks in blue — a shade Andre would have been proud of, come to think of it.

Andre! This was *all* his fault. I really hoped it was true that he'd gotten what was coming to him at last.

"Beautiful girls," he remarked as he completed his lap and came back in front of us. "Now, go and clean yourselves up for me."

'For me...'

Was that a double entendre? I salivated at the idea of his words carrying both meanings. But there wasn't time to dwell on that. The others were falling into line and walking up towards the shower room, where Claire now stood waiting by the door. As we entered, she handed each of us a towel matching our underwear color.

"Don't get your hair wet," she murmured absently. "Only Sandra washes hair."

I nodded, perfectly happy to let my pretty ponytail stay untouched for the moment. The other three hung up their towels on hooks just inside the entrance, then picked out three neighboring showerheads in the middle of the arena. I assumed I ought to take the fourth of these rather than give myself a little space by grabbing one of the spouts on the edge. I wasn't seeing any reason to try and set myself apart. *Au contraire*, I needed to blend in.

So I claimed a spot next to Sabrina, who gave me a beaming smile but did not, of course, say a word. She switched on the water and I watched its droplets begin to bounce off the caramel skin of her shoulders. She was careful to position herself facing the flow so that her voluminous curls remained dry.

Soon steam began to rise. I found a pleasant tempera-
ture and helped myself to copious amounts of soap from
the dispenser. I couldn't remember the last time I'd been in
a group shower, but it was a long way from the most
unusual thing that had happened to me in this building.
More than anything, I was enjoying the chance to give
myself an extended, soapy, all-over clean.

I noticed that Claire had hooked the door open and was
keeping an eye on us. Tommy hadn't gone far. I could see
him in the hallway beyond, where he appeared to be
pacing about and talking on the phone. His ability to
ignore the four naked women showering just a few yards
away in the next room impressed me. Especially considering the way some of them were diligently soaping up
their nether regions, then bending all the way over to
ensure a flow of water rinsed the area clean. I followed
suit, even though I was painfully aware that there hadn't
been a great deal going on down there for me. Not on the
inside, at least.

Once we were done and had thoroughly dried ourselves
off, we were each subjected to a between-the-legs inspection by Claire. She would either nod or murmur something
to the effect that the woman in question would be 'done'
that evening. As she'd already hinted downstairs, I was on
the list for another round with the razor that night.

Claire also took each of our towels off us as we left the
room. I followed the rest back toward where our meager
clothing lay waiting on the floor, wondering what the
routine would be now. Tommy was all the way down at the
closed end of the corridor, still on his call.

Somewhat to my surprise, the others began gathering up
their things in relatively casual fashion. It looked like the

expectation was to get dressed again, out here in the hallway.

But as we were doing so, I heard Tommy's footsteps and voice coming closer behind me.

"Yeah, I think you'll like this latest one," he was saying to his interlocutor. "Come over later and have a look at her. We'll take it from there."

Oh God...

I froze, bracing myself for some kind of strike from Tommy. Though he was behind me, I could sense he was now close enough to hurt me.

But instead, his giant shadow swooped right past me and lunged at Tammy. He hooked his one free arm around her neck and began to pull her violently towards her cell. She went limp and allowed him to drag her lengthy frame, which was still naked but for the stockings she'd managed to put on so far. Her panties hung loose in her fingers.

Tommy was still talking on the phone whilst carrying out this assault.

"Yes...good...I've got to go now. I'm starting work on a new deal this morning, now the thing for Danscombe is done. I'll see you later."

I watched, shocked, as he paused in the doorway to put his phone in his pocket. Tammy, who looked barely able to breathe, looked paralyzed with terror. Then he dragged her inside and slammed the door.

Yet while all this was going on, Sabrina and Lisa were still continuing to dress as though nothing of particular note was happening. Transfixed and shaking in equal measure, I pulled on my own garments. And since the other two returned to their rooms, I knew I was expected to do the same. Claire locked each of our doors behind us, expressionless.

But from my cell, there was no barrier to my witnessing what was happening across the hallway. A scene that gripped me and repelled me, tearing me in two.

Tommy hurled his poor victim onto her bed, where she lay gasping for a moment — before her instinct to clamber to her knees kicked in. Before she was even fully upright, Tommy had lashed out with his right hand and grabbed her long, blonde hair down at the roots.

I could feel her pain as her head jerked backward, the skin of her face taut and etched with fear. By now, Tommy had unzipped his manhood. He then plunged the powerless woman's head onto his rapidly lengthening shaft with unholy force. If he hadn't been holding her in a vice grip by her hair, Tammy would certainly have fallen over.

Watching him repeatedly thrust her mouth onto his cock, just a little more violently each time, brought back the horror of more than one assault I'd experienced in this vicious place. I knew just how much that could hurt, and had no doubt she was feeling the same unearthly agony I'd felt. There was no way to hear anything of the action across the hallway, but I was in no doubt as to the kinds of noises she'd be making. Her chin began to glisten with drool as the attack went on.

Claire appeared at Tammy's door, something resembling a stick in her hand. She let herself in, then stood dutifully beside him as he continued to ram his rod down Tammy's throat. Why didn't she *do* something? She had Tommy's trust; she must have had opportunities to go to the police and put an end to this abuse! My distaste for Claire in that moment roared past even my loathing for *him*.

Steady now, Laura. She's a victim too.

Or was she? Fuck, was I the only sane one in this entire place? I glanced at the other rooms. Lisa and Sabrina were both sitting on their beds, watching the scene. Their expressions were so hard to place: wide-eyed, but not with surprise or shock. Why the hell didn't they look fearful, at least? Because I knew what *I* was thinking: *sooner or later, Laura, you're getting mouth-raped again too.*

I looked back across just in time to see Tommy pull her off his dick at last. But only so he could yank her to her feet and pull her towards the wall facing my cell. I saw his lips issue commands. While her assailant held out a hand for the cane and took it without so much as a glance at his accomplice, Tammy placed her palms on the wall, bent slightly at the waist and closed her eyes.

I could see the cruel flexibility in the cane now as Tommy swished it around with malicious intent: it was light brown, about an inch thick and probably bamboo. I cringed as its first blow fell on her naked backside. Her entire body shuddered, the little triangles of her breasts trembling like jellies, then tightened. Her knees went soft for a moment before she steadied herself against the wall once more.

As Tommy continued to lash her, seemingly for no other reason than to inflict pain, I could see her breathing turn to a series of sobbing pants. Watching her jolting lungs and puffing cheeks was enough to tell me that: I was glad not to have the sound effects.

Actually, it was time to look away now. Watching on wasn't going to achieve anything other than validating the brute as he indulged his dark desires. And it was going to make it harder to stay on track with my plans to enjoy the process of gaining his trust: I hadn't known he was into *this* kind of entertainment. Was there any low to which Tommy would not stoop? Would he *kill*?

I deliberately went over to my bed and turned to face the empty cell next to me. I was tempted to hide under the blanket, but feared it might encourage Tommy to cross the hallway with his fearsome cane. I would stick to staring into the middle distance.

But as I did so, something about Sabrina caught my eye. Her hand! It had dipped into her panties as the violence before her went on.

That woman was masturbating.

CHAPTER 8

*a*fter Tommy finally left Tammy's room and stalked away without even looking at the rest of us, his victim took a minute or two to come to her senses. Then she hobbled back towards her bed in obvious agony. I could see ugly, evil slabs of red across her buttocks and the back of her thighs. Even from across the hallway, they glowed as though they were literally burning.

I'd seen some things in my life — but I'd never seen skin battered into such a raw, shocking state. There was *no way* I could take a beating of that nature. Just no way.

Claire stayed with Tammy as she lay on her stomach, still trembling. She produced what I supposed was some kind of balm and began to rub it into the areas that had been beaten. I hoped hard that it was providing some kind of relief to the poor girl.

But now I was hating on Sabrina. Who gets off to something like that? If anyone deserved to be rewarded with an orgasm, then it was Tammy. I could imagine that having negotiated such an intense thrashing, there might be some pleasure to be had — if you were of a particular disposition. But Tommy hadn't even stuck around for that kind of fun. Surprising, I thought. Could a man like him come purely from thrashing a woman? You couldn't rule it out.

I spent most of the day hiding under the blanket again. But when I emerged for my lunch and glanced across at Tammy, she seemed to be back in her groove. Her welts were morphing into a darker purple, but she appeared to be going about her business — as much as one can do so in a cell with barely any trappings — as if nothing particularly repulsive had gone on that morning. Later in the afternoon, I even spotted her in another unthinkable yoga pose.

I only knew what was morning, noon or night by the arrival of meals, of course. I wouldn't have had a clue if they were messing with us. For all I knew, I was getting breakfast at nine in the evening — and I wouldn't put it past Tommy. Mind control seemed to be an even bigger deal for him than getting his rocks off was, after all. Surely that was what his trick of doing things to people in full view of others was all about?

Meanwhile, I was biting my tongue any time I had contact with Claire, whom I was now struggling to see as anything but a culpable accomplice to the monster. Even when, prior to my makeup session, she sat me down and put me through another shaving routine.

Still, I was going to try and pick her brains. The last time we'd done this was the closest I'd come to getting her to open up. I had to keep up the habit of quizzing her during grooming, even if only to convince myself that I was making progress with my subversion.

"Will Tommy do that every morning?" I asked Claire in an even tone.

"No, every day is different," she replied, not looking up from her work between my splayed legs. "Sometimes you will not see him for a week. He is very busy."

Yeah, it's hard work running a kidnapping empire.

I bit my tongue again.

"Oh, I just thought…"

I trailed off.

"You thought what?"

Aha! I had awakened her curiosity.

"Well, I thought he would be having a lot of sex with us."

I was proud of the tone of voice I'd produced. Without overplaying it, I thought I'd made myself sound like the faces of Sabrina and Lisa had looked as they watched that morning's punishment. Like I now felt repeated sex with us was part of the natural order of things.

"He will if he wants to, of course. But normally, you have to wait. Full intercourse is generally the privilege of the upper floor."

"How many floors are there, then?"

"There is one more level above us, then you would reach the upper floor for the girls. Then there is Tommy's floor. You were there already."

"Oh…well…that doesn't sound too bad," I said vaguely.

Claire stopped what she was doing for a moment and looked up at me.

"But you have to prove yourself."

Or what, bitch?

I quietly took a deep breath to calm myself.

"What's the best way?" I whispered.

"True submission, of course," she said, as if it were the

most obvious thing in the world. "Some girls think they can do it, but when they try, they can't."

Was that a trace of a smile I saw at the corner of her mouth?

"I see," I murmured. "I can imagine that lots of them can't."

I put a trace of emphasis on the 'them'. Just a tiny hint that I had hopes and ambitions in this place. Maybe a subtle, subliminal message she'd take to the top, consciously or not.

But if she picked up on it, she showed no sign of having done so.

Soon after my second daily hair and makeup session, just when I was wondering what the point of it all was — nobody had touched me since I arrived on this floor yesterday morning, after all — came the next twist in my captivity. We had a visitor.

I assumed it must be the guy with whom Tommy had spoken on the phone when we'd emerged from the shower that morning. There'd been something about coming over to take a look at a 'new arrival', after all. So when my kidnapper and another man appeared around the corner at the top of the corridor, I felt a surge of adrenalin.

Sure enough, the pair made directly for my room. Despite the potent mix of worry, curiosity and anticipation reverberating through my body, I remembered to drop to my knees as they approached.

Only when Tommy let his companion pass through the door did it hit me that the man's face was covered.

His mask was really a three-piece job. A Yankees base-ball cap pulled down low over his brow, impenetrable dark glasses and a black neck warmer pulled right up to the bridge of his nose. The effect was an intimidating mix: like a poker player crossed with a polar explorer.

The man didn't share quite the same stature as Tommy — few men could — but he looked athletic enough. He wore tight-fitting jeans, smart white sneakers and a casual pink shirt, open at the neck.

I was glad to see that neither of them was wielding a cane and Claire appeared to be elsewhere. Still, I trembled as I knelt there in the middle of the floor.

"Meet Laura — she's 45 and she's a corporate lawyer. Very smart lady, once you get past the stubborn streak."

Both men laughed at this. I glowered in silence.

"You know the drill," continued Tommy. "Have a good look at her. And if you've got any questions, ask away. I've learned a few things about this one already."

The other guy nodded, then stepped towards me. I felt myself blushing under the intense gaze of another unin-vited stranger. The black lenses of the shades bore into me, like some giant fly giving me the once-over.

After seeming to peer into my soul for several seconds, he moved behind me and stopped. I felt his fingers gently trace the skin behind my ears, swoop across the back of my head and then run through the polished strands of my ponytail. He did this several times. Soft touch after soft touch. I felt myself wanting to purr.

"Stand up now, Laura," said Tommy, his tone somewhat more civil than I'd gotten used to.

The stranger remained behind me as I obediently got to my feet. Then he continued his work. What felt like the backs of his fingers — I could just detect the brittle stiffness of nails, ran down my neck. As he flipped those hands to descend across my collarbone, they crept into my vision. The fingers looked supple and healthy, the nails trimmed tight.

My scarlet glow returned as the unknown man's right hand then swam down to embrace my left bra cup in its palm, while the thumb swooped across the breast itself, brushing the nipple. Somebody had been doing their homework! My breath hitched as he repeated his explorations — but I couldn't help being aware of the other girls.

I stole a quick glance to my left: Lisa was kneeling motionless, her palms flat on her thighs, only watching proceedings from the corner of her eye. And a look across the hallway revealed no antics from Tammy or Sabrina either. Each waited respectfully on her knees. And if, at this particular moment, any of them felt something approaching envy, then I couldn't judge them. You didn't need to be on la-la pills to want a piece of *this*.

I tried to suppress a groan as the guy's other hand joined the fray. Now he was unashamedly trying out both nipples for size, twisting them this way and that. I reminded myself that I could let myself go right now. The moments when I didn't need to *act* like I was into this whole thing were key to the coup I was planning. *So don't fight it, Laura!*

I dared to look at Tommy. I knew it would elicit a tangled rage of emotions in me, but I wanted him to see the lust in my eyes right now. Looking into his was going to pay off later.

And what I saw looking back at me was a new blend of approval and satisfaction. My heart sang. We were getting somewhere at last — and if getting felt up like this was what it took, then the road might be a pleasant one after all. Just as long as nobody reached for a cane or hurled me around by the throat.

Now Tommy's guest moved to stand close to my right hip. I could feel an erection pressing against it as his left hand roved over my butt and panties, and his right finger-tips visited the soft flesh of my inner right thigh. I found myself parting my legs a little.

Then I heard the man's voice for the first time. It sounded younger: mid-thirties, maybe.

"She's *very* responsive, Tommy," he said. "I don't know how you find them!"

It took all my power not to yell out something about sending thugs to people's houses.

My captor just chuckled. Something about the way he did it made me think he knew more than his guest did. It was a thought to file away.

"So…anal?"

He had slipped his left hand beneath my panties now, tripping his fingers across the cleft in my butt one by one.

"Early signs are good," replied Tommy. "Tight hole, but you know how it goes. Would you like some lube?"

A pregnant pause.

"Tempting…but I think I'll leave it at window-shopping for now."

"Are you sure?"

"Yeah…aw, wait, on second thoughts…let's have a little look in there."

"Perfect, won't be a moment," said Tommy with a playful grin. "You stay here with her."

I could feel my pussy's wetness double as these men talked

about my ultimate defiling like I wasn't even there. As Tommy made a quick trip to the makeup room, my visitor hooked his thumbs into my panties and pulled them down. I stepped out of them with shaking legs. Could I handle what was coming?

Then Tommy was back in my cell, brandishing a tell-tale bottle. Both men went behind me.

"Get down on your knees, Laura," I heard Tommy command. "Then bend forward. Rest your head on your forearms...like that, yes...legs wide open now. Good girl!"

Well, we would see about that last part. But at this precise moment, he was dead right. Because I was tingling with anticipation, waiting for the sound of a zipper and denim. I closed my eyes, abandoning myself to the fact that I was as exposed as I could get and there was nothing I could do about it.

But I only heard the squelch of the bottle. Then I felt a huge pair of hands — they had to be Tommy's — spreading my butt cheeks.

I ran my tongue along my upper teeth, slowly.

"Your Claire presents them so beautifully," murmured the stranger. "Never a hair, never a spot, nothing."

"They trained her well in Paris, didn't they?" said Tommy. "She went to the finest grooming school in France before she met me."

Met me? Was he trying to sell this guy the idea that Claire had come willingly rather than been kidnapped? Or was I missing something here?

But I didn't have time to pursue the thought because now I could feel a thumb, thick with sticky lubricant, pressing at my anus. It danced in a circle for a while, pushing a little harder with every spin while Tommy's hands kept me spread wide open. I was squirming uncontrollably now.

Then he slipped past my defenses. He began to probe, bringing the coolness of the gel with him. My mouth fell open.

Gradually I adjusted to the feeling. The more comfortable it became, the more I wished the knuckles resting at my other opening would do something a little more constructive. Maybe that was too much like multitasking?

But what if I...should I *ask*?

Well, it couldn't be a *bad* thing to ask, could it? Especially now that a finger, coated with more lube, had replaced the thumb and was boring its way into places I didn't know I had.

"Uhm...uhh...can I touch myself?" I panted, ready to take a green light from anyone as the finger began to twist left, right and then left again.

Silence behind me: tenterhooks.

"You certainly may," said Tommy, sounding more than pleased with my request. And then to his companion: "I hope this goes some way to answering your question!"

"Oh yes, she's got great potential. I think she'll take another finger now."

"I'm sure she will — she's a *filthy* lass once you get her going. Here, I'll pull her cheeks as far as they'll go."

By now I was already rubbing my clit furiously. Those words...that accent...his powerful hands pulling to new limits...then that second finger...twisting, pushing, invading...

I yelped as I climaxed, fighting not to topple over as my body suddenly went limp. I had no words. My heart thudded as I scrambled for post-orgasmic breath. I felt Tommy's grip slowly relax.

"Seen enough of her for now?" he asked.

"Definitely," said the second man, his fingers already beginning their withdrawal. "We've still got to visit the other slaves, haven't we?"

CHAPTER 9

*L*ife on the twentieth floor began to take on something resembling a pattern. Tommy, sometimes accompanied by cronies sporting all manner of masks, would visit our cell block most days and indulge himself with one or more of the prisoners.

Evenings, when we all looked a million bucks after our appointments with Sandra, were the norm. But there didn't appear to be any set rules, really. Some days, nothing happened at all, though we were dolled up regardless. Others might bring a morning performance like the one I'd witnessed after my first shower here. Across the middle of the day, things were almost always quiet, which matched my conviction that Tommy was still keeping up the pretense of a day job.

With nothing to read, watch or do all day long, I began to understand why none of the girls hid their interest in whatever scenes might play out in the other rooms. But there was certainly more to it than relief from boredom. Having by now experienced that first taste of twentieth-floor action, I knew it was mostly *delicious*. And once you knew what it was like to be chosen, it burned to see someone else get the treatment.

It wasn't as though there was a rotation system. At one point, it looked like Tommy and his chums had forgotten that anybody but the bronzed Lisa existed. This lasted for three or four days. Then, somebody else might be flavor of the week. You just never knew — and that was a clever way of asserting power and control. Tommy made sure sex was your only form of entertainment, and kept you wondering when you were going to get it. Those mind games again.

Well, 'sex' was actually an overstatement. At first, I'd thought it a coincidence that penetration and intercourse had been absent over the first couple of days. But I came to understand that it wasn't going to be a feature of life on the twentieth — just as Claire had suggested. There was *oral* sex aplenty, plus an abundance of 'inspections' and exploratory probes like the one I'd gotten from poker-cowboy. But cocks thrusting between your legs? No, not here. And you didn't have to be a genius to understand that this was a carrot dangling down from the floors above.

And yes, I witnessed more disturbing violence too. But this was always Tommy's department — some things were not for sharing, I guessed. Or perhaps his guests were just ordinary guys rather than psychopaths. Whatever, the sadism never took exactly the same form. I witnessed Sandra being whipped, Lisa having her lush breasts slapped till they looked like cherries, and Tammy being trussed up in a complex web of rope, legs held open wide and a gag in her mouth, so she was powerless to prevent her pussy from being swatted repeatedly with a nasty-looking swish.

I dreaded my turn. I knew it had to come. And when it

did, it was going to be a terrible test. I'd had it easy so far since coming up to this floor: Tommy and his guests had been relatively civil to me. Maybe he would ease me into the kinky side of things with a light spanking?

But the very idea seemed laughable. I'd experienced his capabilities up close and personal, and still shuddered at some of the memories. Though the others seemed to get a kick out of some of these scenes — I learned with time that Sabrina wasn't the only one — I tried to look away as much as possible. Though it wasn't always easy: the car crash kept pulling you back. And I'd be lying if I said my curiosity wasn't growing when it came to some of these dark practices. The other prisoners had an odd habit of wearing a satisfied smile once the pain had subsided. But that didn't necessarily mean I was putting my hand up for being turned pink.

I still wondered if their reactions were down to some kind of drug we were being slipped. But after several days on the twentieth floor — it didn't take long to lose exact count — I was finding it hard to buy into the idea that the bewitchment of these captives could be explained away by some food additive. As far as I could tell, the other women were being served exactly the same dishes I was, and I didn't feel like I was under the influence of anything unnatural. I figured I was smart enough to know if something wasn't right — even if I didn't quite know what that something was.

And the notion that all of them had somehow been brainwashed by Tommy since their capture? Well, I could imagine that if you were here for *months*, being played like this, some effect like that might come into play. But from the few tidbits I was beginning to gather from Claire and

Sandra, nobody had been here for quite that long. And even if they had been, surely they wouldn't all have fallen into some kind of religious fervor at exactly the same time? Their responses wouldn't be as homogenous as they so evidently were.

What about some kind of hypnosis? The thought had crossed my mind almost from my very first contact with Claire. But if they were dangling medallions in front of my fellow inmates' eyes on a daily basis, I'd have seen it. Maybe they'd done it *before* these women came up here, presumably from the nineteenth floor, and achieved a lasting effect. But then, if that was the policy, wouldn't they have tried to hypnotize me as well?

I just couldn't come up with a reason why there was *no* outward sign of resistance from any of them. You could be meek out of fear — I knew that better than anyone — but you wouldn't be walking around with a glow and touching yourself whilst watching Tommy beat your neighbor, would you? Sure, the guy was intoxicating and some of the scenes we experienced or saw were irresistible, but as far as I knew he had also subjected all of us to dreadful suffering too. And he had crossed several lines in bringing us here. Where was their *rage*?

I suppose they could have asked a similar question about me. Ah, but with me it was different! I had a plan! Holding my tongue and behaving myself was part of that plan. Did they all happen to be following exactly the same strategy?

No, something about this whole thing didn't add up.

If only I could have *spoken* to one of them. One or two questions might solve the entire mystery. But silence was golden on the twentieth. You could openly masturbate, you were well fed, watered and pampered — but you couldn't talk to the other girls.

The only chance I could see to try and sneak a word was when we were lined up in the shower in the mornings. Most of the time, it was only Claire who ushered us in. And though she seemed to have more than a passing interest in our quartet of naked, soapy bodies, there were times when she briefly wandered out of the room.

Once, at just such a moment, I caught Sabrina's dark eyes. As usual, she smiled at me. I glanced at the open door: Claire was still out of the room.

"Sabrina…" I began in as low a voice as I could get away with. "Tell me—"

But it was like I'd held up a tarantula in front of her face. She shook her head violently, eyes wide and fearful. Her finger shot up to her lips.

I sighed. So much for that idea. If her reaction was anything to go by, I wasn't going to find willing rule-breakers here.

Solo subversion it would have to be then.

I may not have been allowed to speak with my fellow inmates, but we soon got to know each other in other ways. And, like everything else around here, we had to do so whether we liked it or not.

One morning several days in, for example, Tommy surprised us by bringing two friends along to watch us in the shower. The duo settled into a pair of pine chairs arranged in the dry area, where they had a perfect view of us. As usual, I couldn't say the same for them — each wore a full black balaclava. They wore similar jeans and t-shirts but they were barefoot, which made it very obvious that the taller one was black.

Tommy stood between them, one hand resting on the backs of their chairs, directing operations.

"Laura, get together with Lisa. Sabrina and Tammy, you two team up. Now, show us how you wash each other. You may wet your hair today. And *don't* disappoint my guests."

There was a distinct note of threat in the last line. I hurried towards the jet of water under which my neighbor was already standing, a knot in my stomach. With each day that passed, I was more certain that the time for me to experience pain again was close — but I wasn't going to offer that Scottish prick an excuse.

Lisa returned my smile and motioned me to stand in front of her. I guessed she'd been through this rite before, and was happy to let her take the lead. Soon I felt her firm torso pressing up against my back, then a forearm hooking around my stomach and pulling me gently back towards the streaming water. I blinked as it splashed onto my scalp and spattered my eyes.

Lisa's palms were ever so slightly rough to the touch as she began to soap up my midriff. Then she moved to my breasts, the cascade now sloshing onto my shoulders as she ground gently into me with her slippery hips, offering me to the audience as if I were a prize. I decided that closing my eyes couldn't hurt the show, and neither could letting myself go. *Mmm, enjoy it, Laura.*

Was I becoming bisexual? Well, lines blur at the best of times. I'd never pretended not to revel in this kind of attention from a fellow woman. Full of youthful curiosity, I'd done more than a little experimentation on my trip through

Asia. I'd even gone so far as to lick a pussy or two. Then, probably like all the other girls I'd fooled around with that year, I'd just gotten sucked into the joys of socially approved family life. For a couple of years I would occasionally see a woman and think *I wonder if she's into girls*, but never pursued an inquiry. I was married, after all! And mentioning such fantasies to George had never crossed my mind — what would he think of me? Then, as work had dragged me deeper and deeper into its churning waters, I'd consigned those same-sex adventures to the memory bank. Consciously? No. It had just happened.

But the moment Claire had ventured down *there* with that razor for the first time — never mind her later efforts in Tommy's suite — I remembered something of what I'd been missing since becoming a grown-up. And now, here I was — dripping, warm, wet — being rubbed down by a glowing picture of female health. My back arched into her as her strong, confident hands, fingers splayed to the max, slathered down my sides and over my hip bones. I knew where she was headed.

It felt like a kind of rebellion too. Enjoying myself with one of the other girls was a form of sexual pleasure that not even Tommy could own. Sure, he could stand there watching with his chums. Who knew, he might even butt in at some point. But he could never play a role in the lesbian part. That was ours. It was a kind of solidarity. And that added an extra zing to Lisa's touch.

And the fact that the erratic, unpredictable Tommy wasn't directly a part of this scene almost compelled me to get the most out of it. This man was keeping me here under lock and key, largely bored out of my skull, under the constant, exhausting threat of some dreadful abuse likely to be creative in a way that was all kinds of wrong. Cruel and unusual didn't begin to describe it. After all, the guy made every girl lined up in this shower *eat out of a bowl like a dog.*

All of which made me think I had a duty to revel in whatever sexual distraction came my way. That was sometimes difficult when Tommy was looming nearby, even if it was one of his buddies doing the dirty work. But why hold back with Lisa? From the way she was lingering around the apex of my vagina with her soapy index and middle fingers, she clearly knew what she was doing.

So yeah, *fuck them*, I was going to enjoy this. I threw my head back and let out a little groan as she washed me ever so thoroughly in all the right places. I told myself I didn't care if they were watching or not.

But that last part wasn't true and I knew it. With every day that passed, I grew a little more excited by the idea of being observed doing something sordid. I'd caught eyes more than once whilst things were being done to me — female eyes from across the hallway; impassive male eyes deep within masks — and what might at first have been shame was now turning into a primal pleasure I'd definitely never experienced before. I was discovering that if I could hold the gaze of a third party whilst opening my body to a second, my entire being felt like it went somewhere tribal. It was as though I could hear the echoes of battle and conquest, reverberations from millennia past. Deep, deep stuff. Not a journey my thoughtless teenage brain could ever have taken.

And now, sure enough, I was responding rather well to the audience I knew was looking on. I'd come a long way from the cowering woman that had first arrived on the floor below, terrified of her nude body being seen. That woman who was so ashamed of it that she preferred to get kidnapped than to have it revealed on the streets of New York City for even the most fleeting of moments. And I knew that whatever happened from here, and whenever I got away, this was something I would have to thank Tommy for. Albeit begrudgingly.

And now, my head spinning with all these thoughts, Lisa was kissing me under the gushing hot water. Our tongues writhed, and I could taste the pent-up frustration of living so close yet being unable to speak one word to each other. This naked passion was real.

And as I felt the warm breath of genuine, unquestioning compliance panting at my lips, I knew that the line between myself and the others was only a very, *very* thin one.

CHAPTER 10

*S*o many masks passed through our cell block over that first fortnight on the twentieth floor. They took many shapes and forms: the head of a donkey, spookily realistic mannequin faces, balaclavas, Bedouin headgear. Who were these men, and why did they all insist on hiding their faces from us? If Tommy could be so brazen with his own identity, after all, why couldn't his guests do the same?

I tried to puzzle out what reason Tommy would have to bring men to enjoy his little collection of women in some way. Was he just showing off? I could believe that! Was it some kind of deal-sweetener he used for business purposes? Oh, I could very easily buy that too. But surely not even *he* would play such a dangerous game? One word from any of them and his dark lair in the middle of the city would be discovered by the authorities.

But what if these guys *were* the authorities? You see things like that in movies, after all. And if that was the case…getting him in court one day was going to be hard. I pushed the uncomfortable prospect to the back of my mind.

Maybe it was just the masks, but all of these men seemed to have a certain way of carrying themselves. It's not like every one of them was a perfect hunk, but they all seemed very comfortable in their own skins. Though they were polite enough to Tommy, and even kidded around with him on occasion, you couldn't say they showed fawning reverence. I got the feeling that they were cut from the same cloth as him, at least to some degree. One of them, in fact, even had an unmistakable Scottish twang. The rest, from the few words I heard spoken in my presence, were from my own side of the Atlantic.

Yet none of them seemed to be getting any actual *sex*. Surely Tommy couldn't be playing the same teasing game with all of these guys that he was playing with us? It was yet another thing that didn't quite add up — and I was beginning to get impatient for some honest answers. And yes, some real penetration too! Being used by so many unknown strangers — men whose faces I could only imagine — had created a furious coil of need inside me, despite the fact that I was getting the occasional orgasm.

Then, on what I figured had to be about the sixteenth night, I finally got one of those two things I craved.

It began with what was probably the tamest evening body inspection to which I'd been subjected so far. I suspected I'd seen these two visitors before. Unless people were trading masks and dress sense with each other, then the taller black guy who'd watched Lisa and I go at it in the shower was one of them. And the other was one of the hunkier ones I'd come to know from visits past: there were some serious muscles packing down beneath that check shirt of his. And he was almost as tall as Tommy.

All of which made me gush when my kidnapper took the unusual step of moving behind me, grabbing each of my wrists — not too hard, but enough to persuade — and bringing them together behind my back whilst the other two men looked on, eyes gleaming behind balaclava and mask respectively.

"Let them see your breasts, Laura — push them out nicely for me," he said in that intoxicating brogue of his.

"Yes, Tommy," I said softly.

It was the first time I'd answered him like this, as opposed to simply carrying out the order. But I figured I'd shown I was willing to do things his way by now, and it was time to move this plan of mine along. We needed to get to a point where we could have real conversations.

"Very good, Laura," he said as I thrust out my chest towards the two unknown men. And I noted with relief that there wasn't a trace of sarcasm in his tone.

The black guy stepped forward and took a breast in each of his hands. I could feel my nipples tensing further by the second. Just the thought that my wrists were effectively in Tommy handcuffs was debilitating enough...and now I was being touched by a black man for the first time. I'd never gone there yet, but boy, I'd done so in a few dreams down the years. And now it looked like my dreams might be coming true for a change.

Greedy for that elemental dose of exhibitionism, I glanced across at Lisa. She was watching closely through the glass, of course. As I locked onto her eyes, I noticed for the first time that they were almost exactly the same blue-gray mix as Tommy's. They were *made* for gazes that took you to long-lost places. And I began to drift, moaning.

"Wonderfully soft," I heard the black guy say. His voice was crisp and his tone confident. "Apart from her nipples, of course! Those are my kind of tits."

"Well, gentlemen, my offer stands," said Tommy.

Both the visitors nodded, slowly. Whatever this 'offer' was, they appeared to be accepting it. My heart pounded.

Tommy let go of my wrists, then went to join his two visitors.

"Then we'll take her upstairs for you. Laura, listen to me. I want you to remove all your clothing for us. Claire will be along in a moment to fetch you."

Now that heartbeat went wild. Off the charts, even.

"Should I take off the stockings too?"

"*Everything*," confirmed Tommy. "You'll need to be completely naked."

I nodded and began to do exactly as instructed. The men were already on their way out by the time my panties were halfway down my legs. I could feel a light sweat breaking out on my brow as I pulled off the thigh-highs and placed everything in the usual neat pile on the floor.

My first thought was that I was being promoted. I'd made it to the next floor! I'd been told to get naked because I was going to be given another uniform now — and I was going to find it in a room that had an additional few creature comforts to offer.

But instead of selecting the twenty-first floor, Claire pushed the button marked '23'.

Another twist. I was being taken back to Tommy's special suite. The place where he'd once fucked Claire and then let himself go on my face. That incident felt like months ago already.

Maybe I had to make a pitstop here before my arrival on the twenty-first? My last visit to 'Tommy's floor' had shortly preceded my moving up a level, after all. Whatever the deal was, some quality time with Tommy seemed a strong likelihood. I reminded myself that no matter how distractingly hot things got up there, I needed to remember the opportunity this invitation presented.

Claire led me out of the elevator and then left down the hallway. Hadn't we gone *right* the last time? The sliding doors at each end of the passage looked identical. Was my mind playing tricks on me?

She opened up the entrance in front of us with another light touch of her finger. That was beginning to get on my nerves, actually. How long would it be before *I* was trusted enough to access all areas with the brush of a fingerprint? Or was I just being naive in thinking I ever had a hope of reaching Claire's status? I wasn't blonde and I didn't have an exotic accent, after all.

As the door slid open and we stepped into a long corridor, I knew I hadn't been mistaken — we really *had* taken a different turn up here. Though similar in layout to the hallway leading to Tommy's deluxe suite, this felt entirely different. The vibe was very...bordello. The paint job was a mix of reds and purples. The carpet, plush and forgiving beneath my bare feet, was a dark, brooding gray. The lights, mounted on the wall at regular intervals, hid shyly behind chrome-plated shades. After so much exposure to soulless neon downstairs, the warm glow and soft, sexy colors up here made me want to hang around.

We only needed a couple of steps to reach the first door on the right. Claire stopped, turned and looked me in the eye.

"Have you ever been in a darkroom before?"

Thrown by yet another question I barely knew how to process, I thought for a moment.

"You mean...well, you're not talking about a place for developing photographs, are you?"

"No, not that. I mean like the ones you find in some *clubs libertins*...how do you call them...sex clubs?"

I couldn't help but giggle.

"Sex clubs? I haven't been to one of those, sorry. Do we have those in America?"

"Of course," she said. "But maybe it's true, they are not quite like the ones in France. *En tout cas*, you just have to be prepared for complete darkness. You have to have faith, you understand? When you step in, you will be taken care of."

"Oh, so...you mean...those guys who were just downstairs...?"

"If I tell you, it spoils the mystery," she said, giving me a coquettish little half-smile. It felt like she only just stopped short of topping it off with a wink. "You're not allowed to know, anyway."

I said nothing, but I felt my mouth go dry. I glanced at the plain, unassuming door, then back at Claire.

Wait...was that a hint of *envy* I could see in her eyes?

My imagination, surely!

"So, you are ready...?"

"Uh, I think so? You...are you not coming with me?"

She shook her head.

"*Hélas,*" was all she said.

Fuck, I didn't know much French…but I'd read enough to know *that* word. It meant she'd rather be nodding her head than shaking it. *Hmm, interesting.*

Then she reached over to the door — this one opened with a regular metal handle — pushed it open and ushered me into a tiny, carpeted space. In front of me, covering the width of the entrance to the room beyond, was a thick, black curtain.

Claire began to close the door behind me and the light from the hallway receded. The only way was forward.

Summoning up all the courage I could muster, I found the right edge of the curtain and wrapped my fingers around its heavy, foreboding fabric. Then I pulled it back and went into the ink.

Before I could even take a step, I felt a male arm hook into each of my elbows, as if to guide me. I had no choice but to trust them as they encouraged me gently into the black void, their grip steady and confident. I tried to make out something of the shapes at my sides, but it was hopeless: this was total helplessness and dependency. First I'd been deprived of my clothes; now the sense of sight had been taken away from me.

But, as they led me on, my other four senses became keen as razor blades. It was like I could feel every tiny hair on my skin intertwining with the longer, bolder, manlier ones of my escorts. One forearm was certainly grizzlier than the other. I tried to remember which of the men downstairs had the smoothest forearms, but it was a detail I hadn't registered.

"Get down," whispered a voice in my right ear, and the arms released me.

Uncertain and groping for balance, I dropped to my haunches and then, instinctively, my knees. I could feel a shaggy softness beneath them: some kind of thick rug? I ran a hand across its surface. Its strands felt long, bold, coarse and thick, as though this had been made from the fell of one of those highland cows. *Scotland!* Was *he* in here too? My brain begged to know.

But I was glad to be on what felt like solid ground. If I was going to stay down here on the floor, it meant I didn't have to worry about falling off anything and hurting myself.

Now something thick and fleshy found my face in the blackness, searching. It was enough to unleash a thousand butterflies in my stomach — and they gave me no reason to hesitate. I reached up with my hand, cautious and wary not to squeeze anything I shouldn't. I found taut stomach muscles, then let my hand slide south until it hit an apex. From there I knew my way.

Once I had the girth in my hand, I pressed it against my face for a moment, swooning at the mix of soap and salt assailing my nostrils. I tickled it with the tip of my tongue, tasting that first morsel like a nervous newbie at some pretentious dinner club.

Who *was* this to whom I was giving myself once again? I assumed it was one of the guys who'd assessed me downstairs — but how could I know which one? As the cock in my palm swelled and I got into a better position to swallow it, I moaned at the delicious torture of not knowing.

The air in here was cloying and syrupy. With my sharpened senses, I began to feel certain that we were in a small space. My cat's ears tuned into the heavy breathing around me and told me there were at least three other bodies present. My pussy ached at the thought of a blind orgy. Because that's what this was, wasn't it?

As if someone could hear its cry of need, I felt a hand run down my stomach, then two fingers tripping over my clit and curling into my entrance. They hooked deeper into my wetness, using all of their reach to find my special spot. I bucked as they massaged it, automatically cramming more of the mystery cock into my mouth as I did so.

Then I felt somebody else getting into a standing position next to the man I was busy pleasuring. Though his sighs were getting deeper and I could feel his excitement building, he pulled out and guided my head towards his neighbor. *Oh, sweet Jesus!*

As I gobbled down the latest dick — rougher and longer, but no less succulent — I took my free hand and worked the first one. It was still slick from my mouth. This was *mind-blowing.*

Nobody was telling me what to do. In here, where you could only feel your way around, commands wouldn't even make any sense. For the first time since my capture, I felt I could do what came naturally. And that, it appeared, was to behave like the consummate slut.

As I began to alternate between the two men on whom I was greedily sucking, I felt the fingers slide slowly out of my pussy. I wondered if they were female — you certainly couldn't rule such a thing out in this place. But there was something inherently masculine about the slap on my butt that followed. And I knew that *he* wanted me on all fours.

I obliged, managing not to interrupt my mouthwork as I did so. And then, putting closure to any last doubts as to the sex of the person behind me, a mighty length entered me. I growled as it plowed in, seeming to go on and on until it found my very core. *Fuck!!!*

The thrusting began in double-quick time. And once the owner of the cock in my mouth felt that movement, he responded in kind. They fell into a mesmerizing rhythm, alternating hard thrusts in my mouth and my vagina. Though I could have used both hands on the floor to keep myself stable, I stubbornly kept holding onto the third cock in my right palm. It added to the depravity — and still I wanted more.

I imagined that the man pounding me from behind was, at long last, Tommy himself. There was no reason not to believe it. The grunts were plausible, the dramatic length just about right. Taken to the limit by this thought, I traded one cock in my mouth for another and my climax hit me like a hurricane.

But that was only the first of them. As the romp in the dark went on and on, it became clear that only myself and three men were involved. Having been cautious about booby traps at first, I soon came to understand that there was nothing in this small room but the soft, long-haired carpet on the floor and a few cushions around the walls. There really was no danger. It was *made* for wanton abandon.

But the darkness was unrelenting. Even after I had received each of the men multiple times — on my back, on my side, on my stomach — I couldn't make out so much as a shadow. I hadn't known you could make a room so dark that a person's eyes simply never adjusted. But here I was, being gang-banged in one.

I lost count of the orgasms.

And just when I thought that maybe, *maybe* I was about

to run out of steam, I heard a sound loaded with intrigue. It happened in one of the quieter moments, just after one of the men had come on my breasts. While the second guy was gently tonguing my inflamed pussy, I felt the third one lie down next to me, on his back. I pressed close against him, shoulder to shoulder, wondering if I could dare to run my fingers through his hair. I would know Tommy's tight curls, surely?

But before I had a chance to try and move my arm, I heard his breath hitch. Wait...where was the third guy? All I had to go on was the slight noise of fleshy friction somewhere near my right wrist. *No, surely not!*

The guy next to me groaned again. Yes, now that I listened carefully, that was definitely the sound of a hand job. They *couldn't* have hidden another girl in here all the time we'd been going, could they? And why would they only bring her out now? Had Claire snuck in? No, I'd have heard the door.

I flushed in the dark as the number of possible explanations narrowed to one. And as I heard an *mmm* that was clearly male coming from the direction of my neighbor's dick, my excitement unfurled afresh. As the reality of what these men — whoever they were — were doing to each other now began to overwhelm my thoughts, the tongue on my clit worked itself to a fever pitch.

Now I really, *really* wanted the lights to come on.

But I knew that wasn't going to happen. What if I reached across to help? *Shit*, that would be hot!

Or what if...was it too daring? But there were no rules in here! *Go on Laura!*

Though part of me protested to leave the pleasuring tongue down below, I spun myself off my back and

95

crouched down low at the cock to my right. It was *definitely* being worked. Willing to wait my turn, I kissed the trimmed hairs around its base.

Seeming to feel my presence, the hand opened its fingers and slowed to a gentle rub along one side of the shaft. I took this as an invitation to look after the other, running my tongue up and down it. I could feel the goo on my sticky breasts clawing against his hip bone.

Meanwhile, whoever had just been licking my pussy had found it again, this time lying on his back and getting his head between my thighs. *Welcome back!*

As I began to approach another crest, the hand left me alone with the cock for a moment. I could hear a significant readjustment of body position on the other side of the prone man I was currently attending to.

And then the third guy came back. With his mouth.

As he joined me at the tip, he swirled his tongue onto mine as well. Soon our hot, charged saliva was mingling over some guy's penis. Just when I thought I'd exhausted every possible fantasy in here, *this*!

In my mind it was like this: Tommy, so assured in his masculinity that acts like this didn't threaten his alpha pride, was the one sharing an endless, slobbering mouth-wrestle over a man's cock. And that man was the black guy. The first black guy to have fucked me in my life.

I crashed into another shuddering, spluttering, gasping orgasm as that image crystallized in my brain.

Finally, after what seemed like hours in the darkroom, the guys slunk away. I'd lost sense of where the entrance was, but I supposed you could feel your way to the curtain. Or perhaps they knew some tricks I didn't. Whatever, I was too spent to give it much thought. From having had no penetrative sex, my pussy was now aching from the pounding it had taken. I had trails of drying cum running down my chin and a layer of it caking my tits. The taste of multiple cocks lingered on my tongue. Had Tommy's *really* been among them?

Just when I was beginning to come to my senses, I heard the door open and Claire calling me to come to her. I crawled my way towards the voice, groped for the curtain, then hauled myself to my unsteady feet and emerged into the space beyond it.

"Wait a moment," Claire instructed. "Your eyes need to adjust to the light."

When I finally came into the hallway itself, dim though it was, it felt like I'd stepped onto a bright beach at midday. I also felt a new level of nakedness and exposure. Stupidly, seeing Claire looking at the streaks I sported made me turn a little red.

But she didn't ask any questions. If my intuitions about her feelings on this episode had been true, then I understood why she wasn't volunteering any conversation right now.

"Come. I know you will be exhausted. I'll take you back down to your room to sleep now."

CHAPTER 11

Q/W ithin a couple of days of my darkroom escapade, both Tammy and Sabrina had disappeared from our floor.

At first, I simply thought they'd been taken up for a similar adventure. Their panties, bras and stockings lay piled on the floor, just as mine had. But the hours slipped by, and then a full night. And when Claire came to replace their bedding and toothbrushes, as if preparing their rooms for new arrivals, I knew they weren't coming back.

For Lisa and I, however, life continued much as it had before. My craving to gossip about the latest developments with her went to another level. Now that we had been intimate with each other and were the only ones left here on this floor, my loneliness felt more acute. I felt sure that went for her too.

What I wanted more than anything was simply someone to *speculate* with. What had happened to those other two women? I figured it was either something awful or something wonderful.

Surely Claire could tell me something about where they'd gone? I didn't see why *everything* had to be a secret.

When I raised the subject during the next evening shave, she played her cards close to her chest as usual. So I tried to see if I could leverage her ego.

"Please, Claire," I fawned. "You're the only one I can ask. You know what Tommy is planning, what he's thinking, what he does. You can have real conversations with him... can't you?"

"Of course," she said, choosing a breezy tone of voice that irritated me. And then: "But he trusts me completely."

I let that one slide on by.

"Okay, can you answer just *one* question for me, yes or no. Please?"

"Well, what is it?"

"Tammy and Sabrina...are they still alive?"

At this, she stopped what she was doing and looked up at me. She looked genuinely puzzled.

"That's your question? Are they *alive?*"

"Yep, just that. So, can you give me a yes or no?"

And she actually laughed, shaking her head as she rinsed her blade in the tub of hot water at her side.

"Of course they are still alive! You think Tommy is a murderer? I would not say this to him if I were you."

How the incongruity of her words didn't strike her was so far beyond me that I couldn't resist pointing it out.

"Well, if someone can have people violently kidnapped, imprison them and assault them with canes...you understand how I might think he *could* be capable of anything?"

She sighed.

"Actually, *you* are the one who doesn't understand anything. I sincerely wish I could tell you more."

Checking to make sure she was looking down, I rolled my eyes and gave up speaking for the rest of the session.

Then she took me back to my cell, locked me in and led Lisa off for her pussy grooming, hair and makeup session.

She emerged looking particularly scrumptious, her eyes sparkling in contrast to the understated tones of the makeup she'd been given. Her hair glistened and I could almost smell the shampoo wafting through the partition between our rooms.

Something was up.

Sure enough, about half an hour later, Tommy came down to our cell block. I thought he would be making a beeline for Lisa, perhaps even take her upstairs. If so, was I going to be invited to join? Surely he'd noticed what a fun package we were as a pair?

But our prison-keeper let himself in my door instead. And he wanted to talk.

"I hear you've been asking a lot of questions, Laura?" he smirked.

Claire. I knew it! I'd been too bold with her. And now she'd blabbed.

"I'm sorry, Tommy," I groveled, making sure to keep my tone even and my kneeling pose both submissive and expectant. "I get curious sometimes."

"I see that," he remarked. "You have an inquisitive mind. You're not like some of the others around here. It's one of the reasons I was so interested in you. Why I *am* so interested in you."

I felt a wave of pride wash over me.

And yet it scared me that I was letting talk like that get to me.

"Thank you," I replied.

"And…are you enjoying yourself here?"

Tough one to answer, that. Lying would be transparent, yet I *had* to start selling him on the idea that I was no longer looking to escape; that I was keen on committing to life in this place. And the very fact that he had asked a question like this with a straight face revealed the weakness I hoped would be his downfall. I chose my words carefully.

"It's been a very sexy adventure. You've seen what I am like, Tommy. I can't wait to go to the darkroom again! But I could use some more comfort, of course. A window and some natural light would be nice. And I need something to occupy me — just for all those hours when we don't get fun visits…"

He nodded, looking quite reasonable by Tommy standards.

"Duly noted," he said. "You can have a life like that, I think, but you'll still need to prove yourself a little more."

I could hear my heart cranking up; a pounding in my ears.

"What do I need to do?"

"The same as you've been doing. Sit tight, be a good girl and know your place. The rest will take care of itself. When you need to know something, you'll be told it. Because you're not like the rest."

"You mean…because I'm so inquisitive?"

"No…there's something else that makes you a very, *very* special case."

I was gagging for answers, but I bit my lip.

"Now if you will excuse me, Laura, I have business to attend to next door."

And then I had to watch him leave the room, thrust his hands in his pockets and saunter across to Lisa's cell. His long, powerful legs only needed about three strides to take him there.

I had the feeling he was once again about to do something that was engineered to get under my skin. But still, that had been a positive meeting, hadn't it? Claire might have betrayed my excessive questioning, but it had moved Tommy to come down and have the first real conversation we'd had since my very first days on the floor below. And in spite of himself, he'd said more than he needed to. We were talking. It was a step in the right direction.

Meantime, I could see Lisa looking up at him with reverent, beseeching eyes as he entered her room and stood in front of her. I knew exactly where she was coming from. And I felt a pang of jealousy as Tommy beckoned her to stand, then bent his lanky frame to kiss her. I hadn't seen him kiss *anybody* in here yet, after all. And this was the real deal: deep, long and lingering. Her eyes closed and I could see she was lost in it.

Now that there were only two of us in the block, I felt the impact of this all the more keenly. After all, I was now the only one missing out on the action — previously I'd had three others in the same boat with me. Tommy knew what he was doing — but I didn't quite get why he felt the need to do it.

Then the resentment passed. As Tommy disengaged from Lisa's mouth, unclipped her skimpy bra, pulled down her panties and pointed at the floor, something came over me. Something that stayed with me even as she got onto all fours with her face looking directly into my room.

I *wasn't* going to dignify Tommy's efforts with envy. He didn't deserve that. Also, from the point of view of my longer-term plans, I knew what a destructive path it would be for me to go down. I supposed he thought making me jealous would increase my longing for him and my obedience to him, in order to get what I craved? Well, it wasn't going to work. *I* was the one in control here. And nobody was going to sour my resolution, made long ago on the day they were supposedly ready to release me, to make the most of whatever sexy fun was on offer.

Sure, being in there with the pair of them would be the *best* thing. Especially because I was getting the distinct impression that the twentieth floor was about to see an end to its sex drought. But if tonight was going to be a live porn show with two hot actors instead, I could go with that too! So, as Tommy stripped naked, then knelt down behind her and began to pump her from behind, his tattoo looming over her arched back, I resolved to revel in being allowed to watch.

Having come to understand just how sizzling it was to be observed, it wasn't hard to slip into Lisa's skin right now. Meeting her eyes, drunk on abandon as she took thrust after thrust, was enough to unleash a sudden heatwave of lust right across my abdomen. Tommy was looking straight at me too, his jaw set firm and steel in his eyes. And that produced another billow of desire. It thrilled me to know that I was on his mind even as he pounded this sexy, hot woman.

I got myself into a comfortable position on my knees, spread them, then slid a couple of fingers into my panties. I knew my time for full intercourse with Tommy was going to come — or had it come already in that darkroom? — so there was no need to pine when such enthralling obscenity was playing out before me. Soon I was rubbing myself as furiously as Lisa was getting slammed. I exploded on the double, crying out in the silence of my cell.

As soon as I had my convulsions under control, I looked directly into Tommy's eyes. I guess it was my instinct to show him that the decision to get myself off had been mine and mine alone. That I wasn't embarrassed; that I hadn't been led by longings I wished I didn't have. He'd see that the crashing orgasm had been *exactly* what I wanted.

And though I couldn't swear to it, I was pretty sure I saw that little twitch at the left corner of his mouth. He liked what he'd seen.

Either that, or he liked the idea of what he was going to do to me next. I was fine with that too — just as long as it didn't involve any bullwhips.

Lisa was smiling unashamedly in my direction. She was clearly coming down from an almighty orgasm of her own, but there was more to her look than that. It told me that we'd bonded closer over this. If the whole performance had been an attempt to drive a wedge between us or arouse feelings of spite, then it had surely backfired.

I could be proud of myself.

Tommy didn't bother to put his clothes back on when he'd finished with her. He just gathered them up in one hand and left the room, his cock still proud, stiff and glistening. I couldn't help wondering if I was about to get another visit. But I forced myself not to follow him along the hallway with my eyes. I wasn't going to let him think I was desperate. It would undo all my good work so far this evening.

But I did look up when I heard the click of the door opening. Had *that* moment come already?

"You've exceeded my expectations, Laura. Well done."

"I did?"

"I'll tell you while you suck me clean."

"Of course, Tommy," I nodded. Such commands no longer shocked me in the slightest. And I could find a lot to like about this one.

Tommy motioned towards the chair. Unless you were Tammy, you had to sit on one if you wanted to reach him properly. A woman of average height could only hope to lick his balls if she knelt on the floor. So I took a seat, then slid his wet length into my mouth.

At first, I forgot he was supposed to be telling me something. The taste of Lisa's juices and traces of his spunk, blended together on his meat like a fine sauce on a steak, was a distracting assault on my senses. I knew I was going to carry on with this long after I had slurped away all traces of his exploits.

But then he brought me out of my reverie.

"Your response just now was brilliant. You're really beginning to fit in. You'd never have done that when you first got here, you know that? I think you'd have hidden in the corner, just out of principle. Now it looks like you're getting it. That it's not *about* you."

It was the last sentence that got my mind racing. Still busy with the job of sucking his cock, I had license to process what he'd said. *It's not about you.* Where was he coming from with that? My response had been *totally* about me! I'd made a point of it. The glance I'd thrown him was meant to tell him that.

I gurgled *mmm-hmm* to tell him I understood. Though I really, really didn't. But with his cock in my mouth, I knew I had him in a good place right now. I just had to ask the right questions. To buy a little more time, I transferred his shaft to my hand and began to lick my way over all those hard-to-reach places right down at the bottom. Diligent Laura could be relied upon not to miss a spot, couldn't she?

If it wasn't about me, then…it had to be about *him*, right? But how could he interpret it that way? My brain raced; my tongue slowed. I came up with a theory: Tommy thought I'd tried to channel my inevitable, screaming, raging jealousy in a way that would curry favor with him as best I could. An attempt to lure him away from Lisa and into my cell.

I paused in my work for just a moment, sensing he wasn't going to wreak violent punishment for this.

"*Mmm*, Tommy, how could I hide what I was feeling?" I said truthfully. "It made me *so* horny…"

"And that's what I consider normal behavior, which is very good. A great step. But for you to actively turn to me and put on a show, just so that I could come extra-hard in your neighbor's pussy? That makes you a *very* good girl."

It was just as well I'd gone back to bobbing up and down his shaft by this point, because these words made my eyes open wide with surprise. Good thing he couldn't see them, then.

Oh boy, he actually thought I'd done that for *his* benefit? When I'd really done it almost as an act of defiant protest, albeit one soaked in lustful enjoyment? This man's ego was beyond the understanding of ordinary humans, that was for sure. It ran deeper than I could ever have imagined. He clearly lived on another planet.

But that was a good thing, right? I'd figured that my unbridled, selfish response to a moment designed to test me might show I was keen to hang around for more sex. If his twisted mind had taken that so many steps further, into some wacky world where I'd only been thinking of *his* pleasure, then that was even better. It meant I was closer to gaining trust than I'd expected.

Maybe, just maybe, this was going to be easier than I thought.

"Then I'm very, very happy," I said.

Once again, I'd found words that meant I didn't even have to lie.

"Good answer," he said. "And I think you're done cleaning me up too. Good night, now."

And with that he left the room, still not bothering to get dressed. I glanced at Lisa as he did so. But she was so mesmerized by the rock-hard butt exiting the scene that she literally wasn't seeing me.

We had much in common, me and her, I was sure of that. Yet just like the departed (and apparently very much still alive) Tammy and Sabrina, I was sure she was coming at this whole thing from another angle. Just one of the things I had yet to figure out.

But as I went to sleep that night, I felt the time for both answers and action had come a good deal closer.

CHAPTER 12

The following morning saw a flurry of activity on the twentieth floor as four new inmates arrived. Apart from all the sex play, this was by far the most interesting thing that had happened since I moved up here. Lisa and I watched the newcomers with shameless interest from our cells.

The thing that really puzzled me? All of these women arrived in regular street clothes that showed no signs of having been involved in a struggle. No rips, no frays, no missing buttons. And nobody was wearing glasses at all — never mind special ones that blurred your vision.

Only once Claire had ushered them into their respective cells did they strip down and change into the standard combination of stockings, panties and revealing bra. Yet again, though I sensed a few nerves, not one of them showed the least resistance.

Our cell block was now full, and as colorful as it could get. Tammy's red get-up and Sabrina's pink ensemble were taken over by a petite but vacant-looking strawberry blonde and a slim woman who looked to be of South Asian or Arab extraction. Hitherto empty, the cell between myself and the showers was now occupied by a tanned brunette whose long, highlighted hair tumbled around her shoulders in appealingly chaotic fashion. Her 'uniform' was bright yellow. Looking across into her cell was almost like seeing the sun again! In the third chamber across the hallway, a woman with large breasts, full lips and jet-black hair added a splash of green to the scene.

As each one of them undressed, she handed her street clothes to Claire. The Frenchwoman stuffed them into a series of drawstring bags, then disappeared with them. None of this tallied with what I'd experienced. Watching the new intake, doubting somehow that they had just spent several days in solitary confinement the way I had, I was forced to give serious thought to the bizarre notion that these women were here by *choice*. Could it be?

Was *that* what Tommy had meant when he'd said that I was a special case?

And what if it really turned out that I was the only one in this wacky place that had actually been kidnapped? The very thought of it brought a particular brand of fury with it. It was one thing to have been captured along with several other women, caught up in a web that had trapped many. But the idea that I might be a club of one — singled out as the fool dumb enough to let herself be dragged out of her own home — sickened and enraged me. We'd see just who was the smart one if I ever got him inside a courtroom, that was for sure.

I fully expected Tommy to turn up at the first opportunity and begin attacking these women in his usual rich variety of ways. But we received no visit at all on the first day. Though silence still reigned, high expectation hung over the twentieth floor.

How that tension was resolved, I never found out. Because the following evening after dinner, just when I felt certain something was about to give, Claire came for me.

"You won't do hair and makeup tonight, Laura. You're moving up to the twenty-first floor instead. Come with me."

Startled by the news, I instinctively looked around the room. That's what you usually do when you move out of a place, isn't it? You start figuring out what to pack.

But I had no possessions, of course. Even my lingerie was on loan. I was still a plaything.

"Should I take the toothbrush with me?"

"I will bring it later," she said. "You will have a bathroom upstairs for this. Come, you will see."

I was going to get to brush my teeth in a different room from my cell? *All by myself?* Curiosity and excitement began to swell inside me.

Claire led me back to the elevator, pushed button '21' and took me into a whole new world.

The first thing to hit me was the natural light. We were in an open-plan space again, loosely similar to the floor where I'd spent my first week. There were *plenty* of windows around the perimeter. The day was beginning to fade, but even the gray light of a spring evening — it *was* still spring, right? — was a welcome sight that lifted my spirits. This was going to be an upgrade in more ways than one!

But as soon as Claire showed me my new room, I knew it wasn't quite so simple as all that.

The cell formed part of the central island, its back to the elevator lobby and facing out into the open plan. Less than half the size of my lockup on the twentieth floor, its drywalls were opaque. Only the front partition, which featured a blind of the type favored by managers who wanted to ward off lip-readers, formed a window of sorts.

But the biggest surprise? There were two single beds in the room.

"So, you will be sharing with Andrea," declared Claire. "You take this bed, on the left."

Sharing? The possibility had never crossed my mind in all the time I'd spent wondering what progress in this building might look like. *Hmm.* I wasn't sure if I liked the idea or not. And who was this latest new woman, anyway? Did Tommy have girls running around on every floor of this establishment?

"Oh! Where is she now?"

"She's working. All of you will work. I will show you the details in a moment. But for now, please put on your new things."

She drew my attention to a set of clothes awaiting me on the bed. I stepped forward to examine them more closely. I picked up the main piece, gingerly, and looked at Claire with incredulity.

This wasn't a sexy outfit at all!

This was a gray, drab single-piece dress. It was starched so stiff I could have beat out a rhythm on it. It was like the kind of school uniform nuns made girls wear decades ago. It even had an integrated belt. In a word, it was awful!

I felt I knew Claire well enough now to say this out loud.

"Seriously, *this* is what we wear up here? What happened to…you know?"

The moment the words slipped out, I realized how crazy they must have sounded. I'd only landed up in this prison because I'd been terrified of having my body exposed in any way. For the same reason, I'd been unable to seriously consider escape when I'd had the opportunity. But now, finally confronted with respectable, conservative clothing that opened up a range of new possibilities, I felt like I was being downgraded.

My reaction to the outfit made me acutely aware of just how successfully Tommy had messed with my mind. I could almost hear him cackling at me from somewhere. Another reminder of the danger that lay in wait for my inner rebellion.

"Yes, the twenty-first floor is about dedicated work and service," explained Claire. "It's a quite different way of showing your loyalty to Tommy."

I didn't have to look at her to know that she was saying these words with a straight face.

Fine. You keep a straight face too, Laura.

I shrugged and cleared my throat.

"Okay, I see."

"You have new underwear as well," Claire pointed out.

My eye now fell on the crisp, solid panties and the modest, no-nonsense bra that had lain beneath the dress. Both were monotone white. Neither had so much as a hint of femininity, sensuality or promise about it.

Only a real maniac would even think of changing things up like *this*, I thought.

But then, a maniac was exactly what we were dealing with here.

I removed my twentieth-floor uniform in its entirety, handing the array of alluring blue items to Claire without even needing to ask. Then I pulled on the kind of underwear I'd have been embarrassed to have on my body even at the platonic nadir of my time married to George and working myself into the ground. I stepped into the colorless dress, slid my arms into the short sleeves and fastened the heavy buttons that closed the front. I then secured the belt by means of a button on my left hip. It felt tight everywhere — and not in a good way.

This done, I sat on the bed and put on the tiny black ankle socks supplied. Finally, I twisted my feet into the simple pair of moccasins that had been waiting for me on the floor. The whole get-up screamed of institutionalized, regimented labor.

I stood up in the narrow gap between the two beds once again. I straightened the dress across my shoulders and patted down the hem, which ran almost all the way to my knees.

"Well, I think I'm done. By the way...if I'm sharing a room, does that mean I can talk to this...what was her name?"

"Andrea," repeated Claire. "Yes, this is one of the changes after moving up. You can communicate with the others on this floor."

"Thank God!" I said, not even caring what she thought about it. A bit of interaction with somebody other than my captors could only be a good thing, right?

As she led me out of the door, I noticed that she didn't

close it behind her. I saw that the neighboring entrance was also wide open, revealing a room identical to my own.

"And...you're not locking anybody in their cells here, it seems?"

"Correct. You are all free to move around the twenty-first floor. But only authorized people can open the elevator."

"So, you and Tommy, then?"

"Others could come," she said cryptically. "But usually they choose not to."

"Hmm, okay."

Quizzing Claire tended to get exhausting quite quickly. I decided to stick to following her around the open plan for the moment.

While much of it consisted of the empty offices all too familiar to me from my early days of captivity, some of the spaces around the edge had clearly been refitted and repurposed.

First, Claire showed me what looked like a canteen room. It had a single round table and a handful of chairs. There was a water dispenser in one corner, next to which I gleefully noticed a tray of cutlery perched on a small sideboard. Not only was I no longer going to be sleeping on the floor, but my days of eating like a dog were over!

"This looks nice," I commented. "Will you still be bringing us our meals?"

"No, you will be making them yourselves. The kitchen for the whole building is on this floor. It's one of the places you will keep busy with your new duties."

I laughed in spite of myself.

"Okay...but I am a terrible cook. I don't think anybody wants to eat a dinner made by me!"

"Don't worry, you will be under professional instruction in there. You just have to do as you are told."

At this, she opened a nearby door to reveal what did indeed appear to be a professional kitchen. It was smallish, such as you might find at a humble country eatery, but the chrome-plated surfaces and rows of serious-looking knives hanging up on magnetic racks betrayed an ambitious purpose for the space. I could well believe this was where the tasty meals I'd been fed had their origins.

There was no chef in sight, nor did anything appear to be cooking. I guessed that made sense — it was a while since dinner had been served. But two women, pressed into identical uniforms to mine, stood at the washing-up area away to my left. One of them was up to her elbows in soap suds, with the other seemingly on rinsing and drying duty.

Hearing us step into the kitchen, they stopped what they were doing and turned around to look at us. They each offered a strained, demure smile as Claire introduced me.

"And these are Andrea and Pála," she said.

Aha, Andrea! That would be my roommate.

I immediately clocked that Andrea was somewhat older than the rest of the women I'd seen in this building. I thought she might be in her late thirties. She wore her chestnut hair in a bob cut. It was quite a common style in the corporate environment, but I'd always thought it a little too in-your-face. It smacked of insecurity. And that was exactly what I saw in her eyes as I greeted her now.

The other girl, Pála, had one striking feature I could pick up even from the other side of the room: bewitching blue eyes. They stood out all the more given the lackluster clothing with which all of us were saddled. Her blonde hair was long and straight, the fringe cut low across her forehead. With a name as mythical-sounding as that, I couldn't help but think she had to be Scandinavian.

"We'll leave them to it for now," said Claire. "When the girls are busy, they're quite focused on their work, which is correct. They are all eager to please in any way they can."

Not for the first time this evening, it felt like she was lecturing me. I hoped this wasn't going to be a major part of life up at this rarefied altitude. But I held my tongue, reminding myself that everything she said was another little byte of information for me as I plotted not only my escape but Tommy's ultimate downfall. I was beginning to wish I had something with which to make notes.

Claire then proceeded to show me the laundry room, which was about as interesting as it sounds, and the bathroom. This was more functional than the one downstairs had been. Though the showers were still exposed to the room, there were vertical partitions between them — although these only went up to shoulder height. Opposite the showers was a row of sinks, above each of which hung a wall-mounted cabinet with a mirror for a door.

"You can take this one," said Claire, opening the door to reveal a few basic grooming items such as a comb, hairbrush and tweezers, along with a cheap-looking bottle of shampoo. "You'll be responsible for your own appearance again whilst you are here. And as I said, I will bring your toothbrush up shortly."

I nodded. So, no more sessions with Sandra and, if I had understood correctly, no more intimate shavings with Claire either. Did the lack of such care and attention mean we weren't going to get any…action?

I feared that protracted denial following the tease downstairs was exactly the warped game Tommy was playing now. And I suspected keeping my mind on the prize would be much tougher without the regular doses of exhilaration I'd gotten used to.

On the other hand, there was the 'work' thing. Having something to do could only be a plus, even if it was dull drudgery. Just as I started wondering how busy we were really going to be and how it all worked, Claire led me to a noticeboard strapped to the wall near the shower room.

A typed A4 page listed the precise duties each of us would be expected to perform over what I took to be the current week and the week to come. By the looks of it, there was a fourth woman — Anya her name — whom I had yet to meet. Along with myself, Andrea and Pála, various chores were assigned according to a strict timetable. Not all of them, I noted, could be carried out here on the twenty-first floor.

My eyes skimmed over time blocks during which I would be assigned to meal preparation, washing up, doing the laundry or cleaning the bathroom. More interesting by far were the tasks with a 22 or a 23 next to them. It looked like cleaning the toilets on the mysterious twenty-second floor or making 'the bed' — Tommy's bed? — on the twenty-third would be expected of me almost from the very beginning.

So, girls who made it this far were used as labor slaves to service the upper floors! Some promotion, huh? But it did mean I was about to get regular changes of scenery. It also probably explained where Anya was right now. Drawing a bath in Tommy's executive suite up on twenty-three, perhaps? Then again, she might have been 'refreshing play-rooms' on the same level. Or providing 'grooming assistance' on the twenty-second.

Wait, what day was it again?

That's when I noticed the analog clock ticking away on the wall next to the noticeboard. And below it, an equally tacky date counter. The latter made my head spin: it was already May! We were four days into the month.

Seeing 05/04 in black and white really hit home. If memory served correct, it was April 9th when I'd been forcibly removed from my home. Tommy had stolen just about an *entire month* of my life from me.

My resolve stiffened. I was glad of the fact that I would now be getting regular access to the upper floors. That meant more access to my kidnapper. And, in turn, a faster ticket out of here.

"It looks like you have understood the rotation system quite quickly," remarked Claire. "I think it's all clear, *n'est-ce pas*? You have one day off every ten days. You will see your first one when I pin up the update at the start of next week."

I nodded, unsure of what I was really going to do with a day off under these conditions.

"Will I be able to get something to read?" I asked hopefully. "Or maybe some paper to draw or write on?"

"Not yet, I am afraid," she said, shaking her head. "There are no luxuries on this floor. Maybe you will have some in the future."

She didn't elaborate.

"I will escort you to the other floors when you have duties there, of course, and then bring you back here. All you have to do when you are there is show your fidelity. Not only to Tommy, but to those of us living on the twenty-second floor."

I took a breath, one indignant question on my tongue. But she — or at least her script — anticipated it.

"This is not our decision; we cannot influence it. Apart from taking over the important duties such as food, cleaning and laundry for the whole building, the girls on this floor must show subservience and obedience to the women above. It is how Tommy wishes it to be."

What was I supposed to say when she simply referenced his authority like this? I knew well enough that challenging her blind faith wasn't going to get me anywhere.

"Very well," I said, bowing my head slightly.

"Now, please look at the rules."

She indicated another neatly-typed page on the notice-board. I began to read:

RULES FOR TWENTY-FIRST FLOOR SERVANTS

1. Speak only when directly spoken to by Superiors
2. Adhere strictly to the work plan, unless directed otherwise by a Superior
3. The chef is authorized to direct duties and is a Superior
4. Do not argue with or protest any punishments
5. Wear your uniform, neatly presented, at all times except for sleeping
6. Sleep naked
7. No masturbation
8. No sexual activity with other servants, unless under instruction from a Superior

"They are quite simple, I think? Do you have any questions?"

"Yes, who are the 'superiors' exactly? Tommy and those from one floor up, like you just said? Anybody else?"

"Just the chef, as you see on the board. And apart from your fellow servants and these superiors, you will not be seeing anybody else at all. So it's easy."

"How many superior women are there?"

"Apart from myself, there are two more superiors on the next level. You will see soon enough."

"Okay, I think I have it. Thank you."

I was beginning to feel overwhelmed now. I just wanted to get away to my room and let everything sink in. Was that too much to hope for, I wondered?

"Wait, I do have one more question...is anything expected of me tonight?"

"Once we are done with this introduction, no. Not unless there is some special request from upstairs," said Claire matter-of-factly. "Apart from that, regular duties are more or less completed by this time of the evening. You can shower or visit the bathroom any time from now on, provided you don't have duties."

Continuing around the edge of the floor, Claire pointed out the door to the toilet. Then, after passing another couple of sad, empty offices, she opened up what had apparently been made into a storage room. It was full of buckets, mops, rags and rubber gloves. It was also generously stocked with various cleaning chemicals. At the back stood a clothes rail on wheels.

"Everything you need for cleaning anywhere in the building, you will find here," she said. "And you also have a spare uniform hanging there on the rack. The hanger already has your name on it, so you won't confuse it with the others. Clean towels are on the shelf. You will keep replenishing all of this as part of your duties."

"Got it."

New and exciting though all of this was, I just wanted the tour to end now. Something about arriving on a new floor evidently exhausted me.

By now we had advanced all the way around the back of the central island, but it looked like Claire had run out of things to show me. As she led me back towards my cell, I noticed an identical pair of rooms that would back directly onto mine if it weren't for the elevator foyer in between. It was all very symmetrical up here: four rooms in total, meaning space for eight captives. Only one of the beds, however, looked to be in use on this side. So, just as had been the case through most of my stay on the twentieth floor, we weren't operating at full capacity.

But I'd had enough thinking for now. When Claire finally left me at the door to my cell, all I wanted to do was sit down on the bed and switch off for a while.

CHAPTER 13

I'd barely had five minutes to gather my thoughts when the woman I now knew was Andrea peeked her head cautiously around the door.

Suddenly, I was wide awake again.

The notion of being able to talk to another of the women kept captive here was by now so alien to me that I simply didn't dare to open my mouth. She knew more about the protocols up here than I did. She could go first.

"Hello," she said in a timid tone that bordered on the apologetic. You'd almost have thought she was the newbie and I was the incumbent.

"Hi," I replied, keen to be friendly but still afraid of getting in trouble.

"I'm done for the evening...I heard we're going to be roommates. I'm really sorry, I forgot your name already."

"No problem, it's Laura," I said. "You're Andrea, right? Aren't you coming in?"

She gave a nervous little laugh.

"Oh, right, yes, I will! Sorry!"

Strange woman...

"So, we really *are* allowed to talk to each other up here?"

"Yes," she confirmed, sitting down on the bed and smoothing her skirt over her thighs. "It's not a problem here. We have to cooperate. It's not like downstairs in any way, really."

Well, hallelujah for that! So, she'd been kept downstairs just like I had! At long last, here was someone I could compare notes with. Going to bed could wait a little longer after all.

"Aha!" I smiled. "So I guess there's a lot you can tell me…"

Another twitchy little chuckle. She glanced down.

"I…I'll do my best."

I decided it was time to get comfortable. I kicked off the shoes and scooted properly onto the bed. Adopting a cross-legged position, I leaned back against the wall running down the length of the mattress.

Perched on the edge of her bed, Andrea seemed anything but comfortable. She just sat there on her hands, looking lost. Was she just naturally shy around new people, or did she find me intimidating in some way?

"Great," I said, doing my best to put the jittery creature at ease. "Sorry if I'm too bubbly for this time of night. I don't mean to be exhausting. I'm just so excited to have someone to talk to!"

"No, it's fine, really," said Andrea. "I don't mind at all."

"Have you shared with somebody else while you've been up here?"

"No, this is the first time. But you seem…nice."

Her eyes darted up at me just after she said this. But not in a shifty way. It was like she had said something daring and was seeking my approval. I could see that her lack of confidence was genuine. And wasn't that perfectly natural when you'd been kidnapped and abused? Those freaks downstairs had messed with my perception of what was normal and what wasn't.

Not only did Andrea's painful manner reassure me that I hadn't actually lost my mind in recent weeks, but it also put it at ease in another way. No way could this woman be some kind of agent sent by Tommy to catch me in a trap.

"Thanks, I try to be! I'm sure you are too. Where are you from?"

"Chicago."

"Right…well, I'm from right here in New York City. Not sure if 'welcome' is really the right word for this situation though…"

I didn't want to pepper her with too many questions, for fear that she might scurry off and hide herself in a mouse-hole. I hoped she was going to come up with a more constructive response than she had to my last polite inquiry.

"Why…what do you mean?"

"Well…you know! Being held in a building isn't exactly what most visitors to NYC expect when they come here. I'm sorry this happened to you."

She looked up at me and held my gaze for at least a second — a long time in her world. She looked genuinely perplexed.

"But it's…what I wanted. What we all wanted. How do you mean something 'happened' to me…?"

I began to feel a cold, crawling sensation all over my body.

I searched her face for signs that she wasn't being

earnest. But now, as she hooked her hair behind her ears looking like she was awaiting punishment for something, everything made sense. The latest batch downstairs arriving in street clothes. The way Lisa, Sabrina and Tammy had behaved. Everything.

"Okay," I said, now suddenly beyond caring whether my questions were too revealing or invasive. "Tell me straight, Andrea, please. Did you come here of your own free will?"

"I…I…didn't know there was any other way you *could* come here?"

But now something held me back from blurting out the fact that you could, if you struck it unlucky, also land up in this building by getting kidnapped. And that it was quite an unpleasant experience, to say the least. Since it didn't feel like she had it in her to try and tease information out of me, I wasn't going to volunteer any. If I held a different set of cards to the rest, it might be better to keep them close to my chest until I knew more.

"There are other ways," I said in a soft-yet-firm tone that left no room for further interruptions. "But tell me about your experience."

She hesitated, eyes darting nervously, then spilled the beans.

"It's the same as Pála and Anya and the others that were here before," she whispered. "We applied online…"

I was floored. *Online?* But I forced myself to stay cool. I didn't want my tone of voice to remind her of the fact that this was enormous news to me.

"Ah, right," I replied, trying to sound casual whilst my stomach turned cartwheels. "Which site?"

"You…you really don't know, do you?"

I shook my head, willing her to go on.

"There's a platform on the dark web, especially for people who…want to be slaves."

I could tell she was wrestling with embarrassment at this revelation.

Don't act shocked or judgemental, Laura!

"I'm surprised there's only one," I smiled at her.

She smiled back, a little more confidently this time. I sensed she would continue to talk.

"Well…there's only one that is…reputable. It's called Endgame. You have to pay a large amount to join, and the privacy they offer is total. Every member is *serious* about what they are doing."

"Like Tommy," I murmured.

"Exactly…on Endgame, it's all or nothing. It's not just for a little bit of fetish play…it's for people who want to completely and totally give themselves up, you know?"

I nodded, trying to look like someone who had conversations about this sort of thing all the time. I knew she needed my reassurance to keep talking. I felt overwhelmed — a little queasy, even — but who knew if I'd get another opportunity to learn so much? For all I knew, I might be snatched out of here and thrown back into that threadbare office two floors down at any moment.

"And those people find exactly the right counterparts via the platform, I guess?"

"Yes, they even run auctions for slaves that already have owners."

"Christ," I said, despite myself. "I see why it's on the dark web."

She swallowed hard.

"Yeah…it's easier that way. I mean, everything is done with legal contracts and people sign consent. I've heard it was originally developed by a lawyer with an interest in this sort of thing, in fact. But still…some agencies in some places might ask a lot of questions."

She was right on that point.

"So you went on this Endgame platform in Chicago…? What were you doing before?"

"Oh…I was Chief Operating Officer at one of the *big* companies. I can't say which one, but you'd know it. I was promoted into this really high-powered position, but when I got there, there was so much to deal with. The work was relentless. Emails at three in the morning. That kind of thing."

She was getting onto a roll with her story at last.

"Sure, everybody respected me and I did a good job…but it was such a battle. After three years, I realized I just…*didn't want it*. I started fooling around on the dark web, just looking for an online escape at first. Then I stumbled across this opportunity to disappear for real, at least for a while. Not to have to make any more decisions. And now…here I am."

"Here you are," I nodded thoughtfully. "Here *we* are."

I *knew* I'd seen something of myself in Andrea. And now I'd found it: a broken, middle-aged, female C-Level at a large, evil corporation. Maybe it was a bank, maybe a consultancy. Or perhaps even a shipping giant.

We were the same, me and Andrea. Except for one tiny detail, of course: she had come here by choice and I hadn't.

That night, tucked into a real bed for the first time in almost a month, I dreamt hard. I was in some kind of restored castle, perched on the shores of a Scottish loch. My hands were cuffed behind my back. I was naked, shivering, and standing in a circle with a dozen other women. We all wore leather collars — where had *that* come from? — each connected to the next by a cool, drooping chain. Facing outward from the center, each of us had a turn to be rotated into the firelight. Once there, a larger-than-life Tommy would begin taking bids on each girl. I couldn't see the bidders, they were hiding in the shadows. My memory blurred after that, but the deeply obscene cat-calls stood out. I woke up sweating, the wolf-whistles screeching in my ears.

A little something in Andrea's story had evidently resonated with me.

I hadn't pushed her for any further information the previous evening, fearful that she might turn the quiz around. But, as I'd hoped, she hadn't shown any initiative. Clearly taking charge wasn't her thing — at least not in here. Yet she must have had *some* kind of backbone to make it as far as she did in the business world. I doubled down on my resolve not to lose mine.

And I wouldn't let it happen. I was a 'special case', after all — and now I knew exactly what that meant. And being that kind of exception only gave me extra motivation to resist.

But I still couldn't believe what I'd heard from Andrea. These women had wilfully sought out a platform on the dark web — a place of which I knew nothing — where they could give themselves up in the most extreme, all-encompassing, comprehensive way possible. There really *was* no limit to human depravity, was there?

Meanwhile, I had a new life to ease into. My first full

day began with an automated alarm bell that sounded throughout the floor, though I'd been awake for some time already when it rang. Andrea was quick to rise. For a moment I was startled to see naked breasts and midriff emerging as she peeled back the covers — but then I remembered I was in exactly the same state of undress. I was evidently getting better at going with the flow.

"Morning," I said, stretching my arms above my head and respectfully looking at the ceiling until she'd found her uniform and wriggled into it. "What are you down for today?"

"I have to help the chef with breakfast," she said, flashing me a worried glance. "I've got to get there fast, otherwise…"

I raised my eyebrows.

"Otherwise?"

"There'll be a punishment. He's very strict."

Her very tone sounded like it was cowering. If Andrea had sought out a submissive life here, then nobody could say she wasn't living it to the full.

"I should have checked what I'm down for," I mused, shaking a leg.

"I don't think there's anything for you till after breakfast," she said. "I remember seeing your name on the sheet. You've got a bit more time."

I nodded and wished her luck as she left our cell. Then I sat up on the bed, looked at the uniform I was about to put on, and slowly shook my head. Was any of this *actually* happening?

I pulled myself together and got dressed. Feeling neat and well-presented, if nothing much else, I walked around to where the noticeboard hung. It was terrific to see real daylight again. There was a grayish, overcast quality to the day peeking in through the windows of the scattered perimeter offices, but I didn't care about that. Any natural light was a blessing after my prolonged stay on the twentieth floor.

The next thing to hit me was the clock on the wall: it read six-thirty. Wow, it was *early*! Just like good old times... well, old times at least. Still, I found getting up for work strangely comforting; like I'd been given one tiny part of a normal life back.

That, and the fact that I was actually free to walk around on my own. It was hard to get my head around that. I kept on thinking I'd got it wrong and Tommy or Claire was about to come running after me. I kept on looking over my shoulder. But then I saw a woman emerge from the shower room. She had no escort either. I was good!

This had to be Anya. She was wrapped up in a large white towel. Her hair, the color of straw, was damp and straggly. She had noble features and sharp eyes. Noticing me, she gave me a nod and an awkward hello, then scurried off towards her cell. It all felt a little bit first-day-of-school.

The work timetable revealed that I would be on laundry duty following breakfast, wash up in the kitchen after lunch, then move on to scrubbing the bathroom before another round of dishwashing after dinner. No excursions to other floors on the first day, then. But I would be exploring the upper echelons soon enough.

CHAPTER 14

*D*ay one on the twenty-first floor passed without incident.

Sensibly, I'd been paired with one of the other girls for each of my duty periods, so I always had someone to show me the ropes. Working with Anya, I began my early laundry shift by throwing linen into the machines. Then we moved on to hand-washing lingerie — including the red and pink kits last seen adorning the lithe bodies of Tammy and Sabrina respectively. Where were those two now? Andrea had helped me solve the mystery of how they'd landed up in the building in the first place, but I wasn't clear on whether they might still be on the premises.

The mindless work we were doing offered me plenty of chances to seek out further information from my colleagues. But now, having heard the biggest revelation of all from Andrea, I proceeded with caution. I could now pretend I was here for exactly the same reasons the other girls were, and wait for useful little pieces of information to tumble out of their mouths. Time was on my side.

Anya was Russian, but she had been living in Greensboro for a good few years before landing up in this bizarre establishment. Her accent was a sweet mix of Slavic and American. She was friendly enough — and not as jumpy as Andrea — but certainly not bubbly either. I couldn't imagine either of them touching themselves whilst longingly staring down some sex act in the next room. Did people change in some way when they graduated up here? Was it something to do with the uniforms, the manual labor and the austere atmosphere?

"How long were you on the floor down below?" I asked.

"Who knows for sure?" she said, scrubbing away at one of the heavy-duty bras that went with the dress code here on the twenty-first. "I guess it was two or three weeks, maybe?"

"It's quite different up here, isn't it? I mean…it seemed to be all about sex down there, in a way."

"Yes, it's not so much like there here," she shrugged. "But we are here to serve in any way that Tommy needs, aren't we?"

I could feel my mouth tighten and my nose twitch. I'd waited all this time for a chance to talk to the others, only to find I was surrounded by Claire clones! But why should I be surprised?

I could see that playing along with the robotic pandering was the only smart option. Not just in terms of keeping a low profile, but also for getting information. I'd already let on to Andrea that I was somehow different, but having learned some key truths from her, I wasn't in any hurry to talk about myself more than necessary.

"Yes, of course. It's just a sudden change. But it's really good to have something to do."

"It is," she agreed. "We're helping in a useful way here."

"And we *did* sign away complete control, so we go with it."

I held my breath, suddenly doubting Andrea's explosive revelations.

"Of course," she replied, as if I'd said something wholly self-evident.

In my head, I let out a massive sigh of relief.

"I was wondering, though…did Pála and Andrea come up here at the same time as you did?"

"I came up with Pála, but Andrea was only brought up later. She was already on the twentieth floor when we arrived in the building, and ended up staying there longer."

So it was confirmed: the twentieth floor was indeed the first port of call for the 'regular' intake. My solo cell on the nineteenth must have been a makeshift measure for the lucky one that got kidnapped. Was that so Tommy could try to break down my will without an audience? One that would see for sure that the dynamic between him and me wasn't quite like the one you get in a consent situation?

But if he was concerned about the others knowing that I'd been brought here without my consent, then why had he allowed me to come up here to this floor, where I could talk freely with them? It was only by my own choice that I hadn't spilled the beans about my capture, after all. Did he think they were so dopily subservient that the news that Tommy was a criminal wouldn't bother them?

Well, maybe he was right about that.

"I'm hoping my ex-neighbor Lisa comes up here soon," I said, careful to mix up plenty of leading statements with direct questions. Being a lawyer involved in high-level negotiations on a regular basis, I knew a thing or two about getting information out of people without giving too much away. I could already see those skills were going to come in handy now that talking was allowed.

"She might," shrugged Anya. "What did you think of her performance and her spirit? I know you can't *hear* anything down there, but you can see…"

I could guess what she was getting at.

"Er…yes, I would have given her full marks! It was sexy watching her. I like her, and I'm sure Tommy enjoys her as well."

"Then her chances should be good. But the competition is tough, of course. I guess it can come down to all kinds of things."

Wait, what was she talking about now? It was beginning to sound like graduation from the twentieth floor to the twenty-first wasn't a given. This was obviously something I was already supposed to know. But I hadn't gone through the application process she had — and I wanted to keep her in the dark about that for now.

I'd go with another casual statement and see what came of it.

"There were three of us most of the time I was down there," I volunteered. "Apart from Lisa, there was also a really tall girl called Tammy, and a Hispanic woman, Sabrina. But they were gone before I was brought up here. And I think we've just washed their bras and panties."

"Uh-huh? Well, they haven't been up here. So I guess they didn't make it. They were probably let go."

"Hmm, why wouldn't they make it?" I mused innocently.

She shrugged again.

"Some girls aren't as obedient as they imagine. It's easy enough to be a slave when you're sitting in front of a computer and you're in an internet fantasy. But then they find the reality too tough."

She snorted and shook her head as she said this. Then she resumed her numbing duty with what looked a lot like relish.

∼

Pála was from Iceland, of all places. Apart from being quite strikingly beautiful, she was quiet and stoic. She wasn't bitchy, but I quickly figured out that she wasn't going to be my best source of information either. She didn't seem bothered about saying more than was necessary to get tasks done, and was completely untroubled by silence. Whether that was Tommy's sorcery, the Scandinavian way or both, I couldn't be entirely sure. But I could tell that she was fundamentally on the same page as the other two up here. Service was a calling to be cherished. Even if it involved getting down on your hands and knees and scrubbing the shower tiles.

So much for my companions. It would be an overstatement to say I was surrounded by zombies, but not a million miles from the truth either. I hoped and prayed Lisa would be promoted here sooner or later. She'd seemed like a fun, bubbly girl — and one whom I'd already gotten to know far more intimately than this crowd.

Then again, I'd seen the rules. If Lisa made it up to this story, we'd have to restrain ourselves. I still took it as read that we were being watched, one way or another.

And what of the man in our midst? The chef, evidently an external day worker like Sandra downstairs, introduced himself to me as I entered the kitchen with Andrea for washing-up duty after lunch. He was almost bald, with little more than stubble covering his scalp. This seeped into bristles of a darker tint around his chin and jawline.

Though he wasn't big in stature, his biceps and forearms looked like those of a boxer. There was no trace of a belly behind his apron, and I strongly suspected he had abs of steel. But I certainly wasn't going to poke him in the stomach to find out — he had an intimidating air about him. And, as the noticeboard had made clear, he was also a 'Superior'.

"You must be Laura," he said with a curt nod. "I'm Simon. I'm here three times a day to take charge of the cooking. I believe you'll be giving me a hand tomorrow. I hope you're not going to be as clumsy as your friend Andrea over here."

I dared not glance across at my roommate, who naturally suffered the insult in silence.

"I hope the same," I replied, assuming the situation qualified as being 'spoken to by a superior'.

"Good, then I'll leave you two to clean up. I've got no reason to hang around here any longer tonight."

I looked Andrea in the eye once he'd gone out of the door. But she only met mine for a moment before dropping her gaze to the floor. She looked weak, defeated and hopeless.

Just what was this chef capable of apart from cooking, I wondered?

CHAPTER 15

I got a swift answer to the chef question the following morning.

When I walked into the kitchen, it already looked quite different from the tranquil oasis in which Andrea and I had washed up the night before. Heat was on the rise, and I could hear something bubbling. Simon was already bustling around, metal clanging on metal as he did several things at once with utensils and pots.

I didn't have the benefit of another girl to guide me this time. But I guessed that was because Simon would be more than happy to take control of proceedings.

He seemed to sense my arrival, not even turning from what he was doing before he began to issue commands.

"Come here and stir this pot," he said in a tone that left no room for negotiation as he beckoned me over to the stove. "Here's the wooden spoon. I trust you know what porridge is supposed to look like? Don't let it stick to the bottom. Tell me if anything doesn't seem right, got it?"

Though it didn't sound like a difficult assignment, the nod I gave him was a nervous one. He had a way of making me feel like a scared little schoolgirl — and the uniform I was wearing only exaggerated that effect.

Helping to prepare breakfast was weird enough without Simon's abrupt manner. In some small way, I felt like I was now on the 'other side'. If not exactly poacher turned gamekeeper, I was playing an active role in the running of this bizarre prison. The thought that the other 'prisoners' were in fact there on a voluntary basis eased my conscience somewhat, but part of me still felt like a traitor. People were going to have to eat this meal on the floor like animals. It was just *wrong*!

But they wanted that, Laura. They paid *for it.*

So I was distracted when Anya presented herself to pick up some breakfasts for delivery.

"Get two trays ready, Laura," barked Simon. "The ladies upstairs are hungry. Move it!"

I looked around the room in a panic. Trays...how should I know where those were? Ah yes — I'd helped wipe them down the previous day! We'd stacked them right beneath the big sink.

Trembling, I walked across to fetch them, watching Simon for any sudden movements. He'd been scooting back and forth across the kitchen area the whole time I'd been there, apparently preparing multiple meals. Bacon was frying, eggs were being poached and sauce hollandaise was being stirred. I could see an accident coming if he spun around to grab something in a hurry.

I picked up two trays and brought them over to the large, empty surface beyond which Anya was waiting. Then

I hurried back to my porridge pot, wary of leaving it alone for more than a couple of seconds.

"Now I need two big plates."

I knew exactly which shelf the plates were on too. I thanked my lucky stars that I had an eye for detail — and that I'd paid attention the day before. This chef did not seem the forgiving type.

I returned to hover near him, uncertain how to proceed.

"I have the two plates," I said.

"Good, give me one of them," he said, gruff as a grumpy grizzly. "And keep watching that porridge."

The fact that he still knew what I was supposed to be doing whilst occupied with so many tasks of his own only made me shakier. His presence seemed to swell as he spoke.

I held out a plate with my left hand. He grabbed it without even needing to look. His confidence and his ability to multitask were daunting. I got the feeling he *never* made mistakes. Which made me fear a fumble of my own all the more.

With one hand now free, I reached back and used it to stir my pot. The second plate remained in my right hand, ready to hand to him when he needed it. Right now he was constructing what looked like a gourmet breakfast of eggs benedict, crispy bacon and fried tomatoes. He grabbed some sprigs of chive and parsley from a container, then sprinkled it over the food. His hands working on fast-forward, he then added two understated slices of what looked like sourdough toast. Only now did I notice the toasting grill he'd apparently found time to keep an eye on whilst cooking everything else.

In a blur of activity and with minimal help, Simon had

created something worthy of any respectable restaurant kitchen.

So, this was how the women on the twenty-second floor dined? My curiosity to visit it was running riot already. But right now, it seemed that privilege would fall to Anya. Simon passed me the laden plate, his hand hovering there for the next one. I gave it to him with utmost care, only letting go of my grip once I was certain his fingers had clasped around it. Then I turned to place the full plate on a tray.

Anya was waiting patiently behind the counter. I caught her eye for a second, but something in her look told me now wasn't a good moment to try and chat. Then she left the room with the first tray.

I returned to my porridge whilst Simon busied himself with his next work of art. I assumed this huge pot was breakfast for the sex slaves below, and probably for us worker bees as well. Like everything we'd been fed since getting here, it was good, hearty food. But certainly not in the same league as what I'd just seen heading for the floor above.

Once we'd sent the second five-star breakfast plate on its way, Claire appeared. Unobtrusive as always, I might not even have noticed her arrival if it hadn't been for the bright red of the loose blouse she wore. Simon had his back turned to the door as he bent over his work, but seemed to have a sixth sense for the presence of an expectant waitress.

"How many do we have today, gorgeous?"

I gathered the chef's flattering words were for Claire, not me.

"We are full downstairs," she replied, with just a hint of a purr in her tone. "Six breakfasts."

"You heard the lady, Laura," he said. "Six slaves to feed down below. Bowls are on the shelf over there. Grab a ladle and serve up."

Okay, I could do that.

Feeling Claire's eyes following my movements, I went to the shelf, watchfully took up six bowls, then placed them on the counter next to my bubbling pot. I sourced a ladle easily enough, filled the bowls one by one, then turned towards the serving area.

Claire had stacked six trays in a pile.

"You can put all the bowls on the top tray," she said. "I will divide them downstairs."

"Of course," I said, somehow more wary than usual around her as well. Maybe it was just the vibes Simon was putting into the room. But there was also that weird new rule about deference to the women from upstairs.

And then it happened.

As I put the last of the bowls down, with very little space left on the tray, my knuckle caught the edge of its neighboring portion. I couldn't react fast enough to prevent it from toppling over. As boiling porridge splashed onto the back of my hand, I instinctively yanked it up and out of the way. In turn, this sent several flecks of the stuff flying through the air.

And, as fate would have it, these landed squarely on Claire's rosy red blouse, right across her slender midriff.

I cringed.

"I'm…I'm so sorry, Claire…it was just so hot, I reacted automatically…"

But she didn't have to get mad at me — because Simon did it for her. I heard a deep, resigned intake of breath behind me. Then he growled.

"*What* has she done?"

Now I froze, terrified. I could feel that he had turned around by now, and could see perfectly well what had transpired.

"For *fuck's* sake! She's lost a bowl! And look at your top! Is that *respect?*" His voice was like thunder now. "Answer me, Laura: is that *respect?*"

"No," I whimpered, turning sideways to him and hanging my head. "I'm sorry. It was an accident."

Neither that fact nor my apology seemed to appease him in the slightest.

"Well, I'm *fucking* tired of hearing that," he roared. "You servants need to learn to pay attention, it's as simple as that. Claire, shall I deal with her right away or finish making your breakfast?"

I was trembling all over now.

"Let's finish first," she replied immediately, with no apparent malice in her voice. It sounded like she was keeping things on an even keel as usual.

"Fine," said Simon. "I'm almost done with your breakfast. She serves that bowl again, then you take it downstairs. And I'll be done with your meal by the time you get back up here."

"*Bon,*" said Claire once again. "Please finish, Laura. I will be back in a moment."

And then she whipped off her stained top, exposing the inevitable white bra and sculpted torso. She looked less than untroubled by having to do this as a result of my clumsiness. Then she left the kitchen, presumably to dump her blouse in the laundry room. With shaking hands, I cautiously re-filled the bowl I'd knocked over. I found some kitchen paper and wiped the worst of the mess off the tray.

All the while, the words 'deal with her' seemed to echo around me. I could sense the steam coming out of Simon's ears behind my back. The sizzle of the bacon and the bubble of the egg-water paled in comparison. My heart was pulsing in my throat as Claire came back and took the tray.

We plated up Claire's breakfast in brooding, pregnant silence, then set it on another tray, ready for her return. Seemingly done with breakfast service at last, Simon wiped his hands on his apron.

There was no doubt he was going to 'deal with me' now.

I gulped as he went over to the pot in which the wooden spoons were kept. He selected one of the chunkier specimens, with a nasty kind of intent that I wouldn't have associated with cooking. The spoon's wood was dark and it had three long slits cut into its center.

I began to quiver.

"Okay, I don't need to explain what you did wrong," he said with menacing calm. "Put your hands on the edge of that serving counter. Make sure that breakfast tray is *well* away from you."

I did as he ordered. Despite the heat that had risen in the room, both from Simon's rage and all the cooking he'd done, the metal surface felt cool beneath my palms.

"Now take a step back, but keep your hands where they are."

Obeying his command put me into a bending position.

My senses were on full alert. I became keenly aware of the dampness in the air and the sweet smell of perfectly crisped bacon.

Then I flinched as the chef grasped the hem of my skirt with his hand, his knuckles kissing the back of my right thigh for a moment. I could feel my unattractive underwear

143

exposed as his powerful fingers tucked it into the belt. I could feel a tightening there, and knew there was no chance of the skirt falling down of its own accord. It was securely stowed.

Next, Simon seized the broad strip of my panties and jerked it up towards my spine. As this part of my underwear disappeared into the furrow of my butt cheeks, I knew they were now as good as bare.

Simon was evidently not a man to hang around when he had set his mind on something. With barely a moment's delay, I heard a swish of air behind me. A fraction of a second later, a loud cracking sound.

There was a tiny pause before I felt the pain on my left butt cheek. It started like a harmless pinch, but then it welled and welled, like someone was holding a hot iron there and refusing to let it go. And just as it reached its zenith, and I instinctively knew it was on the verge of subsiding, the first smack on the right side landed.

A new agony unfurling whilst the first released its grip with tortuous languor was enough to bring the tears.

I shuddered with sobs as he continued to hammer out this alternating beat. Left. Right. Left. Right. His rhythm was calculated to perfection, a new sting landing every time the last promised to lose its edge.

It was sheer torment. But what could I do apart from take it? I could hope to outsmart Tommy and his cronies — but brainpower wasn't going to help me here. I knew I could never be a match for a thick-set man with a weapon.

After several vicious strokes on each side, I noticed Claire returning to the room, still dressed in only her jeans and bra. As far as I could tell from the quick glance I took with my tear-drenched eyes, she looked mildly interested in proceedings. Ignoring the tray we'd set for her, she walked around behind me and joined Simon.

The moment she was by his side, he seemed to step up a gear. Then, just when I didn't think I could handle anything more and began wondering if begging for mercy could win me a reprieve, he moved to the backs of my thighs.

I wanted to howl as the first blows landed. Though the two spots on my butt that were billowing with red-hot pain were now spared, the distress on my legs was even sharper. But at least he was working his way down each side, rather than digging the same furrow deeper and deeper.

I'd known all along that a moment like this could come, though I'd never thought anybody but Tommy would have been the one issuing the pain. Now that the time was actually here, my strategy of playing a long game didn't seem so smart anymore. If punishment like this was going to be a regular thing, patience might not be an option.

But I was hanging on for now.

I didn't hear a word exchanged between the pair behind me as the lashing on my legs continued. But I could imagine Claire standing there, watching the beating as though it were a perfectly acceptable part of the world she lived in. Which for her, of course, it was.

Then, with one final crack and not a word of warning, it was over.

"I think that will do for today," declared Simon. "It should switch her on for next time, though I'm not getting my hopes up. Honestly, Claire, I don't know where you guys find some of these women. I'll do my best to set them straight, though, of course. As always."

I didn't care about the insults. The only thing that mattered was that he'd announced we were done. If Claire said anything in reply to Simon, I missed it as my body took stock of the damage. Sniffing and panting as I tried and failed to wriggle out of the lingering pain, it certainly didn't cross my mind to move.

While trying to recover and return to my senses, I was vaguely aware of Claire walking around to the front of the counter and gathering up her breakfast tray. She'd be taking it upstairs to eat in peace, I supposed.

Then Simon released my skirt. Even the hem hitting the back of my thighs felt like a cruel little aftershock.

I waited for the sweet release of dismissal from the room.

"Come on, stand up! You're not done yet. You think your colleagues should miss out on breakfast because of your misdemeanors, huh?"

"No, of course not," I said as I straightened up, choking back another round of tears.

"So serve up porridge for yourselves, then get out of my sight."

I couldn't *believe* he was making me continue work after what I'd just been through. My legs were in shock and I could hardly stand. The least he could do was let me run back to my room and collapse. This sadistic twist felt like the cruelest part of the whole ordeal.

Even though it still felt like I'd been attacked by a thousand bees, I robotically carried out my orders. I had no interest in eating any time soon, so I just dished up three bowls of porridge for the other girls on my floor. Then I took them through to our small dining room on a tray.

As each of them thanked me, I got the feeling they knew what had just happened. They could see it from my tear-stained face if nothing else. Though I felt they were on my side right now, I still didn't want to be with anyone.

Then I ran to my room and lay down on my bed in the only way I could without searing pain: curled up on my side.

CHAPTER 16

"*H*e did *that* to you?"

Andrea nodded as I contemplated the foul, ugly marks she was revealing. A stormy sunset of purple and black. It was a hideous testament to a punishment she'd taken across her backside two days before my arrival on the twenty-first floor.

"Okay, okay…I've seen enough!"

She let her skirt hem fall back into place and turned to face me once again. She'd found me here in fetal recovery mode after finishing her breakfast.

"What did he use?" she asked.

"A big wooden spoon."

She nodded, biting one half of her lower lip as if there was something she didn't want to tell me.

"He has…other things too."

"Worse things?"

Andrea nodded again, clearly uncomfortable at being the one to have to make this revelation.

I said nothing, just stared vacantly at the wall. I wanted to know and I didn't want to know.

"Do you want some...ointment?" she volunteered. "It's a really good idea."

"I didn't know we had any. But yes please!"

"There's some in our bathroom cabinets. I'll get it for you and rub it in, if you don't mind? We've got a few minutes before morning chores begin."

Ah, of course. More chores. No rest for the wicked. I rolled my eyes.

A couple of minutes later, I was lying stomach-down on my bed, my panties down around my ankles and my skirt hitched up once again. Andrea was massaging something cool and soothing across my buttocks and thighs. As the balm seeped into my tortured skin, I felt something like a will to live make a reappearance.

"Awww, thanks, this was a good idea! It feels almost...nice!"

"Any time," said my roommate. "We have to take care of each other when things like this happen."

"I hope it won't be too often though," I said. "I think I've got my limits when it comes to this stuff. If he keeps doing that, I'll snap."

"I also thought that after my first time," she said, wiping her hands on a piece of tissue. "But it grows on you."

With my face still pressed into my pillow, I was free to raise my eyebrows at this without Andrea noticing.

I'd done well to avoid the topic of my unusual status since our first conversation, and so far it seemed she was either too forgetful or too shy to pursue it once again. Probably the latter: timid creatures like her probably didn't feel it was their place to inquire. If I was here, then it could only be with Tommy's blessing. In which case, why would she question my presence any further? For her, after all, anything was good in a world where Tommy called the shots.

But...*it grows on you.*

I knew what BDSM was and I understood that Tommy and his ilk got their kicks from it. I'd seen enough evidence of that before today. But I'd always thought it was something the women involved merely endured, out of devotion or a keenness to please. But now, this remark from Andrea. Did some part of her genuinely get off on the beating? Did *all* of them get off on it?

Maybe they did. But I couldn't agree with her that it would happen to me too. I'd tried a few things back in my heyday, but this wasn't one of them. Getting thrashed had never appealed. I wasn't going to learn to like being savaged by the chef. Especially if he was planning on upgrading to more powerful weapons the next time I made an innocent mistake.

And yet, as I tripped through a fitful sleep that night, I dreamed of unknown men taking turns to cane me in a shadowy room. And I was awake well before the alarm call, itching to touch myself.

The next morning, after my shower, I caught sight of my wounds in the full-length mirror for the first time. They shocked me and surprised me in equal measure.

I was shocked by their raw, evil appearance. And taken aback by how large the abused area actually was. I thought Simon had concentrated on the same spots with every blow on my butt cheeks? Now I had my doubts about what my senses had told me in the moment.

But I was surprised — and almost pleasantly so — by the fact that they looked as mean as they did. Now a very dark red, they appeared to be on track to catch up to the marks Andrea had shown me. I'd been assuming she'd endured something far more fearsome than I had — but these ever-darkening bruises suggested I'd at least been playing in the same ballpark. That was good news on some level.

The war in my mind took on a new intensity as I dried myself down and began to step into my uniform. On the twentieth floor, I'd survived monotony and mild discomfort by keeping my eye on the short-term sexual attentions with which I was provided. My disdain for my prison and its keepers had been relatively measured in comparison to my first days in solitary confinement — but so too had been the lustful moments. With the prominent exception that was the hard, repeated fucking I'd experienced in the darkroom.

Now, contemplating the wilful damage that had been done to my body, I could feel an indignation and a hatred I hadn't known since the first hours after I'd been dragged into this building. And it was Tommy in the crosshairs of these emotions, not Simon. I knew who the ringleader was. To my mind, it was the Scotsman who had ultimately beaten me.

But there was a flip side to it as well. Something new. Something with a keener edge. I felt it in my stomach as I sealed up my mundane outfit and twirled to examine the rear view in the mirror. The marks of my punishment clearly extended beyond the bottom of my skirt. Anyone who happened to walk behind me would have no doubt as to who had been a naughty girl and how she had been dealt with.

I tried to keep myself from thinking those thoughts. Tommy didn't deserve them, not for one second. It was one thing to get on board with the sex demands, but quite another to give a tacit green light for this kind of violence. I would *not* let this 'grow on me'.

Yet as I went about my business that morning, my emotions continued to swing this way and that.

Then, after lunch, I got my first glimpse of the floor above.

Claire and I made the short elevator journey there in what felt to me like awkward silence following my *faux pas* at breakfast the day before. But she hadn't mentioned the incident and might easily have forgotten it already for all I knew.

And when the doors opened to reveal the lush new world that was the twenty-second floor, my mind suddenly had better things to think about.

"This is where the marked ones live," she said matter-of-factly. "Come, I will show you the toilet you have to clean today."

What she'd said about being 'marked' came flooding back to me. I hadn't been able to make sense of it then, all that time ago, but now she'd revealed that it was a sign that you lived on the twenty-second floor. Which, at first glance, looked a lot like a life worth living.

Instead of the usual foyer, the elevator opened directly onto a bright, smart open plan. Here, for the first time, I saw coherent decor and design harmony. The soft cream carpet was devilishly inviting. While the daylight was more than enough right now, free-standing lamps were there to provide illumination when necessary. Elaborate, vibrant plants — small trees, really — stood in corners, adding the first touches of greenery I'd seen in weeks. Every room seemed to have a purpose, too: not an abandoned office in sight.

The first thing I really noticed, though, was the array of glass-fronted rooms directly ahead of me. Three of them. With floor-to-ceiling windows and transparent partitions to their neighbors, they were effectively 360-degree fish-bowls. What else could these be but a place to wash?

But these were not the functional washrooms I had come to know on the lower floors. Covered in large tiles the color of dark stone, they were straight from the pages of an interior design quarterly costing $20 a copy. The quartet of showerheads were fixed to the ceiling. Set in a square formation around the middle of the room, they were of the wide, generous kind that created a rain effect. A low, tiled wall in the middle of the room held the silver-and-brass taps and a variety of other water-gushing installations. And, neatly lined up along its top, a large array of bottles. You could tell from a distance that they hadn't come from the discount shelf at the local drugstore.

But it looked like the women up here were also allowed to indulge in something even more luxurious than a shower with a sweeping view of NYC. Because the rooms on either side of the central one looked to contain full-body bathing installations. I guess you could call the one on the left a wide tub and the one on the right a jacuzzi. Both were set up to face the city skyline; both had what looked like a minibar fridge within reach of the tub; both had free-stand-ing, heated towel rails in equally easy grabbing distance.

There was no doubt about it: I had penetrated the lair of

Tommy's elite. Even if only as a maidservant armed with a mop, bucket, rags and other tools of the trade.

"Wow," I said in a low tone, unable to entirely cut out a note of envy in my tone. "Not bad!"

"Please don't speak unless I speak to you," said Claire politely. "Remember the rules, particularly when you are up here. Otherwise, I will have no choice but to inform Tommy."

I nodded. I'd clean forgotten. And it was easily done with Claire, because until now there had never been any hard-and-fast rules where she was concerned.

More than that, she didn't exude dominance or authority. I'd never been afraid of her. But she *was* in a position to 'inform' Tommy about anything she liked — and that gave her clout.

I hadn't seen the man once since being moved up to the twenty-first floor. And I got the distinct impression he kept his distance from those of us who called it home. There hadn't been any visits from masked strangers either. In fact, the only man we'd had any contact with on our level was Simon. The thought crossed my mind that the only way to access Tommy at the moment might be via a misdemeanor. I filed it away.

We took a left turn from the elevator, passing the open doors to what at a glance looked like bedrooms. I longed to take a look inside. I was desperate to know what the other two 'marked ones' looked like. Were all the women up here petite and blonde like Claire?

It only took a moment for me to learn part of the answer. After we passed the second room, we came to a cozy alcove. It was lined with bookshelves on three sides. A pair of suede armchairs loaded with cushions, each with its own reading lamp standing sentinel, completed the picture. It was the perfect little library.

And there, standing with her back to us as she examined books, was another of the chosen ones. And she was neither tiny nor blonde. In fact, her long, straight hair was black as pitch. It shone with vigor — no doubt nourished by all those exclusive products I'd seen in the bathroom.

Sensing our presence, she turned around. She smiled, revealing a perfect set of teeth nestling in a wide mouth.

"Ah, Kimiko," said Claire. "You can carry on with your browsing. It's just another new servant."

Kimiko? That name could only be Japanese.

She was beautiful as only the women of her country could be. Classic perfection. But she was certainly taller than average. Her figure-hugging black dress, complete with high heels, only exaggerated the effect.

"Well, it's always interesting to see them," she said, continuing to smile. And now she was looking me in the eye. "Another pretty one, I must say."

I blushed despite myself. Remembering that I wasn't supposed to talk, I tried my best to thank her with my eyes.

"This is our erotica library," explained Claire. "You'll be dusting the shelves here at some point, I am sure. But the books are only for the residents of this floor, as of course you understand."

I nodded, a ripple of thrill running down my spine. A private, residents-only erotica library? *Hot. As. Hell.* Maybe a little more so because it was forbidden to me. That, and the fact that I'd been longing for something to read for a matter of weeks now.

"Some new books have come in, Claire," she said, her accent marked but her English perfect. "*Escort in Training* is here at last! I'm stealing it first but you can have it after," she winked.

"*Naturellement*," Claire replied. "I look forward to that. It sounds like a very unique story. But now I must take Laura onwards."

She led me further around the floor. The next thing we passed was something akin to a series of museum display cabinets. Solid walls behind but glass at the front. I didn't get a good look as we walked past, but couldn't help noticing a few touches. One of these miniature rooms was dominated by two pieces of wood attached to the wall at the back, in such a way that they formed an X roughly the size of a person. Others featured leather cuffs or metallic buckles, some fixed to the wall by chains and others screwed into place.

Claire chose not to tell me anything about these installations. We then passed what she pointed out as the hair and makeup room. Finally, we arrived at a door in the corner of the open plan.

"The toilet is here," she declared. "Please, go inside."

She followed me into the room. Inside, beyond a pair of broad sinks, it was further divided into two stalls split by a solid wall. Each looked spacious, with light brown mosaic tiles dotting the floor. The plumbing must have been integrated into the wood paneling behind the bowl and seat.

"Your duty today will be to thoroughly clean all surfaces in this room. Obviously, scrub the toilets first. These must be *completely* spotless. You have all the materials you need, and rubber gloves which you may use. When you have done this, and the sinks, you will mop the floor, then polish it by hand so that it is dry and safe for the marked ones. Do you have any questions?"

I took this as permission to speak. A chance I wanted to take, now that she had piqued my curiosity once more. Something was nagging at me.

"Just one, if I may? Although it's not about the cleaning, exactly."

She gave me a look that bordered on the sympathetic. Though she was going through her motions as always, I was starting to think she was in a relatively relaxed mood today.

"Go ahead, what is it?"

"You talk about being 'marked'. I'm just really, really curious. Where exactly are your markings?"

"Ah," she said, raising her eyebrows. "That's a good question."

She thought for a moment, then did something I would never, ever have expected. She beckoned me into one of the stalls.

"Come, I will show you," she said. "Close the door."

She put down the top seat of the toilet, then began to unbutton her jeans. I held my breath as she pulled them off, amazed at how forthcoming she was being right now. Then, in just her lacy white panties and a black t-shirt that no doubt had a white bra beneath it, she sat on top of the toilet and stretched her toes out towards me.

"Pull down my panties," she said.

I put down the bucket and mop I'd been carrying, got down on my knees and obeyed. She lifted her tiny butt just enough for me to get a grip and pull. As her feet slipped through the holes and I placed the garment on the jeans she'd thrown on the floor, she brought her heels up to the edges of the toilet seat and leaned back slightly. As her legs fell open, I could see *everything*.

At first, nothing struck me in particular. Then she

pointed her forefinger to the very top of her vagina, to the skin just north of the hood covering her clitoris. It was the tiniest of tattoos. A galloping horse, its body just a fraction of an inch above the epicenter of female desire. Its flying hooves, meanwhile, actually flanked the clit itself.

Yet the stallion — it *had* to be a stallion — still displayed tone and texture. You could see its muscles flexing and the hairs of its mane rippling in the wind as it ran. The precision that must have gone into this thing blew my mind. It had to have taken a master artist, a very long time and a great deal of restraint from Claire.

"This is how we are marked," she said.

"It's *incredible*," I murmured, assuming my right to speak still applied. I had to force myself to tear my eyes away from the thing. "And it's permanent?"

I was pretty sure I knew the answer, but I wanted to hear it from her lips.

"Of course. This is exactly the point."

I shivered, aroused.

Then the naughty, lascivious look I knew all too well from those video broadcasts with Tommy came across her face. And she let loose another surprise.

"And now, Laura, I want you to lick my pussy."

CHAPTER 17

*H*ad the pride of showing me her marking gotten to Claire? Passion had appeared in her eyes the moment she revealed that spectacular little tattoo to me. That look I'd only ever seen when she knew she was about to get some. And judging by the sudden, unexpected command she'd just issued, that rule held firm.

And I thought I was supposed to be cleaning the toilet!

Whatever. Maybe she'd allowed herself to be distracted in a moment of weakness. But I was supposed to bow to the whims of superiors. And right now, this was a whim I could totally get on board with. The fire in my belly told me so.

Her pussy looked sweet, pink and decadently inviting. For all the time she'd spend grooming mine since my arrival in this place, I'd never been required to study hers. But it didn't surprise me to see that it was perfectly hairless, the skin flawless on all sides.

She pushed her pelvis forward towards me on the toilet seat, holding herself steady by the ankles. Her inner thigh bones reared up as her legs splayed a little further, awaiting my tongue between them.

I scooted forwards, my skirt not quite long enough to protect my knees from the hard, rough tiles of the toilet floor. I checked behind me to make sure the bucket and mop were well out of the way. A quick push with my heel, just to be on the safe side. As I bent towards her cleft, I could feel the tiny claws of my hem dragging across the bruises Simon had left. It was more of an itch than a pain by now, but I was acutely aware of what was being revealed there. Not that there was anybody behind me. Should I have locked the door?

Just focus, Laura. You've had enough fucked-up moments in here, so enjoy this one!

Her pussy was glistening; I could smell the scent of her arousal as I came nearer. I thought about starting slowly, teasing the soft, milky skin around her lips — but she'd given me a specific instruction. So I swirled my tongue inside my mouth to make it wet, then landed it at the very bottom of her groove, touching down soft as a feather.

My chin rested on the toilet seat as I made my way up her opening. Her lips were parted evenly all the way up, leaving a neat half-inch of niche for my tongue to follow. Her tangy taste accompanied it all the way. The thought of Tommy's cock pounding this hole in the very recent past flooded me with a new lust as I reached her clitoris.

I wanted to touch myself, but I remembered that masturbation had been forbidden. *Better not...*

I dived under her hood to tickle her bud for just a moment, then let it snap shut again. Face to face with the tiny stallion that said she belonged and I didn't, I dared to kiss it. A million thoughts clattered around my head, but none could trump the excitement of naughty sex. Naughty *lesbian* sex. While I was supposed to be working! And it wasn't even my fault, because I'd been *told* to do it.

I repeated the entire move along her pussy. Time after delicious time. Her sighs told me I was doing something right, and I resolved not to change anything until she told me to. Soon enough, I began to notice moans coming from my own mouth as well as hers.

I dreaded the thought that I wouldn't be allowed to pleasure myself or come, but for now I could only go with it and savor what I was doing. This was a beautiful, *stunning* woman — French, too, if you don't mind — and she was getting off on *my* tongue. I had plenty of doubts about her. We certainly weren't chums. But this was about our hungry bodies and nothing more. I lost myself in it.

Even so, I don't know how I didn't sense Tommy's massive presence behind me.

Claire didn't seem to have heard his approach either, because it was *her* little flinch that prompted me to lift my head out of her crotch and look around.

All I could see at first was two thick trunks of thigh in black suit pants. But I didn't have to look up to know who it was. *Shit!* Had I been caught doing something I shouldn't?

No, not if we were playing fair. Because I'd only been doing what I'd been told to do by a 'superior'. If anyone had done wrong, then it was Claire for leading me astray. Then again, when had fair play ever come into this arrangement?

I stayed frozen where I was, waiting for somebody to say something. I wasn't even allowed to talk, after all.

"Tommy!" said Claire, a note of surprise in her voice.

"I see you're putting the latest servant to good use

already," he said, seemingly at pains to keep his voice steady. "Very pleasant viewing, I have to say."

What emotion was he hiding? I couldn't place it. Something was about to snap — you could feel it in the air.

"So, does she lick pussy well?"

"Ah, she was doing a fantastic job…"

I blushed at the praise.

Another silence as we awaited Tommy's next words. Suddenly I became very aware of the hardness of the floor pressing at my knees.

"Well then, we should let her finish, shouldn't we?"

"If you wish, Tommy, of course."

I was just about to turn back to continue servicing Claire — for whom I could sense the interruption had come at a frustrating time — when Tommy spoke once more.

"However, I will be fucking her as she does so."

My head began to spin.

"*Mais*…but are you sure? She's a—"

Tommy cut her off, impatient.

"I *know* what she is! I make the rules around here — and I break them if I want."

Was this something like *discord* I was hearing? What rule were they on about?

"Of course, Tommy," she mumbled, totally back in her role after that hint of protest. "Here?"

"No, that won't work, she's far too low down," he rumbled. "Get up on the sink outside and I'll go in behind her."

Claire responded by putting her feet down on the floor, then gently pushing my shoulders away to make space for her to stand. I heard Tommy turning around behind me, and knew there was now room for me to get up as well.

As we stepped out of the stall and Claire hopped onto the countertop between two washbasins, adopting a similar feet-up position to before, I caught sight of Tommy's face in the mirror. His jaw was set firm and determined. It wasn't the expression I associated with an explosion of anger — it was more like he was in conflict with himself.

I was sure the rule Claire had referenced was something to do with the deliberate austerity of the twenty-first floor. That servants weren't supposed to be serviced, as it were. But there could be no doubt Tommy was going to go through with this. He was already unzipping his trousers. I was transfixed, my juices flowing hard. My need was almost painful.

He didn't seem to like me staring at him in the mirror.

"Come on!" he hissed, grabbing my hair by the roots and shoving my face into Claire's vagina. "Eat her out again!"

Why did exploring her with my tongue feel another ten times sexier when Tommy forced me to do it? It had been hot enough before. Now I was on the verge of a seismic event.

And that was before he reached under my skirt with both hands and pulled down my workaday underwear. I felt it drop to my ankles and knew that stepping out of the panties was the right thing to do. I widened my legs, bending further at the waist as I smooched Claire's clit and waited for Tommy's entry.

I couldn't stop myself crying out as he pushed his way into me from behind. I couldn't be sure if it was truly my first time with him, considering the darkroom mystery, but I was happy to believe this was the case. He hit my limits without a hitch — and I knew he had so much more to give me. If only I had the space!

Knowing the thrusts to come were going to destabilize me, I groped behind Claire with both hands, looking for somewhere to hold on. I wedged my fingers into the space between her butt and the countertop on which she was perched — and only just in time.

After a moment twitching inside me like a bull pawing at the ground with his hoof, Tommy went for it. From a standing start, I was suddenly taking a pounding the like of which I had never known. Lisa had taken it hard the other day. But as hard as *this*? No, this felt like another level. This was earthquake territory: it actually felt like the walls were going to come down around us.

I quickly began to shudder and quiver as he slammed into me, always seeming to find another gear just when I thought he couldn't. There was no way I could pretend to do any focused work with my mouth while this was happening, but my tongue being repeatedly rammed onto her clitoris seemed to be doing the job for Claire. I knew she was close.

We were *all* close. The French submissive, the New York lawyer and the Scottish kidnapper were all groaning now, guttural and animal.

I could only hope I was on the right side of the rules. They'd said no masturbation and no sex with colleagues — but they hadn't said no orgasms, had they? In any case, I was reaching the point where I had no further say in the matter. My body was going to do its thing.

As Tommy approached the precipice, I felt a strange sensation deep inside my pussy. Something I couldn't hold back. It was almost like I wanted to pee, but not quite the same. It startled me, delaying my orgasm for just a moment while Tommy released his load and Claire squeezed my head between her thighs in a way that meant only one thing.

My hips were bucking and this thing inside me was building. Like some crazy beast that wanted to get out.

"Please...Tommy...I need to...I have to...there's something..."

I didn't know *what* I needed to do, exactly, but I hoped he got the message.

He pulled out.

Now that hurricane was ramming at my ramparts from within. I was convulsing, white-water rapids churning inside me.

Then I felt the liquid. It wasn't Tommy's cum, but something else. A powerful jet splashing down my thighs, calves and ankles. I could even hear it pattering onto the floor. Had I just...*squirted*?

What else could it have been?

Oh my God.

I thought that was something *other* women did?

Fuck!

I lost myself for a moment, a fearsome mix of post-orgasmic bliss and embarrassment. I liked my head being exactly where it was, tucked between Claire's thighs. As long as I was there, I didn't have to face up to anyone.

I had no idea what sort of reaction I was going to get.

"Well, Claire," said Tommy at last. "It looks like we have our first squirter."

"Vraiment? C'est formidable!"

Judging from her tone of voice, it sounded like she was taken aback. But in a *good* way.

"Someone's been absolutely gagging for my cock," I heard him say.

Ah, there it was. That sneering arrogance again. It snapped me out of my comedown. I coolly noted another moment of post-sex weakness from Tommy. And next time, when Claire wasn't around, I was going to use it against him.

For now, it was enough that I'd responded as I had. I was sure it could only represent a breakthrough in my plans. And there'd been no acting required. I allowed myself a little grin before I began disentangling myself from Claire's sated pussy.

I didn't mind that there was still a remnant of that smirk on my face as my eyes met Tommy's in the mirror. I knew he'd take it differently from the way I meant it.

For the first time that I could remember, though, he didn't hold my gaze. He seemed annoyed with himself again, and keen to leave the room.

"She's made my trousers wet," he said bluntly as he stepped out of his shoes, socks and pulled off the pants. "And this floor will need an extra-special polish now. Have you briefed her already, Claire?"

"Yes, Tommy," she replied, sitting up on the edge of the sink counter. "She knows what to do."

"Good, then you can go and fetch me another pair of trousers from upstairs. Be quick, I've got a meeting to get to. I'll take a quick rinse in the shower here. Meanwhile, this slut of a servant can start cleaning up all the mess she's made."

CHAPTER 18

*T*he incident with Tommy in the upstairs bathroom only kept me going for so long. Then the pain and drudgery of life on the twenty-first floor set in and weighed me down. As he made himself scarce for first one week, then a second, I felt more and more certain that what had happened had been a case of my kidnapper going off-piste, caught up in the moment. Just like he'd done with Lisa downstairs.

Yes, I was occasionally required to attend to the whims of the 'marked ones' when my chores took me upstairs. Claire had evidently been well within her rights to make me eat her out, doing so again on more than one occasion. And Kimiko interrupted me one day as I vacuumed the floor of the twenty-second floor's exclusive little gym, requesting a full-body massage.

But Kimiko's neighbor, a posh-sounding English brunette named Kate, was the dirtiest of them all. My first encounter with her came on the day I had to top up the beans in her coffee machine — every room up here had one, of course. Once I was done, she cast the book she'd been reading to one side and told me to stick around for a moment. Then she got on her hands and knees and told me to lick her asshole.

Before very long, she wanted me to stick my tongue right inside. Then she was handing me a bottle of lube and requiring me to jam two fingers in. She began to touch herself as I did this, exploded quickly, then dismissed me.

This was the kind of one-way traffic I became used to. I was never expected to climax, nor touched in a way that would lead me to do so. Though I generally enjoyed the experiences — particularly tasting Claire's fantastic pussy — they weren't really a lot different from the manual labor that took up most of my time. As I was figuring out, life as a 'servant' — the term seemed to apply the moment you made it to my current level — was all about degradation.

The twenty-first floor was obviously designed to make you feel worthless. That you were only there to keep the building running smoothly and occasionally pleasure the women above you in the pecking order. The key difference from the previous floor was that you weren't allowed to pleasure yourself and that Tommy was generally conspicuous by his absence.

As far as I could tell from my conversations with the other servants, we were all having much the same experience. Even if they seemed happier to go along with it than I was.

I had plenty of time to ponder the psychology of it as I scrubbed toilet bowls, made beds and ironed shirts. I tried to imagine that I'd come here voluntarily, like the rest had. I was a qualified, experienced, highly-remunerated lawyer with her own home in a smart part of town — and I'd now been reduced to spending my days doing jobs that required rubber gloves. This after an initial spell downstairs that had featured sex events on an almost daily basis. Yes, there had been a high level of discipline and boredom, and, as a rule, no intercourse. But we'd been dressed to impress, at least, and there was always some sort of fun with Tommy — or the other men he brought here — to look forward to. And you were allowed to masturbate to your heart's content. What did it feel like to be 'promoted' here after that? Would you be questioning your decision to start playing with fire on the dark web?

I suspected that was exactly what the powers-that-be wanted to know by switching it up like this. Downstairs, you proved your devotion to Tommy, your insatiable lust and your ability to withstand pain of the sadomasochistic variety. If you were among the best at that — though I wasn't sure what exactly went into making the cut considering the passion I'd seen from Tammy and Sabrina — then they wanted to see if you were still so keen on the whole thing when your servitude took on a different form. When you weren't allowed, or even asked, to look particularly sexy. When you didn't have to kneel because you weren't on the sex agenda anyway. When Tommy was so distant that he couldn't even be bothered to carry out your punishments, instead letting the chef take care of reprimands and order.

To my mind, the explanation was that this was a sterner, stronger test of just how invested you were. With hindsight, it had been relatively easy downstairs. Apart from the grinding boredom, what red-blooded woman would have had a problem with it? Then again, maybe I'd lost my sense of perspective since landing up here.

I clung to the notion that Tommy had faltered in that bathroom upstairs. That I had enough of an effect on him to make him break protocol. If that was the case, it couldn't be long before I was whiling away my time browsing for new erotic books. I'd noticed a couple of vacant bedrooms on the elite story, after all. It wasn't a full house up there.

And from there, my way out of here would be easy, surely? Those women, I had gathered, could access all areas of the building and weren't under any kind of surveillance. Having jumped through all the hoops to climb so high, they had shown they could be trusted.

Or was it more complicated than that?

Meanwhile, we gained another colleague on the twenty-first floor: Lisa. We hit it off just like I had sensed we would during our silent coexistence downstairs. She was from southern California, where she'd grown up on the beach. And she had the personality to go with it. I loved being around her, even if all we were doing together was scouring pots and the like. The sexual tension between us had to remain just that, of course. The rules pinned to the board were clear on that point.

Although I wasn't going to go so far as to reveal my unconventional route into this building, something about the way I'd interacted with Lisa so far made me feel I could trust her and be honest with her. And because she was a more natural human being than the rest, seemingly able to get into this whole adventure without turning into some kind of robot, conversation flowed better with her.

"So how does a fun-loving beach chick from California end up scrubbing underwear for fun?" I asked her as we tackled another load of Tommy's clothes soon after her promotion to the twenty-first floor.

She laughed, her eyes twinkling.

"Hmm, how can I put it? Life back home was great, don't get me wrong. I never worked too hard and there was always a party to be had. There was plenty of sex on offer too…in fact, I was in an open relationship until quite recently. I'll be honest — I was spoiled! But my mind and my body wanted *more*. Do you know what I mean?"

"I think so. Like an extra-kinky kick?"

"Yeah, things got a bit too easy for me, you know? I didn't have any challenge, and after a while, sex got kinda…boring! Then, one night, I stumbled across a porn movie where a girl was tied to a chair and gagged…man, it was *hot*! That's when I started looking into this alternative scene…like, how could I get myself in that situation without it being lame?"

"You mean it wasn't so easy to get someone to…tie you to a chair?"

"Well…I knew a lot of sporty guys back home, but I was pretty sure the classic sports jock wouldn't have a clue about that kind of thing. Same for the surfers. None of them would even have been able to process it if I'd told them what I was exploring, so I kept it to myself. I tried a couple of specialist dating sites to see if I could get to know some dominants. Had a couple of fun sessions, but still…it *was* lame."

"Why?"

"Going into that role for an hour or two just felt engineered," she shrugged. "I know it works for a lot of women, that 'just in the bedroom' thing. They want to be responsible moms and colleagues most of the time, just escape and hand over control now and then.

Maybe it's just me…that I'm an all or nothing kinda girl.

I quickly got to wondering if something more…*extreme* was a thing. Like, *really* handing over control. And not just for an hour or two."

It was still strange to hear these words from a girl like her, who had so clearly been part of the cool crowd all her life. A life so many others would have envied. The grass really is always greener on the other side, I thought to myself.

"So you ended up going down a rabbit hole?"

She laughed.

"Yeah, who would have thought I would figure out how to use the dark web? I mean, it's not hard or anything, but that kind of thing was for computer geeks, I always thought. *So* not me! But that's where you had to go if you wanted to find the really hot stuff."

I nodded thoughtfully.

"And is this as hot as you'd hoped?"

Her eyes went wide.

"Hell yeah — so far! Don't you think it's been awesome?"

I bit my lip, uncertain what to say. My question had clearly aroused her curiosity. And not even to Lisa was I ready to reveal just how 'alternative' my path to this place had been.

"A lot of the time," I smiled. "Yeah, I've had some pretty memorable moments. With you too, of course."

She winked at me. "Well, what can I say? You were one of the sexiest neighbors I've had in my life."

I blushed. Despite the irony of our silly uniforms and the ridiculousness of our situation, I couldn't help feeling pride at such a compliment from a girl in her twenties.

"It felt like you've been with women before, somehow… am I right?"

"Oh, yeah, going way back. I've been bisexual since high school. So being here, caged up with all these beautiful girls…that's been even hotter than I'd thought it might be!"

"Except there's hardly been much chance to touch them. And now it's not allowed at all."

"Mmm, but if we make it all the way, then it's party time! We just have to keep thinking about *that*, right?"

Another confirmation that this thing had been set up as a kind of knockout competition. For the rest of them, at least. Was I automatically a part of that?

One of a hundred questions I had lined up for Tommy. If and when I could catch him in a prolonged post-coital glow.

"Yeah," I chimed in. "Have you seen the marks on the girls upstairs, by the way?"

"Oh, I haven't had any chores up there yet," she said. "Did you?"

"Yeah, I've been up a few times already. Wait till you see it! It's another world. But these little tattoos they have… my God, they're amazing. Really, *really* tiny…and just here."

Her eyes widened as I pointed to my crotch.

"Oh my God, you mean…that's where the marking goes?"

"Mm-hmm," I nodded. "A galloping horse, basically on the clit. It's incredible."

"Stop it, Laura, you're making me horny!"

Yeah, I was making myself horny too.

"Okay, okay, let's change the subject."

"Right," she said. "What about you? You're a lawyer! How do *you* end up doing this? I can't even imagine!"

What could I say? I was a terrible liar, but could I volunteer enough vague, carefully selected truth to satisfy her? *Think quick, Laura!*

"Hah, I could say the same about you! Well, I got divorced a few months before landing up here, that's one thing. It was a bad scene, the guy cheated on me with a much younger woman."

She nodded sympathetically.

"I got *way* too much into my work after that. I neglected my relationships and even failed to speak to my kids much."

"Wait, you have kids? But…"

I knew what she was thinking. Volunteering for this when you had offspring would be a heck of a move.

"Yeah, but they're in college. They've left home. Yep, I'm *that* old, Lisa!"

"Okay, I'm with you now," she laughed. "I just thought you looked too young to have old kids! It was easy for me, of course — I'd quit my relationship and just gotten out of a job. I told one very close girlfriend where I was going and put her down as my emergency contact, but apart from that I just spun the line that I was going on a long trip somewhere."

These people had put down *emergency contacts*?

Little nuggets like this pushed my buttons like nothing else. Where the fuck was *my* get-out? What about *my* welfare if a situation arose?

Well, Tommy *did* have my cell phone, I supposed. And he knew my employer inside out.

A pang of guilt ran through me as I thought about the way my kids had been lied to following my disappearance. Spring was undeniably turning into summer now, and the likelihood that they might be putting in an appearance at the house soon was increasing. *Would they notice anything?*

I had to pull myself together. This wasn't the time for such thoughts.

"Well, hey, it really is a long trip. New York is the other side of the country for you! Nobody needs to know exactly what you're up to."

"Exactly," she grinned, her eyes full of life and lust.

"Anyway, so that's about it," I said, returning to my back-story. "There was a big sex drought after the divorce…well, before the divorce as well, actually! I'd certainly never explored anything in this direction. And now, here I am."

Well, I hadn't told any lies! And this threadbare version of the truth seemed to satisfy Lisa. As far as she was concerned, the mechanics of how I'd landed up here were the same as they were for her and all the rest. I didn't need to spell them out.

"Yep, here you are! And since you asked *me* the question…is it as hot as you'd hoped?"

I felt my skin crawl. *Hoped?* Ugh, there was so much I could say to that word. Part of me was crying out to spill the beans to her — but I knew that doing so could be fatal to my plan to gain Tommy's trust.

"Hot? Hmm, well…I recently learned that I can *squirt*. Does that answer your question?"

"I think it does," she smirked.

And still I hadn't told a lie.

CHAPTER 19

*T*owards the end of May, my big chance came.

I'd done chores on the twenty-third floor before. I'd gotten to know Tommy's living quarters a lot better. But he'd always been out when I'd polished the taps of his bathtub, vacuumed the floor of his suite or replaced the shirts in his walk-in closet. He never left anything personal around — doing the chores here was more like servicing the hotel room of a transient business traveler. I suspected the other half of the floor, where the darkroom was, would be a lot more fun for snooping. But I hadn't been allowed back in there thus far.

But today, according to our calendar, was Saturday. And when Claire brought me up to Tommy's private suite to change the bed linen in the morning, there he was. He sat at the varnished wooden bureau, writing something, his back turned to us. He appeared deep in concentration.

Claire knocked respectfully on the open door.

"The cleaner is here, Tommy," she said. "Can she work, or would you prefer her to come back later?"

My kidnapper didn't turn around. He just grunted that I could get going, but ought to be as quiet as possible.

"Do the dusting, polishing and change the bedsheets," she whispered to me. "Leave the vacuuming for now, and anything that makes a noise. I have to go out for a while, but if you finish before I am back, wait on the floor just inside the door."

I nodded my understanding, then got to work under these new and curious conditions. I'd never been in a room with Tommy before without being the center of attention — even if this had involved submitting to some pretty twisted perversions. Now, it wasn't even clear that he knew who was moving about behind him as he switched his attention between a sheaf of papers and his mobile phone. After all, Claire had only referred to me as 'the cleaner'.

Such was life as a worthless servant, interchangeable with any other. I was getting used to it. And when I caught sight of myself in the mirror on Tommy's dresser, I realized how being deprived of my daily beauty treatments could make me buy into that notion. I'd done my best to keep myself looking good — as much for my own sanity as anything — but Sandra's professional touches and the glow that comes with regular orgasms had worn off. I saw a plain woman looking back at me. And what else would you expect of someone who wore a stiff uniform like this and spent her days carrying out mostly menial acts of servitude?

Tommy genuinely seemed unaware of my presence while I performed my duties as noiselessly as I could. I began with the quietest jobs, hoping he might lighten up later. The polishing and dusting of surfaces and lamps kept me busy for a while. I took it slow, taking special care around anything breakable. Particularly that decanter, which looked to be of fine crystal and filled with a liquid I suspected was some venerable whiskey. I ran my cloth over the tiny camera lens on the window frame with distaste. I was sure this was the device they'd used to taunt me while I'd been in solitary confinement. I was no fan of that thing.

I didn't dare approach the desk and chair where he was poring over whatever task was keeping him so engaged.

Then I moved to the bed, where I knew the chances of being completely quiet were slimmer. I carefully laid all the pillows to one side, removed the summer quilt, then untucked the pair of fitted sheets as noiselessly as I could. As was often the case, I could see clear traces of sexual activity on the linen. This was where the marked ones were brought to play, I knew. Though they all had their own rooms one floor below, I wondered if any of them ever spent the night with their distant 'boss'.

I managed to replace everything without earning any kind of reprimand for making a racket. Then I gathered up all the dirty sheets in my arms, took one look around the room to see if I had missed anything, and slipped out into the antechamber. I was done with the work I'd been asked to do, but there was still no sign of Claire.

Well, I'd been told what I needed to do in this situation. Wait on the floor. I folded the linen up into a neat pile. Then — and I don't know if this was force of habit, some faint hope or a mix of both — I chose to kneel. With the soft stack of laundry as a cushion, I knew I'd be able to hold the pose for some time.

I hardly dared breathe. I had no reason to expect either thrills or punishment. But the mere fact that Tommy was just through the next doorway, alone, meant a certain potency hung in the air. Yes, I was a mere servant. One who'd done her work soundlessly and without any errors. I knew I should consider myself invisible as I knelt there and awaited deportation back to my quarters.

Yet I'd seen Tommy break his own rules before. Could I get lucky once more? It was a delicious possibility that I couldn't shake from my thoughts. I reminded myself that it wasn't just a case of my being horny for more of what I'd enjoyed in the bathroom downstairs — but that we were *alone* up here. Maybe I could get him talking. And trusting.

My ears pricked up as I heard him talking on the telephone. I couldn't make out everything he said, but I was able to catch a few snatches when he put extra emphasis on his words.

"...no further discussion..."

"...our final offer..."

"...you're making the right decision..."

It sounded like another of his business deals was turning in his favor. Or was it something more sinister?

"...pleased to hear it..."

"...so we have a deal..."

After what must have been the usual pleasantries at the end of the call, I heard Tommy ring off. Then, obviously delighted with the outcome, I heard what sounded a lot like a deep breath, a stretch, and a satisfied sigh. Whatever had been stressing him so much while I'd turned down his room had now clearly been dealt with.

He began to whistle a tune I didn't know. I sensed he might be about to move. And now, after perhaps twenty minutes of waiting, I asked myself if he actually *knew* I was still hanging around out here. Claire had only whispered the instruction to me, and Tommy had barely seemed aware of my presence as I'd serviced his suite. So my pulse fizzed as I heard footsteps coming in my direction. Was I going to come as a surprise to him?

A moment later, I saw his hulking frame from the corner of my eye, striding towards the bathroom. Then he spotted me — and yes, he was thrown off guard! Sure, it was only for a split second — but I could swear to it. He stopped his whistling.

I looked up at him, my hands clasped behind my lower spine.

"Still here, I see?

The note in his voice betrayed pleasant surprise. No doubt he was still high from his call. In the last minute or two, he'd won another boardroom battle: I felt I could reach out and touch his swollen ego. *You might just have lucked into the perfect moment here, Laura...*

"Claire told me I should wait here once I had finished my chores. I'm...at your service."

Some primal instinct made me add those last words. They slipped out as if on autopilot. My heart thudded as I wondered how he would react. Would he, after all this time, sense sarcasm or play-acting? *Was* I play-acting?

No. And that was a good thing.

As long as I didn't let him drag me too deep under his spell. To derail me from my plans.

"Quite right," he said, clearly blind to the possibility that anybody might try sarcasm, even though I'd done exactly that when he'd held me in the solitary cell. "And on your knees too, just in case. Exemplary behavior."

"Thank you, Tommy."

He seemed to hesitate for a moment. Then, giving me the once-over with his eyes, he straightened up, growing another inch taller. I saw that curl at the edge of his mouth. He took his time over a deep breath through his nose.

"Stay right there while I use the bathroom."

I nodded, feeling my pussy begin to throb as I did so.

He disappeared around the door into the bathroom, leaving it ajar. I heard his shoes clipping across the tiles, followed by the sound of a zip opening. Then a firm, steady stream hitting water. It went on for several seconds. My thoughts went to places I don't even want to tell you about. Another sigh of satisfaction, then the zip closed again.

The toilet flushed.

Footsteps. Running water. Footsteps.

"Well, you've caught me in a celebratory mood, Laura. I'm not interested in foreplay right now, I can tell you that. Stand up!"

I scrambled to my feet as fast as I could.

"Now follow me into the suite and get undressed fast. I don't care how or where, just get it all off. Then I want you to bend over the edge of the bed with your legs wide open. Make sure I can see your cunt nice and clearly."

I trailed him into the main room. My fingers were shaking as I tried to get the tight, awkward buttons of my dress open. Tommy stood watching me as I fought with them, his arms folded and his foot tapping impatiently. God, that c-word had sounded so *fucking* hot coming from him! The vowel was mangled and it shot out of his mouth like an arrow from a bow. My *coont* was his.

I was naked as fast as I could manage. I threw my uniform, slipper-shoes, socks and underwear onto the floor without a moment's thought. Then, still under his vigilant gaze, I approached the foot of the bed, placed my palms on the quilt I'd only just arranged, and put my forehead down between my wrists. Finally, I slid my backside as high as I could and splayed my legs.

A breath of air on my wet sex told me I'd followed my instructions to the letter.

Then I heard that zipper once more and braced myself.

"Fetch me a whiskey, Laura. And you can pour one for yourself too."

I didn't like whiskey at all, but now wasn't the time to unsettle the ship. Tommy was *offering me a drink*. As he came back down to earth, I knew I had to switch on and play the game. Even though I was feeling equally light-headed following an orgasm in which I simply couldn't hold back the screams.

I walked to the sideboard on unsteady legs, gingerly removed the lid from the crystal decanter and poured a modest amount into two glasses. I returned to the bed and presented him with his. Then, still half-expecting him to tell me to get lost or punish me for impertinence, I climbed back onto the mattress with him.

This was Tommy like I'd never seen him before. Now dressed in only his open shirt, he lay on his left side, prop-ping himself up on his elbow. Everything was perfect in his world. He'd just screwed over some company, then he'd dumped his load in some willing woman's pussy and now he was nursing a tipple in his right hand. Like a boxer senses his opponent is a blow away from a knock-out, I knew he was as softened-up now as I would ever find him. Claire might return at any moment. I had to get him talking — and fast.

I sat cross-legged on the quilt, still absolutely naked. I didn't dare to try and mirror his casual pose. He seemed happy with the arrangement, raised his glass and took a sip. I copied him, trying not to screw up my face at the taste.

"Not your thing, huh?"

I evidently hadn't hidden my disgust as well as I'd hoped.

I smiled.

"Not usually," I admitted. "But since you invited me to try…"

"You'll get used to it," he said airily. "If we bring you over to my place in Scotland, there won't be much else to drink."

My head spun. He was volunteering *big* information about his plans here. Maybe all I had to do was show the interest that would keep him going.

"Oh! There's a place in Scotland too?"

"Of course!" he said, raising an eyebrow. "You think I'd abandon my country? That's where my family estate is. It's the center of my universe."

"Of course, that makes sense! It's just…well you've been in the United States as long as I've known you…"

"Incorrect, young lady," he said, looking amused. "It doesn't take all that long to cross the Atlantic with the right plane. You don't know where I go for all those days when you don't see me."

Wow, I wasn't even trying to throw hooks out here, but he was biting anyway.

"Well, I guess there's a *lot* I don't know, Tommy. And… I'd really like to hear more about your life."

"It's not that complicated, really. I'm a freelance negotiator. Companies bring me in to push deals over the line, just like happened with Danscombe. Most of my work is here in the States. That's why I keep the place in New York."

"You mean this entire building?"

He nodded. "Plus a hotel room when I'm in town."

"Wait, do you *own* this place?"

"Aye, took it over last summer. Very useful for my purposes. Most of my work meetings are only a short cab ride away."

"Okay, but…"

"But?"

The look on his face was inviting me to push further. Fine. I'd take on the elephant in the room.

"Well, there's…I mean, so this thing with all the women…it's just a hobby?"

"Indeed, can't be all work and no play, can we? Though taking care of you lot does take up a lot more time than golf or pottery, I'll tell you that."

I wasn't sure *taking care* was the first phrase I would have used. But that was a thought to keep to myself right now.

"I can believe that. It's quite the elaborate setup you have here, if I may say so."

"You may."

I hadn't *literally* been asking him. But, of course, he took it that way. Breathtaking. I felt ever more convinced that he believed my submission was complete. It emboldened me.

"And is it true what the other girls say — that they're all here vol…because they found you on that website?"

I'd almost stumbled. I had to choose my words *very* carefully now. I didn't want to hint that I classed myself in a different category in terms of my willingness to be here. It suited me if he kept believing that I'd come around to their way of thinking *despite* the fact I'd been kidnapped. Mentioning the episode would hint at my lingering bitterness.

"Yes Laura, it is," he said, speaking more slowly now. "We've had a steady flow of applications since the moment I began. I'm having to be quite selective now. You'd never believe how many dirty, servile sluts there are out there."

He looked me right in the eye, as if he'd issued a challenge. I looked down at the sheets, all in a mess after our romp. But new questions were stacking up in my head.

"When you say 'we'...who exactly do you mean?"

"Oh, Claire and I, of course."

"Aaaah, so you mean...*she* didn't sign up on the dark web to be here?"

Tommy chuckled at the very suggestion.

"No, she's been with me from the very beginning. I met Claire at a yacht party on the French Riviera. I didn't know it until we were a couple of weeks into our relationship, but it turned out she was a seriously kinky little minx deep down. She's from a wealthy Parisian family and could have had anything she wanted in life. But conventional luxuries and regular partnerships were already boring her senseless. She was looking for something *different* when she met me. And it turned out we were on similar wavelengths..."

"But...I'm confused. If you'd found each other, why did this whole project with all these other women begin?"

"Ah, well, I wasn't interested in being a one-woman man, you see. I don't know if I could ever get used to that — and why would I? I told her this from the start. It suited her just fine. As I said, she wanted to go *completely* off-piste.

And the idea of being one of many submissives, and making sure the others were prepared for me, quickly began to turn her on. She'd been secretly interested in women for a long time too, which helped. So I had her marked, and we took it from there. First in Europe, and now in America too."

"I see," I mused. "I really like the marking, by the way. I saw it up close."

"I'm glad you find it appealing. It's taken from a photograph of my favorite horse back in Scotland. He's quite the potent one, so I thought I'd do him the honor."

I nodded, plotting my next question. He took a sip of whiskey but kept on looking me in the eye.

"If you keep on being such a good girl, you'll be getting a stallion of your own soon too. Don't worry."

I forced myself to hold his gaze, choking back all the words of protest welling up in my throat. Declaring people were getting stallions was all good and well apart from one small detail — one of them hadn't signed up for this game.

"That sounds nice," I murmured, hoping it sounded more convincing to him than it did to me.

"And now, Laura, I'm going to require your services again. You'd better put your drink down."

I glanced at his cock, which was rapidly showing signs of life once more. What had it been, twenty minutes?

I pushed some of the more rebellious thoughts to the back of my mind, shelving a dozen questions for the next opportunity. I placed the whiskey glass on the side table and gave him a willing, enquiring look.

"Lie down on your stomach now."

I did as he asked, entirely failing to shake the image of *that* marking on *my* pussy. And the longer it lingered, the slicker I became inside.

But I couldn't yell out my latest orgasm as Tommy fucked me from behind, this time with his full weight on my body. Because he clamped one massive hand over my mouth as he pumped, pulling my hair tight with the other.

No further questions for the moment, Your Honor.

CHAPTER 20

*T*he more I talked with the girls on my floor, the more certain I became that I was enjoying unusual privileges where Tommy was concerned.

"I've hardly seen him at all," admitted Andrea as I casually brought up the topic before bed one evening. "I mean, sometimes he's been around when I've done chores...he was even in the shower once when I cleaned the bathroom!"

"Oh, really?"

Her mouth curled downwards as she continued, as though there were some sour and disappointing taste in there she couldn't get rid of.

"Yes. But I was told to get on with my work...and he paid no attention to me."

She looked hesitantly across at me with her shy doe eyes. I got the feeling servant life was having its effect on Andrea. And I knew what she wanted to ask, of course.

"It was more or less the same for me when I went to clean his room," I volunteered. I couldn't bring myself to tell her he'd had sex with me on multiple occasions. It wouldn't make her feel any better, would it?

She nodded glumly.

Andrea was beginning to have a tough time here, no doubt about it. I couldn't quite put my finger on why. It was clear enough she wanted to devote herself to Tommy. But she seemed too jittery to really let herself get into it. And because she got distracted easily, she was getting more abuse from Simon than most. She always had traces of his violent rebukes somewhere on her body.

The next evening, as I washed up the dinner dishes with Anya, I asked her if she would tell me about her latest adventures upstairs. She'd opened up quite a lot as our period of shared servitude had gone on.

"Oh, those women have been using me plenty!" she said with a wry smile. "I think every day this week, one of them has made me do something to her. Have you had anything with the English one?"

"Kate? Yeah…she's wicked, isn't she?"

"She made you lick her *everywhere* as well?"

I nodded.

"I heard a rumor that Tommy finds her accent hot," she whispered, looking over her shoulder to make sure nobody else had slipped into the kitchen.

"Really? How does *that* work? The *Scottish* accent is the hot one! She just sounds like your regular London girl."

"I know, right? But I guess that could count as exotic for a Scotsman…"

"True," I said, thinking back to my previous business trips to Great Britain. "It's a long way from the Highlands to the River Thames!"

She laughed, handing me a heavy-duty wok for a final rinse.

"Yeah! Anyway, she keeps me busy enough. And Kimiko and Claire don't seem to be getting bored of me either. She loves reading, that Kimiko, doesn't she? She made me hold a vibrator on her clit whilst reading some erotic book the other day."

But she didn't say a word about Tommy. He hadn't been near her, had he? Still, I had to have it confirmed.

"Lucky you like it," I teased. "It makes a change from scrubbing and ironing, don't you find? Although, of course, Tommy would be…"

I stopped short, shaking my head as if the longing was too much. As I'd hoped, she picked up the slack.

"Exactly! I know it's kinda hot knowing you're being used by his special women…like you're still serving him in some indirect way. But I'm missing *him*…and missing cock, I guess."

"Orgasms too," I sighed.

"Those as well. But if that's the way Tommy wants it, that's the way it has to be. We're not here to argue."

I still couldn't get over the reverential, almost religious way my fellow servants spoke about the man who'd kidnapped me. Sure, they'd signed up for this of their own accord. And yes, Tommy could do things that made your toes curl in double-quick time. But still, I couldn't see myself ever falling for his charms in same the way they had. Maybe when I was *with* him, sure — but not whilst I was drying off the guy's dinner plates!

It was just another of the things that set me apart in this place, of course. Unlike Anya, I'd gotten away with a couple of *howling* orgasms, with a surprise squirting episode thrown in. Where was all of this going? Was I close to a move upstairs? Or were there still tests that would have to be passed?

I recalled Tommy's hint that I was well on my way to being marked with one of his galloping Highland stallions. He hadn't been in an equivocal mood when he'd said that, so I had reason to believe I really was making good progress towards the next floor, more revelations...and my chance to get the hell out.

This last thought shook me out of the reverie I'd slipped into since Anya's last remark. Now I remembered there was something else I wanted to get straight from the others.

"Anya, you've spent a lot of time upstairs. It seems to me like those three women actually get to leave the building — they're 'out' a lot, aren't they? What do you think?"

"Oh, they *definitely* leave the building! Jogging is certainly allowed, because it keeps you in good shape. And they each get a credit card, don't you know? And they're expected to use them on looking good for Tommy — and for his friends, sometimes. I've seen them coming back with shopping bags, sometimes twice on one day!"

"Wow! So they're completely trusted...to come back?"

She gave me a quizzical look that bordered on the suspicious. As if I'd said the nuttiest thing in history.

"Why *wouldn't* they?"

Why wouldn't they? Well, let's say they'd been, oh, I don't know, *brutally kidnapped*. But I couldn't tell her that. I'd almost given myself away again. The last thing I needed was any of the others thinking I was some kind of insurgent. That wasn't the image I was going for.

"Of course they'd come back," I chuckled. "Just kidding!"

Anya didn't seem to find the idea particularly amusing.

"Well, I guess we're done here," she said in an even tone, handing me one final plate to rinse and dry. Switching to silence, she busied herself draining the soapy water from the sink, then swirled it out until it sparkled.

You wouldn't *come back, Laura...would you?*

～

My troubled mind kept ticking long into the night, and I didn't sleep well at all. But in the morning, something came along to yank me back into the here and now.

We were halfway through breakfast, and considering our tasks for the first part of the day, when Simon burst into our dining room in a rage. He brandished aloft the wok I'd held in my hands not twelve hours before.

"Which of you *useless* servants was responsible for washing up the dinner dishes last night?" He glared around our humble mess. "Don't make me go outside and look at the list..."

I was terrified. What had we done wrong? I'd paid as much attention to that darn wok as anything else, hadn't I?

I forced myself to my feet with all the relish of a slave about to be paraded before a crowd of rabid hicks. There was no point delaying the inevitable. After a short delay, Anya followed suit.

"Look at this!" Simon yelled. "I'm trying to get started on lunch and I find crusty old pieces of carrot on this pan? I bet you two were talking shit the whole time instead of paying attention to your work. Clearly I've been going too easy on some people around here. That changes *now*. You'll begin by stripping. Get moving, *both* of you!"

But Anya was the one responsible for the washing part!

My face creased into a frown and I wanted to protest. But I knew that this would be a terrible idea: as far as Simon was concerned, the entire team had let him down. Resigned to my fate, I began to unbutton my uniform.

Pála, Lisa and Andrea didn't know where to look as Anya and I shed our clothes right there at the table. Simon was the picture of impatience. They tried to keep eating their breakfasts, but that was only ever going to be awkward. I was as keen to get this over with as they were, and was butt naked in no more than twenty seconds. I'd had some practice at fast undressing by now.

On this occasion, however, I wasn't sure how much I was going to enjoy what followed.

"Come to the kitchen, quickly now. I'm supposed to be preparing lunch, not dealing with miscreants!"

Simon showed the way through the door and tracked us to the kitchen. I could feel his green, angry eyes on me as I walked.

"It's such a shame I have to keep making a mess of you girls," he goaded. "You're so shapely, both of you. And your skin is so perfect. Anyone would think you *want* a bunch of bruises, the way you behave."

But that was as far as the flattery went. Once we were into the kitchen, he ordered us to sit back to back on the unforgiving linoleum floor, with our knees up. Then he got to work with the ropes.

About an inch in diameter, these were coarse and tightly wound, like the kind you'd see used to moor a modest fishing boat. First, he wound a length around our middles and pulled it tight, binding our bodies together. The rope pushed at my breasts from beneath, no doubt causing them to protrude weirdly. I could already feel

Anya's worry from the stickiness of her skin as her back clung to mine.

Simon's next move was to connect my bent knees to whatever shelf supports or table legs happened to be nearest. Nothing was going to slide around because all the fittings in this kitchen were firmly built into place. As became abundantly clear when he tightened these latest bonds: my legs had no choice but to spread. Then, for good measure, he secured my ankles such that I couldn't even dream of bringing them together.

He worked fast and accurately, his hands seemingly at one with the ropes as he fashioned the knots he needed, tightening each one with an uncompromising jerk. He'd done this before, no doubt about it.

"Your turn now," he said to Anya, revealing that she was going to get exactly the same treatment. Each time he pulled a restraint tight, I could feel the twang as if it were vibrating through my very own body.

Then, with a final bewildering series of knots, he somehow managed to bind her left wrist to my right, then raise our connected arms and secure them to some spot above shoulder level. He repeated the move on the other side. When he was done, we had spread our wings as well as our legs. We were as open as it was possible to be.

Finally — and ominously — Simon slipped a loop of rope around our necks. For a moment I feared the worst. But he didn't pull that one too tight, thank God.

I was unable to move any part of my body more than an inch. I could feel it was the same deal for Anya. We were sitting ducks, powerless to do anything except await whatever he planned to do to us. Then to endure it and submit to it.

I ran my tongue across my dry lips, hoping to moisten them.

"Very well, let's make this quick and painful," declared Simon, straightening up to tower over the pair of hapless females trussed up on the floor beneath them. "We'll start with my hand and then move on to the fly swatter. Tits and pussy, alternating, one-two-three. I hope you're ready. Because I certainly am."

Oh God, he was going to hit us *there*? I'd only ever heard of Simon attacking people from behind. I didn't like the sound of this new tactic one bit. I shuddered at the thought of him channeling his brute power into places like *that*.

He began with Anya. When his hand cannoned into what must have been her left breast, both of us rocked and swayed, effectively weightless with our arms and legs being pulled away from us. She endured the next hit in silence, but grunted in discomfort when he landed a blow down below. It sounded sickly, wet and thick, that slap.

Instinctively, I tried to close my legs to protect myself. But that, of course, was an impossibility. And now Simon was moving around to issue me with the same treatment.

He squatted down as he got set to attack my breasts. When he began his takeaway, I saw that he was planning to do this back-handed. I winced, certain that this was going to hurt more than the open palm. *Wham!* It was the follow-through that did it. Making sure he accelerated to the bitter end of the stroke, his fingernails dragged across the battered area, like an army pouring acid on enemy crops. I bucked and choked, whimpered and lurched.

I could *not* go through with this.

Wham!

He'd switched hands now and landed his first assault on

my left breast. Left-handed and back-handed. With awful accuracy, he bulls-eyed me directly on the nipple. *Fuck! Ow!*

But I was going to *have* to go through with this, wasn't I? I had absolutely no choice in the matter.

Now Simon swung his hand around. He was still squatting between my legs, his intent as dark as his chef's whites were bright. I looked pleadingly into his eyes, but met no trace of sympathy. Mercy was the last thing on his mind as his pupils dropped towards my open center. He pulled back his palm, ready to strike.

Slap!

I clenched my teeth, bracing every sinew to stave off the wave of pain coming from between my legs. As it rippled out from my core, I lost my nerve and my fight. My head tried to collapse forward, but the rope began to choke me, forcing it upright again.

And so it went. Simon circled us like a vulture turned predator, attacking our breasts and vaginas with awful, metronomic precision.

By the fourth round with his hand, however, I began to feel something different. I didn't want to acknowledge it, but there was a delicious anticipation mixed with the apprehension as he prepared to deliver his next vicious slap — especially when it was between my legs.

"My fingers are coming away wet!" he declared after completing a quartet down there, confirming my worst fears. "You're not supposed to be *enjoying* this! I think it's time for the swatter. That will get you both hopping."

And he was right. I'd never known any pain so excruciating as that of the fly swatter landing on my nipples. Simon's accuracy was a terrible thing that soon had both of us screaming out loud the moment each hit landed. We were quickly soaked in sweat, our arms aching from being held aloft, a succession of cries mingling into one great howl of suffering.

With this latest instrument of torture, the pussy hits were more tolerable than those on the nipples — but not by much. Every time he completed a strike, I prayed it would be the last. Yet every time he lined up for the next, that twisted need was back. It had me twisting my pelvis to give him a better angle. I just couldn't help it. I wanted to come. How *warped* was I?

It grows on you. Andrea's words were ringing in my ears now. I'd been wrong and she'd been right. It was beyond my comprehension — but it was true. I *had* to keep a lid on this, or I'd never leave this place.

After about a dozen complete sets on each of us with the fly swatter, Simon stood up and took a step back to survey us. We were *finished*. Panting, dripping, stinging — and finished. Thank God he understood this.

"Well, you're lucky I need to get back to work. But if there's a next time, I swear I'll double up on that. Understand?"

"Yes, Simon," we mumbled.

He released our limbs one by one, allowing us a moment to shake them out. It was worse than getting off a twelve-hour flight in economy class. Everything hurt from being stuck in one position for too long. But at least the throbbing where he'd beaten us was slowly beginning to subside.

"You can get up now, you two…oh, look who's here! If it isn't the most gorgeous of them all!"

Claire, of course.

She smiled at the compliment, though I could tell she was largely unmoved by it. Simon was attractive in his own steely way, but I knew by now that Claire had no genuine interest in 'other' men. Though I also knew she wouldn't hesitate to fuck one if Tommy demanded it.

"Ah, I heard I would find them in here with you," she said, running her eyes up and down our naked, freshly-tortured bodies with no apparent signs of shock or surprise. "Are you done with them?"

"For the moment, yes," he sighed. "Until they screw something up again. Which won't take long, I'm sure. Did you have something in mind?"

"Yes," she said, holding out two pointed, glassy objects in her right palm. "I've been told they need these inserted."

"Aha, their time has come, has it?"

"I believe so," she replied, pulling out a bottle of transparent, slimy liquid from her back pocket. "Come now to the other side of the kitchen counter, please. Bend over, place your feet apart and stand on the tips of your toes."

CHAPTER 21

*T*hat day, more than any other, it felt like I was someone else's property. Truly owned. Which was strange, because I hadn't seen Tommy at all. But mopping, scrubbing and stacking with a butt plug wedged firmly in place, my pussy and breasts still smarting from Simon's handiwork all the while, had a subjugating effect the likes of which I hadn't yet felt. As the brains behind this whole game, Tommy didn't need to be present to get under your skin.

Though I'd never experienced a butt plug before, Claire was patient and skilled enough to make the insertion fairly painless. The turnip-shaped toy settled comfortably enough and didn't hinder me much as I went about my tasks. But putting my underwear and uniform back on was a nightmare. Every movement tingled. I was quite sure that the evenly-spaced strips where Simon's fingers had struck my breasts were turning a shade darker by the minute.

The big question was what exactly awaited us, and when. Simon's words had hinted at some significant event

— something for which this butt plug was necessary. During the course of the day, I learned that Lisa had also been fitted with the same device. So there were three of us waiting with bated breath.

At around five o'clock, which was usually the time for a brief unwind before dinner, Claire came for us. She found me hanging out with Lisa and Anya in the twin cell the two of them had shared since Lisa graduated to this floor.

"Is everything good with you ladies? I'll be taking you upstairs for a while. If you need to use the toilet, go quickly now."

A knot began to coil in my stomach. I wasn't used to inquiries as to my wellbeing, nor suggestions that it might be a good idea to make use of the restrooms. Innocuous though Claire's words actually were, they carried an ominous weight. It felt like a particularly challenging ordeal lay ahead of us.

I felt ready and willing for just about anything...*except* another dose of sadism. This morning's punishment had been enough to work up the kind of twisted passion I'd sworn I wouldn't succumb to...but my body surely couldn't take another beating so soon.

We all took up Claire's invitation to visit the bathroom, after which we convened just outside the elevator. She awaited us with something draped over her forearm... sacks! The kind of hessian ones used to haul potatoes. She proceeded to hand one of these to each of us.

We darted worried, furtive glances at each other.

"Please put these over your heads, *mesdames*. Do not worry, the fiber is loose so that you can breathe. There are also some additional holes cut into the bags to make sure there is no problem."

I could sense the uncertainty and surprise in our group at this latest development. Though we'd all experienced our share of new things in our time here, I was pretty sure blindfolding hadn't been on the menu for any of us. And this didn't look like harmless bedroom blindfolding either — clearly we would be making our way to unknown places *whilst deprived of our sight*. The flashbacks to my abduction began almost the moment I reluctantly slipped the bag over my eyes.

Claire then approached each of us to bunch up the slack at throat level and tighten a knot around it, creating a pony-tail of sorts. I felt it drop between my shoulder blades.

"Not too tight? Can you breathe?"

"It's fine," I murmured, still uncomfortable with the memories this was bringing back.

Then she adjusted the bag's position to make sure none of the additional breathing holes were placed near my eyes. I was aware of light beyond the material thanks to its loose weave, but that was as far as it went in terms of vision.

She steered us into the elevator one by one. Now the trauma of *that* evening mingled with a raft of new possibilities. Was this the final examination? The one where they took me back outside to strip me in Times Square and see how I handled it? Or where Tommy fucked me in the middle of Broadway to put my devotion to the test?

No, it couldn't be! The sacks were too obvious. Unlike the mysterious glasses I'd had forced on me all those weeks ago, these would attract attention. The cops would come running.

Still, I felt a strong sense of relief when I felt the elevator moving upwards. Judging by the length of the journey, I was pretty sure we were heading for Tommy's floor.

And when Claire marched us out of the lift and turned us to the left, I knew very well that we were headed for the mostly uncharted 'other half' of the twenty-third story. The hallway with the darkroom. I hadn't been back here since that memorable night — and wasn't sure Anya or Lisa had been here at all.

But why the blindfold? I'd seen this part of the building before, after all.

Once we were into that warmly-lit corridor and Claire had guided us into one of the rooms on the right — one with ambient light, this time — the reason became clear. We had visitors again.

Claire lined up the three of us in a straight, tight row. I knew I was in the middle because my elbows were touching those of a companion on either side. I just couldn't say which one was Anya and which was Lisa.

I heard Tommy's number one woman move away from us. Then came the voice of the man himself. And it wasn't us he was addressing.

"Gentlemen, here they are. As you know, this is a rare privilege — only a few of my acquaintances are invited to test the new trainees for their anal skills. I'll remind you once more not to speak out loud. Depending on how tonight goes, some of them could be back in their day jobs by next week. And I hardly need to remind you of your own reputations. As always at this stage, it's best that nobody recognizes anybody."

Day jobs? I'd just managed to clear my mind of the crazy morning when I'd stormed out of mine. Thanks, Tommy.

"Now that they're in servitude rather than on display, they're not as groomed as they would be downstairs," he went on. "In the past few weeks, they've been learning that they're nothing more than a servile collection of holes to be used and enjoyed by others, you understand? That's why we've given them the sacks and you're not required to wear masks. Tonight, their faces don't matter: it's all about that one particular hole you'll be trying out for size. I'll present them to you in a moment."

Tommy's footsteps came closer. Judging from the clip his shoes produced and the echo in the room, we were probably standing on wooden floorboards. It didn't feel (or sound) like there were a great many soft surfaces in here, that was for sure.

"Hold up your skirts, ladies. Nice and high, all the way to the hips."

My elbows jostled with those of my neighbors as I followed the instruction. Now I felt Tommy doing some-thing with the girl on my left. I heard a rustle and his knuckles brushed my hip...ah, he was pulling her panties down!

"Ahh, there we are. I recognize those cheeks! Welcome, Anya."

"Thank you, Tommy," I heard her whisper. It wasn't loud enough for anyone else in the room to hear, I was sure of that.

"Step out carefully now," he went on. "Left shoe first... now the other...that's it, good girl. Now spread those feet so my guests can see how you've readied yourself for them..."

I couldn't help but be impressed that he'd recognized a member of his private collection from the shape of her backside alone. I was on full alert for his next move, but he went around me to my right. He repeated the procedure on the girl I now knew had to be Lisa. I felt her upper body move a little away from mine as she too made room to widen her stance.

I was last to end up pantiless, slightly bent at the waist and baring my butt plug to the audience. Which, going by the volume of the appreciative murmurs, consisted of perhaps five or six men. I wondered if one of them was the guy who had so thoroughly inspected me down there that distant evening on the twentieth floor.

"As you can see, gentlemen, these hopefuls have been nicely loosened up for you. I'm told they've been plugged up all day, whilst doing their regular chores around the building. So don't hold back on them; that's the last thing I want. This is a critical examination for them. If they can't take a thick, substantial cock up their arses, they'll have no further business with me."

Jesus, this was starting to sound scary.

I'd never done this with even one man — never mind multiple men. I had no idea how it was going to play out... but a part of me *was* getting very curious.

But at least I didn't have to feel pressure the way Anya and Lisa did. They would *not* want to get thrown out on the basis of what happened in this room. Me? Well, if Tommy wanted to let me go because of something that occurred in the coming minutes, fine! Though we both knew that wasn't going to happen. Special case and all that.

"A final word to you ladies. I've chosen men who will challenge you with both their length and girth. But I want to see you offer them everything you've got. Then we'll see how worthy you really are."

Arrogant cunt. Turned on as I was by the situation, I still had time for that one powerful thought.

"Claire, over to you. Secure them and then open them up."

A few gentle pushes from his right-hand woman later, my wrists were bound by a pair of what felt like leather cuffs, pulled ultra-tight and fastened by buckles. These, in turn, were hitched to some solid fitting high on what I supposed was the wall in front of me. For the second time that day, my arms were effectively helpless. But though they were pinned above my head, the rest of my body was free to move.

Once Claire had secured all of us in what I assumed was a similar fix, she began pulling out the plugs. Again, she was tender about it, yet still it was a shock to feel the thing pop out. It felt like a huge, gaping cavity had taken its place. And when she smeared that void with another huge helping of lubricant, it felt like an Arctic wind had whipped its way inside.

But that was the gentle breeze before the storm.

"Gentlemen, their holes are ready for you," announced Tommy. "Please, ride them as hard as you can. Claire will be on lube duty throughout — and she's more than willing to lend you a hand if you need a little refresh."

I shook my head inside its potato sack and afforded myself a wry, disbelieving smile. Just when you thought Tommy and his crew couldn't come up with a scene crazier and more depraved than the last, they did. Did it get me going? Hell, yeah! But part of me was still terrified as I heard the men approach *en masse*. I was sure there were only a few of them, but such was the menace in their footsteps that it felt like the great African wildebeest migration was heading my way.

And just like a herd of galloping animals, they ran riot

over me. *Fuck*, what an introduction to back door sex! I yelped in lustful suffering as they lifted my skirt and went in, one by one. Some stayed for only a minute or two, then moved on. Others pumped relentlessly, endlessly, for what felt like several minutes at a time. Each cock I took in my anus felt bigger than the last. Yet I never reached breaking point. I surprised myself. I could take this.

And they were bringing me really, really close. But after the squirting incident, I was wary of letting go in a situation like this. It had only happened that one time so far, but it was a possibility…and who knew if I'd be punished for making a mess? I decided it was best to keep my thoughts on the safe side of the line. Easier said than done when you've got a succession of big guys using your most intimate orifice for pleasure they certainly weren't trying to hide.

The men maneuvered me into various different positions, depending on the stature of the guy concerned. Some needed me bent perpendicular at the waist; others took me almost upright. One of them, perhaps the tallest, lifted my feet off the ground and pinned me right against the wall.

It was a particularly violent ride with him. He actually grabbed my ankles and pulled my calves parallel to the ground, so they flanked his waist. Then he pressed his way into my anus, hard and insistent. I never ached to touch my clit more than I did at that moment — but this was both forbidden and impossible.

Another thing that happened whilst the unknown man was doing that to me? The relentless rubbing of my forehead on the wall and his chest on the tail of the sack gradually caused the thing to slip out of its original position. And then, like some rare eclipse, a hole passed directly in front of my right eye. I could see the whitewash of the wall against which I'd been slammed.

By another stroke of fate, the guy then suddenly chose to flip me. I hadn't quite realized I *had* the ability to turn around — but it turned out the cuffs didn't prevent it. Which is how he was able to slide out, drop my legs for a moment, spin me, then get his elbows under my knees and straighten up. *Christ!* This was some kind of wild position he had me in now. I was suspended, my hips slightly higher than my shoulders. He pushed his way into my butt with renewed intent. Once more, I fought back the urge to let my desire run free.

I couldn't quite twist my head in such a way that I could see him properly. My limited vision from this angle, coupled with the fact that another jolt would rock through me just as I was trying to focus, made him agonizingly difficult to pinpoint. All I could really make out was a tall, black outline. But maybe it was better that I wasn't looking directly at the guy. If he noticed an eyeball gazing up at him, the cat would be out of the bag — so to speak. This was one hole I wanted to keep to myself for as long as possible.

Though his brutal, powerful efforts were extraordinarily distracting, I needed no second invitation to take in what I could via my right eye. The hole might slip away at any moment, plunging me into blindness once again. So in between every thrust, I sneaked a peek.

I could clearly see the scene to my immediate right. If I hadn't lost my bearings, the bagged-up girl in action was Anya. And the man currently assailing her bent figure from behind?

No! No way in hell!

I checked once.

This peephole had to be playing tricks on me.
I checked a second time.
Yes, it was him!
How in the *universe*…?
Andre!

CHAPTER 22

*T*hank God the hole in the sack over my head slipped away from my eye after that. If I'd looked at my former colleague having his way with Anya any longer, I'm pretty sure I would have passed out.

I'd had some fucked-up shit to process since being in here. But this was beyond both comprehension and rational explanation. So much so that the moment I was sightless once again, I began to wonder if I'd imagined it. Weirdness on that level only happens in dreams and fantasies, doesn't it?

Maybe the pounding I was taking at the time, coupled with the fact that I was suspended in mid-air with my head thrown back, had put me into some kind of trance. One that had taken various incongruous pieces of the last few weeks and thrown them together into a ridiculous, trippy scene.

Because it *couldn't* have been Andre!

Tommy and Andre had been enemies from the moment they'd squared up in the boardroom on the morning I'd been kidnapped. I still recalled the spark in the air as the two alphas had tried to establish early supremacy. That was a battle Tommy had won with impressive ease. And if what my kidnapper had told me was true, things had unraveled for Andre from that moment on. Having taken out his frustration on me and caused my 'breakdown', he'd been suspended by Kerstein and the Danscombe deal had been lost. Tommy was his nemesis. They wouldn't be in the same room together for *anything*.

Or had the *entire* thing been a setup by the pair of them? I could totally imagine Andre being into the same kinds of kinks Tommy was. The idea of him running an establishment like this one wasn't a lot wackier than the Scotsman doing so. They could be formidable partners in that sense.

But it didn't add up. Why would Andre play any part in his negotiating partner disappearing, getting himself into major trouble and losing out on a massive bonus? There had to be a better explanation.

And I certainly *wanted* there to be one. Because if Andre *knew* I was one of the three women whose faces were hidden behind rough, brown hessian, then I had a whole new level of bitterness and shame to deal with. I'd have another courtroom revenge to plot and another guy to be put away.

No, if that was really Andre I'd spotted, then I didn't want to believe he was aware of my role in the scene.

But I didn't know *what* to believe anymore.

The rest of the session passed in a blur. After catching those glimpses of Andre — so vivid, so *not* like a dream — my mind checked out. Not even the bizarre thought that one of the final few anal invasions was almost certainly *him* really hit home. When time was finally called and Claire led us downstairs, I was in a stupor.

But that went for Anya and Lisa too. I almost forgot just how intense the sex itself had been. But seeing their dazed faces once Claire untied and removed their sacks reminded me that we'd just done something extraordinary. Their hair was all over the place. Their jaws hung limp and their eyes looked empty. I think all of us needed a bit of time to ourselves.

We showered in shocked silence before proceeding to dinner. Pála and Andrea were curious about our latest adventures, of course, but I wasn't in the mood to talk. The intensity of the day — though Simon's brutal punishment felt like a week ago now — had chased me down, caught up with me and wrestled me into playing dead. Even without the Andre sighting, I would have hit a brick wall by now. So I stared vacantly out of the dining room window as I chewed my food, leaving Lisa to tell of what had been done to us. Though even *she* wasn't quite her usual bubbly self.

The only thought I was really capable of as I fell into bed that night was that this thing needed to resolve itself sooner rather than later. The claustrophobic not-knowing had swollen uncomfortably in the light of what I'd seen upstairs.

Or at least what I *thought* I'd seen.

I woke up feeling tender back there. But the ever-present reminder of my violation brought with it a tiny nugget of need. One that I couldn't shake off all day.

Just another reason I had to get out of here. I knew other girls had had it worse than me, but the lack of a chance to let myself go was driving me to the edge. I hoped for any assignment on the highest floor, because I'd seen how that could lead to rare pleasures. But for the next couple of days, the timetable had me trapped down here. Where nothing but bad stuff ever happened.

That evening, once again at around five, I was surprised to see Claire turn up with the accessories we'd got to know so well the day before. *What? Another round?*

"Come on, we have to continue your examination, ladies," she said as she herded the same trio together.

More nervous looks. None of us had reckoned with *this*. We'd all survived the previous evening with no more than a mild discomfort to show for it. But *again*? So soon?

I spoke up, deliberately flouting the rules: "But...will it be the same as last night?"

She eyed me coldly but chose not to call me out. Perhaps she knew her answer was as good as a punishment.

"Of course! Your anal test is in three parts. Tommy needs to be sure that you can handle his needs on a regular basis. You must make it until the end of the third session tomorrow evening."

I gasped. Three nights in a row of *that*? Were they *insane*?

"Please, ladies: here are your bags. You know what to do."

The procedure was exactly the same as the first evening. From the way Tommy spoke, I understood that this was a new group of men. And when the first of them went in, I almost screamed blue murder. No amount of lube could prepare me for the sharpness of the chafe.

But then, once I let myself relax a little, I was surprised to discover that I handled it just fine. Within a minute or two I could hardly tell any difference to the night before. I would never have guessed it, but it looked like I was some kind of champion anal slut! More ready than she thought to take a back door pounding multiple nights in succession. And *that* thought got me even hotter under the collar than I had been on the previous evening's excursion.

Moreover, my sack worked as it was supposed to. I wasn't distracted by any surprise Andre sightings.

But I could tell that things weren't going so well for at least one of the others. Towards the end, her cries took on a hideous note. It sounded like pure pain and suffering had surpassed her sexual pleasure.

Then the screams just…stopped. And way too suddenly to be good news. What had happened to her? *Was it Lisa?* Worry overcame me. I strained to hear what was going on above the slap-slap-slap over somebody's thighs on my butt cheeks.

I heard Tommy's voice. He wasn't far away so he didn't need to shout. But it was loaded with purpose and urgency.

"I think she's out, Claire. Undo her wrists, quickly. I'll take her weight."

Out? As in *passed out?*

Jesus, I hoped it was nothing worse than that, at least. My panic subsided as I heard Claire and Tommy calmly discussing plans for the woman to lie down in the next room. For the remaining pair of us, meanwhile, the orgy continued with no less vigor and fury.

But now my lust turned to undiluted outrage. Tommy had allowed this poor woman to be anally abused to the point that she'd lost consciousness? The brute! He was *so* going to do time when I got out of here — and I'd make damn sure he was in a block where somebody did that to him!

The voice of reason reminded me that she'd signed up for this. I knew that disclaimers had been signed. But still, he had a duty of care! And I was uncomfortably aware that the victim could just as easily have been me. And he sure as hell didn't have *my* signature on any waivers. Another timely reminder that Tommy was a violent, dangerous criminal who shouldn't be allowed to charm his way out of trouble. As the only one who'd legally been wronged, it was my calling to make sure of it.

One more day of this Laura. Just hang on.

Once we were back on the twenty-first floor with our sight restored, I established that the one missing was Anya.

I gave Claire an enquiring look. She knew what I wanted to ask — and surely that I was going to ask it out loud if she didn't take the initiative.

"Anya will be okay," she explained. "She just lost consciousness for a short while, but she is already awake again. Unfortunately, the test was too much for her. She will be given the option to continue as a servant — but she will not be able to be marked."

Game over.

Callous. Brutal. Final.

My heart went out to Anya. This was a harsh, hard place. And no matter how often I got distracted by new, twisted pleasures, I *couldn't* let myself forget that reality.

The following evening, thank God, Lisa and I completed part three of our assignment without any distracting incidents. Nobody fainted. We killed it.

And as the third anal gangbang in as many days played out, a part of me felt proud to be among those who were clearly going to make it all the way. A woman who could take everything that was thrown at her — and put inside her. Pushing my limits, and discovering that they were far beyond where I thought they were, was a sexy kind of liberating.

As on the first two nights, I ended up with a chafing where my wrists had been tied, sore muscles in the arms that had been held up and an extremely raw feeling down below. I was ready for a break, and glad we were finally getting one. But these three days, beginning with Simon's hardcore abuse on the kitchen floor, had taught me that I was made of sterner stuff than I would ever have believed. Stern enough that the next phase of my plan ought to be a piece of cake.

CHAPTER 23

ommy came to fetch us himself.

"It's time to hang up your uniform, Laura," he said with a genuine smile as he leaned in the doorway of my cell. "You and Lisa are moving up. You'll have your stallion by tomorrow."

It was the morning after the third part of our *extremely* thorough examination. Tommy betrayed no signs of sarcasm or an imminent let-down. I knew that 'upstairs' could be no empty promise: I'd been there myself and I'd seen the vacant rooms. This was for real.

Remarkably, we were now into the second week of June. I had arrived here, kicking and screaming, in *April*! It had taken the better part of two months, but I had finally gotten to where I needed to be. I'd climbed a mountain and the end was in sight.

So I didn't need to fake any pleasure.

"Thank you! I can't wait!"

The only awkward thing was that Andrea was there in the room with me, being completely ignored. She had a faraway look in her eye as I took off my uniform under Tommy's watchful eye. It was like she knew she was doomed to failure. I hoped for her sake — and for Pála's — that this wasn't the case. I wished nobody any ill here. Especially not after what happened to Anya.

"Er, I'll see you around, I guess," I said as I got set to walk out of the door. I didn't know if that was true. But she would still be up on the next floor to clean, wouldn't she? Theoretically, I supposed, I'd be able to require *anything* from the servants when I saw them around — just as the likes of Kimiko and Kate had been doing with me until now. But that would be just plain weird as far as I was concerned. I'd been in the trenches with Andrea and Pála for weeks. We'd knelt on floors together; scrubbed underwear side by side. I wasn't going to rub their noses in my promotion.

"Bye, Laura," whispered Andrea. "Yes, I'll see you…"

"Let's go and fetch your friend Lisa now," said Tommy.

I followed him, completely forgetting to feel shy or embarrassed at my nudity. This place had certainly changed me in that regard. Just as he had promised.

I hung dutifully outside Lisa's room while she was told the good news and made to undress. I was brimming with excitement that we were being promoted together. She'd come up to this floor later than I had, but seemed to have impressed enough to be fast-tracked. I was certainly going to be glad of her company upstairs. Being thrown amongst all those established favorites was intimidating enough without being the only newbie.

Lisa emerged in her birthday suit, also grinning from ear to ear. I almost wanted to chastise myself for celebrating when I was still a prisoner — but all things are relative and every jailbird needs those little victories to keep her going. Besides, this move *did* come with the promise of imminent release.

In both senses of the word, come to think of it.

Sure, I might have had some major strategic plans to execute, but my short-term priority was going to be grabbing an orgasm as soon as I had the chance. So I was going to indulge myself for a short while on the twenty-second floor. I'd earned that right. *Then* I was going to get out and see my kids.

I wasn't sure of the details of how that last part was going to work — but I knew I'd figure it out. I'd plotted my way this far, after all. And Tommy seemed to have forgotten that I might even *want* to escape.

Your arrogance is going to cost you, Mr. Sexy, I thought to myself as we crowded into the elevator with him.

Surprisingly, he kept his hands to himself as we took the short journey up. Instead, he stretched, as though he hadn't completely woken up yet. He became ridiculously tall when he did that. He dominated the small space like a lion in its lair. His scent seemed to hit us harder than before. It made me feel even more naked in comparison: I hadn't had any perfume since my days on the twentieth floor.

"Welcome to New York high society," he quipped as we stepped out onto the classy, luxurious twenty-second floor we would now call home. "Sandra and Claire will be looking after you this morning. You're no longer plain worker servants I'm happy to take or leave. I *care* how you look now that you're up here. You'll always look your best — and you've made it this far because I know you'll want things to be that way *without* me having to ask."

"Of course we will, Tommy!" said Lisa.

I was happy she spoke for both of us. Even now, after all this practice, I wasn't sure I could muster up a tone of voice like hers.

"You'll get settled in and spruced up during the day, then you'll have your official induction and marking once I'm done with my work this evening. I'll leave you two at this point. The shower is your first port of call, then you'll head for the makeup room. You know where everything is by now."

We felt like intruders as we walked over to the incredible twenty-second floor shower room. We'd only ever known it as a place we had to scrub, clean and service. To ensure a constant supply of fresh towels. To replenish soaps and lotions.

"I'm just waiting for someone to ask what the hell we think we're doing!" giggled Lisa as she cautiously turned on one of the cascades.

"Yeah, me too!"

I got myself under the neighboring stream and caught her eye. It was a view for a queen. Steam, soap, a stunning woman…

"Are you thinking what I'm thinking?"

"You bet I am, Laura! But maybe we'd better wait?"

"Yeah, I know…though I'm so tempted to join you under there and have a little tickle."

"I'd love that. But…just until we know the rules…till we know it's for real…"

"Agreed, let's be good."

We washed ourselves thoroughly from head to toe. It was one of those showers you just didn't want to leave. On this side of the building, the nearest skyscrapers were definitely far away enough that I didn't think you had to worry about anybody staring in. Though if I was honest with myself, the concerns I'd had about that in my first days of captivity were almost alien to me now.

Claire and Sandra were waiting for us in the makeup room. Though the Frenchwoman welcomed us warmly by her standards, she wasn't a whole lot more fun than she'd been at any point so far — even though I understood we were just about equals now. Never mind, that was *her* problem! And Sandra more than made up for Claire's lack of sparkle. She spoke with a freedom she'd never displayed downstairs.

"Welcome, girls! Congratulations on making it up here! It's a very select group...but I can see why you've been chosen. So naturally beautiful, I hardly need to do anything!"

I blushed at the makeup artist's words, and Lisa batted away the compliment: "No, Sandra, you're a magician! We need you!"

"But the first step is to shave them," interrupted Claire. "Girls, you'll get your marking later so we have to make you perfectly smooth, especially in that area."

Sandra nodded and pointed to what looked like a pair of large sinks installed at ground level. Each of them had a broad ledge at the back and a swooping front with a particularly low middle. A pair of taps and a hand-held showerhead were neatly fitted at their flanks. I'd seen these before on my cleaning rounds, but never quite figured out what they were for.

"Take a seat, ladies," said Sandra. "Enjoy your upgrade. We don't use buckets and stools up here!"

Wow! These basins were specifically designed for genital grooming procedures!

"Just when you think you've seen it all!" I laughed. "By the way, we *are* allowed to talk again up here, right?"

"Correct," Claire confirmed. "Unless Tommy forbids it for some specific activity, of course."

It wasn't hard to concoct a few scenarios where such a rule was in place. But I tried to keep these from my mind as we took up our positions in the special shaving tubs. Thoughts like that wouldn't be helpful at all, sitting there with our legs wide open and all that close-quarters touching. I settled onto the ledge, placed my calves in the niche evidently carved out for them, and put my feet on the floor. Sandra squatted down in front of me while Claire took Lisa.

Boy, it was good to be spoiled again! Particularly when this procedure needed doing so badly. We hadn't been issued with any shaving gear on floor twenty-one, so things had begun to look more than a little tangled down there. Now, with two perfectionists taking all the time they needed, we gradually became as smooth as ostrich eggs.

"Who will do the tattoo?" I asked Sandra.

"That'll be Tommy himself, won't it Claire?"

"Of course," she replied. "Tattoo art is one of his hobbies."

"Mmm," murmured Lisa. "That's very appropriate, somehow."

We exchanged smiles. I had to admit, the idea of Tommy doing his own marking seemed entirely fitting. And very, very steamy.

That evening, Tommy did the deed.

And not without ceremony, of course.

Once we'd been transformed into knockout super-models by the incredibly talented Sandra, we'd been shown to our rooms and introduced to our extensive new wardrobes. *Real clothes!*

"This is just a selection to get you started," she said, almost apologetically. "You'll have time to go shopping later this week."

This week! The thought gave me the jitters.

Claire helped each of us pick out something appropriate for the occasion. I landed up in a figure-hugging blue number and black high heels, while Lisa got an emerald-green dress. It had a lower hemline, but also a lower cut at her cleavage.

After Andrea delivered lunch to our rooms — awkward! — we were shown into one of the display cabinets that had made me so curious whenever I'd been up here. There was a larger one in the middle of the row, in which a pair of high bar chairs was the only furnishing. Claire told us to settle in and wait.

And there we sat for most of the afternoon. All glammed up, bathing in the warm, yellow light. Just like rare and valuable museum pieces. And a part of me couldn't help feeling treasured.

At one point, Kimiko and Kate stopped to have a good, long look at us. It was hard to make out what they were saying, but the expressions on their faces were decidedly wolfish as they pointed to various parts of our bodies with approving nods.

"This must be what hookers in Amsterdam feel like," I murmured to Lisa out of the side of my mouth.

"Yeah…but it's kinda nice, isn't it?"

"Never thought I'd agree with you on that, but yes!"

Both Lisa and I were too wound up and full of anticipation to get bored before Tommy's arrival, that was for sure.

By the time he *did* appear in the early evening, Claire had overseen a few changes to the setup in front of us. Andrea and Pála had come up to help her. It was beyond strange to watch my *very* recent colleagues creating the scene — including carrying the reclining chairs that would presumably be used for the procedure itself. I felt embarrassed to be glittering under the spotlights whilst they continued to labor away in their sad, stiff uniforms.

But they were long gone — and probably stuck on some menial task downstairs — by the time of our captor's grand entrance. The lights in the space beyond the cabinet had been lowered so that we were even more dramatically in focus. Kimiko, Claire and Kate were already waiting on a semicircle of chairs facing our window, all smartly presented in black one-piece dresses, as if heading for an upmarket party. Each already held a glass of fizzy liquid in her hand. The champagne bottle nestled in an ice bucket, perched in turn on a small table draped with a white cloth.

It was into this small but expectant crowd that Tommy emerged. And...*wow*. I'd seen him in jeans and polo shirts. I'd seen him in business wear. But until now, I'd never seen him in full evening dress. Everything shone, from his damp, gelled hair to the lapels of his tuxedo to his polished black shoes. A tartan bow tie added a touch of Scotland to the breathtaking ensemble.

Could he *really* be such a bad guy?

I reprimanded myself for even asking the question. The passage of time had a strange capacity to take the edge off an ugly experience. To make you doubt yourself, even. I had to watch my thoughts like a hawk.

Claire leaped up to pour Tommy a drink, which he then proceeded to clink with the three members of his select audience. Then he gave a short speech, introducing us to the existing members of the stallion club. Unlike our earlier lady visitors, his voice was booming enough to penetrate our display case.

"Lisa and Laura have shown constant lust, and supreme patience during long periods of sexual denial. They've displayed an aptitude for obedience. They've shown that even humble labor, in and of itself, gives them daily satis-faction…"

I tried to keep my expression neutral despite this last outlandish comment. It might have been true for Lisa — but for me? He seemed to be ignoring the fact that I never signed up to be his slave. And if it hadn't been for those couple of slips during which I'd been allowed to have sex and even climax, I doubted I would have survived my time on the last level without breaking.

"…like all of you special ones, they are naturally bisexual, adoring the female touch without any affectation. They have endured extreme pain with their heads held high, and been aroused not only by the strikes but also the marks they've carried for days afterward."

I felt a shade of red come across my cheeks. I'd vowed not to let it grow on me! But clearly I'd failed — and hadn't been able to hide the fact either.

"Finally, they have also shown they have the necessary capacity to both handle and thrive on prolonged anal pene-tration. As you all know, only my marked ones are entitled to this form of sex from me."

He went on to tell something of our personal backgrounds, with the air of a man giving a eulogy. According to him, I 'used to work' at Kerstein — I certainly didn't 'work' there. It was no surprise to hear that he and I weren't on the same page with regard to my plans to reclaim my life — or at least those parts of it I was interested in getting back. Lisa, on the other hand, looked quite comfortable with the way he was speaking about her activities and relationships before coming here to hand her heart, soul and body over to Tommy.

Finally — and here the audience really sat up and listened — he detailed a few of our sexual quirks and talents.

"...Laura loves to begin touching herself with a few tugs on her left nipple..."

He'd paid close attention, I'd give him that.

"...and you'll be delighted to hear that we finally have a squirter in our midst. I know you will *all* be making it your goal to witness that as soon as possible. And I'm looking forward to seeing each of your gorgeous faces getting doused by her unstoppable releases in the near future."

So, he thought I could do that on demand, did he? I wanted to shake my head behind the glass pane. The man knew no bounds.

"Ladies, that concludes my presentation of your newest sisters. Cherish them just as you cherish each other already. You all know where your priorities lie. And now, we'll proceed to the marking."

He turned the key in the front of our cabinet, swung the big door open, then helped each of us climb down to the floor. When he held out his hand to support me, I could almost have been fooled into thinking Tommy was a real, genuine gentleman.

He closed the door behind us, then indicated the pair of tattoo studio recliners that flanked the display case.

"Underwear off, skirts up to your hips. Then lie back and get ready to be marked. I see both of you have had tattoos done before, so you'll know what to expect."

We both nodded, though it wasn't quite so simple as he made out. One look at Lisa, the California beach babe, was enough to tell you she was well acquainted with the procedure. For me, it was a little different. I'd picked up a regrettable scrawl on my skin when I'd been in India. Some Sanskrit proverb; the kind of thing traveling kids go for. Luckily, perhaps guided by some sixth sense, I'd picked a fairly inconspicuous spot for it: just below my armpit. It had been a painful choice, as I recalled. How was *this* going to compare?

"Claire, music!"

His sidekick responded with a couple of swipes on her phone. Then the slow, steady beat of a drum filled the space we were in. After a few seconds of this rhythm, the evocative sound of bagpipes joined in. I hadn't known there was a sound system up here. But the quality of this one was predictably superb. This was just the soundtrack for losing yourself in a task.

Tommy reached for the small bag of tools stored beneath the chair and got to work on me first. My breath hitched as he took my clitoris between his fingers and thumb for the first time, pushing it from side to side as he sought the canvas for this incredibly precise, detailed piece of true art.

And it felt like I held my breath all the way through.

Apart from trying to control my lust in the face of continuous brushes on the apex of my pussy and tiny pricks of metal all around its upper hood, I was terrified of making any sudden moves. Not only would it be likely to hurt, but it might spoil the integrity of my rampant stallion.

And though I had every intention of getting away from Tommy's harem, I *did* like the tattoo. The fact that it stood for something I didn't entirely buy into didn't bother me. I was a lawyer: the only thing you could draw or write with truly binding consequences was an autograph on a contract.

After about forty minutes, Tommy straightened up and looked me in the eye.

"You're done, Laura. I've marked you. You're now officially one of mine. Congratulations."

Where words like that would have come across as sour and sarcastic in the early part of my stay here, he spoke these with sincerity and a straight face. I knew it was all based on an out-of-control ego and misguided assumptions, but I allowed myself to take it in the spirit he intended.

"Thank you, Tommy," I replied.

He moved over to Lisa's chair and repeated the procedure. In the absence of any other instructions, I waited where I was, keeping my legs open and my fresh, titillating new tattoo on display to the select audience. Then, when Lisa had also been marked with a stallion, Tommy addressed the audience once more.

"And so three become five," he said in the solemn tone of a priest. "In America, at least. I know you ladies would like to have a closer look, but the stallions need to settle for a day or two. But as always, I will allow you to help me with the final part of their initiation."

"Mmm, thank you, Tommy!" said Kimiko.

"Yes, this is my favorite part!" added Kate.

Claire was already busy adjusting the recline of the chairs, bringing the backrests below parallel with the floor.

"Flip over, both of you," commanded Tommy. "Butts up nice and high."

Heart thudding, I turned onto my stomach. My torso was now sloping diagonally downward and my butt was the apex of my body. Clutching onto the headrest with white fingers, I was surprised to find that the chair felt comfortable and stable even in this position.

I heard Tommy's voice somewhere up above me.

"All right, Kate, I'm happy to have your assistance here. I'd like you to lube her up, then hold her cheeks apart so as to give me a nice, easy entry."

"Of course, Tommy!" sang a breezy English voice behind me.

Then, with the help of my new neighbors on the twenty-second floor, Tommy welcomed us to the club by means of hard, rough anal sex.

CHAPTER 24

*I*t would be suicide to get too comfortable.

And getting comfortable was dangerously easy on the twenty-second floor.

Instead of sharing a poky cell, I now had a spacious, tastefully furnished room of my own. After so long preparing meals for others, receiving mine on a tray was now standard procedure. My staid uniform had been replaced by a varied wardrobe that ranged from the outrageously sexy to the comfortably respectable. I could take long soaks in a bathtub overlooking the city. I had a wizard on standby to make me look better than nature ever intended. My neighbors were nothing but a delight.

And I had books at last! The genre may have been limited to erotica, but it certainly wasn't trash. From *Delta of Venus* to *My Secret Life*, everything I read got my brain ticking as well as my juices flowing.

On top of all this, my room had a private, one-way intercom system, at the other end of which was an irresistible hunk of testosterone. One who'd made me squirt once again during that welcome ceremony on the reclining chair. After hearing Tommy speak about it the way he had, I'd figured there was no need to hold back if I felt that strange swell return. Thankfully, the performance had gone down very well with all concerned — and I didn't even have to clean up after myself this time. One of the servants from downstairs would take care of it.

After being allowed one full day to find my feet in this new environment — and to end my coffee drought in a decadent haze of Guatemalan Arabica — the intercom's buzz woke me early on my second morning as a marked woman. Tommy's voice summoned me upstairs.

Thrillingly, I was now able to take this journey myself. My fingerprints had been registered and I could operate the elevator independently. I hadn't dared to ask Claire whether I could access *every* floor — but she'd confirmed that I could certainly take the trip skywards and make my own way into Tommy's suite.

"But only if you're summoned, of course," she cautioned. "Don't get the wrong idea just because things are comfortable now. None of us can make spontaneous visits. But we all have to be ready to serve Tommy at any time."

Well, I had been summoned now.

And since he'd told me to come 'as I was', I wore nothing more than the delightfully wispy nightdress I'd found in my closet. My feet were bare.

I found Tommy in his enormous double bed, in which he was evidently just waking up. What time was it, anyway? I hadn't quite registered what the digital clock by my bedside had read. But by the looks of the sun just above the horizon, this was an early start.

"Ahh, Laura. Get under the covers and wake me up with your mouth, will you?"

More than willing, I pulled back the sheets at the bottom of the bed and slithered up the gap between his splayed legs. I could feel the presence of his stiff member before I even wrapped a hand around it. After a night's sleep, there was little trace of a scent. Just clean, undiluted masculinity.

Enjoy this while you can, Laura!

One command led to another, and soon Tommy was pounding my freshly stamped pussy like a jackhammer.

"Ride on top, Laura. I want to see that stallion whilst I move inside you."

Well, I wasn't going to say no to that rare opportunity. As he got into his stride, I too locked my gaze on the tiny little horse galloping around my clitoris. The sight almost made me explode on the spot. Then, when he began to thrust with such force that I couldn't keep myself upright, I had to steady myself by propping my palms on his steely shoulders. Though I'm not sure he even felt my weight there.

Soon enough, feeling my entire body jolted by the power of only his hips proved too much. I screamed my pleasure. And just a moment later, he released all of his, hot wave after hot wave. We collapsed in a heap, and a minute or so passed before I could speak.

"God, Tommy…that felt so *natural!*"

He looked amused.

"Why shouldn't it?"

"Well…there were a lot of, you know, *rules* before. I wasn't even sure what they were half the time!"

He rolled onto his back, stretched expansively, then

interlocked his fingers behind his head. After a deep breath, he began to speak.

"Rules are only necessary for training purposes," he explained. "They're more of a test of your dedication than something to give me direct pleasure. The dedication itself is what ultimately brings me joy — but by the time you've been marked I *know* it's there. All of you marked ones would scrub toilets for me if I asked you to. I don't need proof of it all the time. At this stage, I'd rather have you pretty and waiting for me when I need you. Or anyone I choose to share you with, of course."

I sensed a willingness to talk. Another opportunity to probe the Andre thing — among much else.

"Oh, so...the thing with masked visitors can still happen? Or does it work differently now?"

Quizzing him felt so much more natural now that I'd become one the elite. Having jumped through all the hoops to reach the top, surely anybody in my position would want to know a few things? I was less concerned about arousing suspicion than before — but reminded myself that caution was still my friend. I knew how quickly Tommy could snap. And just one betrayal of any intent to escape — even being found fooling around with elevator buttons I shouldn't — would see the wealth of trust I had earned go up in smoke.

"Certainly! Well, you'll be fucking and servicing acquaintances of mine as required. On the lower floors, where a new arrival's destiny is uncertain, we're careful with identities. But now we'll usually go ahead without masks, because I know the marked ones are here to stay. Unless, of course, the guest in question still wishes to hide their identity. That's up to them."

"Mmm, well, it sounds hot either way," I said truthfully. "So...we're talking about some well-known people, are we?"

"Mmm, sure," he nodded.

"How do you know them? Through business?"

He turned his head to look me in the eye.

"You might say that. *Aye*, you might say that."

I could tell from his face that he was enjoying the fact that he knew something I didn't. A *particularly* enjoyable something. And all doubt that my Andre sighting had been a figment of my imagination vanished from my mind.

Andre's name was poised on my lips. It felt like they were burning. But I ignored the heat. *Leave it, Laura.* I couldn't have known about Andre without having snuck a peek. And admitting I had done so would reveal me as subversive.

"And the darkroom would be another option for somebody like that, I guess?"

"You're spot on with that, Laura. You enjoyed it in there, didn't you?"

I nodded enthusiastically.

"You heard, I guess?"

"From the others, you mean? No need — I was there!"

"Ah...I'd been wondering about that. Did you...I wasn't sure if you'd actually..."

I widened my eyes and nodded in the direction of his cock, which still hadn't subsided from its recent efforts.

"I did indeed. You're a lucky girl. I broke my own rules more than once for you, you know that? Most girls don't get sex until they make it up here."

I blushed.

"I know, I know...and thank you. So Lisa was also lucky down on the twentieth floor?"

"Ah, she's a sexy fox, that one. Such a fun lass, so natural in the way she gives herself. She was always going to make it. But I think she'd have had to wait like everyone else if it wasn't for you being in the cell next door. I wanted to see how you responded."

"And you liked what you saw?"

"I knew you'd be jealous in that scenario, but you came up with a clever and creative way of offering yourself, Laura. A pretty mix of intelligence and lust. That's you in a nutshell."

The compliments were sending my mind into a tailspin. As I smiled my acknowledgment, I fought not to let them derail me.

"Can I ask something else about what happened in that darkroom?"

"Go ahead."

"There was this one moment when it seemed like... hmm, how can I put this...well, I was the only girl in there, wasn't I?"

Tommy nodded.

"I thought so. Well, it seemed a lot like one of the guys was doing something to one of the others...sucking, if I'm not mistaken...did I imagine that?"

Tommy just winked at me.

"Next question!"

He might have had his guard down, but he still knew how to tease when he wanted to.

"Fine! Something's been bothering me from the start... about that screen I had in my room at the very beginning. When I was...all the way downstairs."

"Oh, that. What about it?"

I felt my pulse quicken. Had I ventured into dangerous

territory by mentioning my initial prison cell? By refer-
encing the fact that I'd been brought here by force and
hadn't forgotten it?

Why did I need to know all this stuff, anyway? Getting
out of her was all that mattered, not satisfying my curiosity!

"Well, it seemed like you could see me through that
screen. I was kinda worried that I was also being broadcast
over the internet or something."

"God no!" he said in a shocked tone. "Listen, we have
agreements in place about that sort of thing. Everything
that happens in this building is private until you're marked,
at which point I've taken full ownership of you. It's all in the
contracts, and they're watertight."

I coughed.

The edge of his mouth curled wickedly.

"I know, Laura. You didn't sign a contract. And it's far
too late for that now. But all's well that ends well, I'd say."

He *seriously* thought we could just brush that whole
violent kidnapping thing aside on the basis that I was now
fucking him with evident relish? A guy as intelligent as
him? Wow. I mean...just wow!

Leave it, Laura. Let him think that.

Still, I couldn't leave this conversation hanging where it
was. Quite apart from my curiosity, it would be completely
unnatural for me not to ask further questions. And I still
felt the need to play along and reassure him that his stallion
had not been misplaced.

"Like you say...it's worked out well," I said coquettishly,
reaching over and resting my fingers gently at the bottom
of his shaft. "But I'm curious, of course...how did it
happen?"

He cleared his throat. I flinched for a moment, fearing it

might be the start of a dangerous growl. That I'd pushed too much. But it was nothing more than the cue for a monologue.

"Look, women were never any challenge to me in life. It was always too easy. It was the same for Claire with men, really...we both needed so much more, in our own ways. That's why we started this whole game with all the submissives. But then, I suppose, *that* got too easy. I had this long waiting list, and nobody ever wanted to leave. We'd been fooling around with the idea of a kidnapping. Of training someone from the ground up. But it was really just a vague fantasy until that day I first saw you at Kerstein."

I hardly dared to breathe, for fear it would make him clam up. I nodded and ran my thumb up and down the side of his cock, just to offer some gentle encouragement. It did the trick. He kept talking.

"Something about you struck me that day. There's a look in the eye of the kind of woman we've gathered in this building — and I spotted it in yours right away. I knew you were a divorcee, too, because I'd done a fair amount of homework ahead of the negotiation. Some of those juniors at Kerstein were only too happy to spill beans in the bedroom," he chuckled.

Ironic, I thought.

"Anyway, I wouldn't have done anything if those girls hadn't messaged me to tell the story of how you'd ended up storming out of the building. A fight with Andre, I believe it was?"

I nodded ruefully, knowing it would bolster his belief that I didn't want to go back to an outside world full of painful memories.

"When I heard that news, I figured you had disappeared

as far as your employer was concerned. If we could act that same day, before you had a night's sleep and went back to your desk, we'd be able to link your absence with a work-related breakdown. And, of course, winning the deal would be easier — your professional reputation precedes you. Not that this was necessary, because Kerstein was going down sooner or later anyway. But arranging for your disappearance certainly added a fun twist."

Fun?

The loathing bubbled up again. But I bit my tongue.

"Anyway, look, I have to get up," he declared with a sudden purpose about him. "I'll look forward to your services again very soon. I'm thrilled you made it to the top."

"Oh, can I ask one last thing?"

"Quickly, then."

"What are we going to tell the outside world? I mean, my family will want some sort of explanation if I'm gone forever, and—"

"We'll handle that. Very few of the women in here want their kids or their parents to know what they're up to, unsurprisingly. We always figure out some yarn."

"But...what about those of us that stay? I mean...doesn't someone like Kate want to see her mother and father from time to time?"

"Of course she does! I've already given her leave for that purpose. Kimiko too. Good girls get to ride private jets... once they've been here long enough. So don't worry about it, Laura. Just keep doing what you're doing and we'll figure it out."

He was *still* convinced I had abandoned my life to him, wasn't he?

An ego like that was beyond mortal comprehension. But it was the only thing I had working in my favor. His twisted belief system, which rested on a lifetime of feminine fawning, meant I still had his trust. And right now, that was the only thing that mattered.

CHAPTER 25

"*L*aura, do you fancy popping out with me?"

It was the end of my first week on the twenty-second floor. I'd just finished a light lunch of shrimp salad. And Kate had appeared in the doorway of my room.

The moment I'd been waiting for.

I felt the panic rising. Suddenly, I had the chance to *leave the building*. Yes, I'd known it was coming — but not when or how. Nor that I might have somebody come along with me. So I hadn't been able to lay any plans for how I was going to get away. I looked around the room, wondering what I should take with me for a possible escape attempt. Then I looked at Kate, afraid she could read my mind.

"Hey, it's normal to be nervous! You haven't been out of here for a few weeks. That's why we wouldn't send you out alone just yet. But if you're ready, I'll take you for a little outing."

"Of course, of course, I'd like to! Sorry if I looked a bit panicked. It's just a bit of a shock, that's all."

"Not to worry," she smiled. "Shall we go in a quarter of an hour or so?"

I nodded, grateful for the chance to compose myself.

"Wait, Kate! What are you wearing?"

"Oh, nothing special! Don't overthink it. We're not going nightclubbing! I'm sure we'll do a little shopping, though, so don't put on something too hard to wriggle out of in a cubicle!"

I liked Kate. She was the most direct woman I'd ever met when it came to matters sexual. And by now, she'd returned a few of the favors I'd given her when I'd been the maid from downstairs, so any ice was well and truly broken. She always said whatever she was thinking, and that made me trust her. I guess I felt good around people who didn't display any shyness: opposites attract and all that.

Although I wasn't really shy anymore, was I? Well, that depended! In here, where it was in some ways a safe environment, I had certainly flourished. But what would it feel like out on the familiar streets of New York? I was about to get the answer.

Kate led us into the elevator, pushed that '-1' button I'd hit all those weeks ago when I'd been offered a naked release, and we were on our way. My heart pounded and my head spun with thoughts of freedom and terror. Was I really going to run away from her as fast as I could just as soon as we were in a crowded part of town?

But if I did that, what then? I had clothes on my back, but I had zero money and no keys to get inside my house. Nor had there been any mention of having my phone returned. I could break into my house through a window, maybe, but that's exactly where my captor would expect me to go. He'd take a taxi there and be there waiting for me — this time without any goodwill to my credit. My options were limited to running to the office, really. And I didn't like *that* idea one bit: they thought I'd had a nervous breakdown. Explaining the real story, on the other hand, would be awkward and embarrassing, even though none of it was my fault.

What if I made a dash for a police station? Hmm, why not? It was the logical move — I wanted to get Tommy put away for his crime, didn't I? And the police could protect me from being scooped up by my kidnapper again. But now that the prospect was realistic, I wrestled with the idea. He'd seemed almost contrite this morning, hadn't he? And while he was certainly deluded on some level, I'd got the sense that he knew he had crossed a line with the kidnapping.

And what about the other women in there? They were *happy* in their own ways. They'd gotten what they'd signed up for. Was it fair to Lisa, Kate and Kimiko — I couldn't quite put Claire in the same category, knowing she'd been complicit in the crime — to snatch Tommy away for jail time that wouldn't undo what had been done to me? Was it fair to the hopefuls downstairs? Would it be…selfish of me? Or was I just trying to find excuses for not doing it?

I yelled at myself for even entertaining the idea of not reporting him. It was my civic duty! My duty to all women who'd been victims of such crimes, and might be in the future! I'd never be able to look myself in the eye again if I made that move.

You WILL report him, Laura.

Okay, but I didn't have to do it *today*, did I? Kate had said I wouldn't be let out alone 'just yet' — which suggested I'd be able to get out on my own at some point. That would obviously be much easier from an escape point of view. When I got sent out with one of those credit cards I kept hearing about, *that* would be the day for it. Money would give me a bunch more options.

I resolved to be good and stick with Kate for this first excursion. My time would come. Just a little more patience.

I tried to block those terrible memories as we stepped out into the cold little foyer which evidently served as the main entrance for all concerned. I almost barged Kate out of the way when she opened the door leading out into the quiet side street where I'd last set foot in the outside world. But going up the steps to the sidewalk, I felt woozy.

"Do you need a moment, Laura?"

I stopped halfway, heaving breaths and nodding.

"It's okay, it's normal. Take your time."

If this reaction was normal for any of the women kept in the building for weeks on end, then I was thankful for that. I had to assume that Kate knew nothing of the dark time I'd had in this very spot — and I wanted to keep it that way.

Gradually, the weirdness morphed into joy. Like the day when all this craziness had begun, it was sunny. Only now it was summer, not early spring. The sensation of warmth on my back slowly brought a smile to my lips. Breathing real air — even if it reeked of good old NYC taxi fumes — made me feel part of the world again. This felt *good*!

"How about we go grab a coffee *al fresco* somewhere? I think it'll do you good!"

"Let's do it! We'll walk, I hope?"

"Absolutely, it's a great day for it. Just enjoy being outside again, okay? Ease into it."

We headed towards the Hudson. I couldn't wrap my

head around the idea that I was taking a stroll through New York once again. I pushed worries about what would happen if I ran into somebody I knew to the back of my mind. What were the chances in a city this big, anyway? And I owed it to myself not to worry about what people thought. That thinking had cost me dear on the night of my abduction. If there was one thing I was sure I wanted to take away from this thing, it was that.

The half-freedom was a weird kind of liberating. I knew that I *could* take flight but was choosing not to do so — yet. At one point, an NYPD patrol car passed us. If I threw myself in front of it and told my story, there would be nothing Kate could do. Nor even Tommy. But the plan all along had been to do this the way *I* wanted to do it — and I was sticking to that plan to the very last.

We never really did get around to doing much shopping. We stuck to walking around town and coffee at trendy sidewalk cafes. And I won't lie: there was a thrill in sharing a secret that no passer-by could possibly have guessed. To them, Kate and I were just a couple of regular, working women catching up for a chat. Even if we *told* them we were part of a 24/7 sex collective catering to the whims of one man, we would have been laughed out of town.

Still, who knew what secrets of their own our fellow coffee enthusiasts might have had? They all looked so innocent. But I was now more than ready to believe some of them were involved in depravity I could never have imagined a few weeks ago. Like prowling the dark web in search of ways to sell themselves like slaves.

When we got to paying for the cappuccinos and slices of cake we enjoyed, Kate's credit card came to the party. Or, rather, the credit card she'd been given.

"Hey, can I see that? I'm curious!"

"Sure," she shrugged.

The name on the card gleamed up at me. And it wasn't Mr. Tommy So-and-So, of course. It was a business card, issued to TM Highland Limited. I guessed those were probably his initials. I hadn't gotten as far as taking in his surname during the single, intoxicating professional encounter we'd had, but I guessed the 'M' could well stand for Mac-something.

"I'm just wondering, Kate, do you know Tommy's surname?"

"I've never actually asked," she laughed. "Somehow, I'm quite happy with not knowing it...don't you think? Surnames belong to the everyday world, and we don't need to worry about stuff like that, do we? We live a simpler life."

"I suppose you're right! I never thought about it like that."

"I can tell you that Tommy's from a very wealthy family, though."

"Well, I'm not surprised to hear that. I get the impression he's gotten what he wanted from a young age."

Kate nodded.

"True, but I understand that his father was *very* strict. The family fortune is enough that Tommy could have lived very comfortably without working, but his old man had worked his way up in the world and insisted that Tommy found a way to earn a living."

"Do you know if his dad is still around?"

"He is, but they don't talk much. It's a tricky relationship and there are things for which Tommy won't forgive him. I've not found out what those are — and I've been marked for over a year now!"

"He might share it with you one day. He's quite forth-coming after sex sometimes, don't you find?"

Kate grinned.

"You noticed? I'm always happy to listen if he wants me to! But it's not always like that, of course. Sometimes you're sent packing straight after he's done with you. At the end of the day, though, if he's happy, I'm happy."

"Of course," I smiled. "And what about Claire? Do you know much about her?"

"Ah, she's from a very rich family too — she and Tommy have that in common. Her dad owns half of Paris, by the sounds of it. She's an only child and had anything she wanted from day one. Obviously, being as beautiful as she is, she never struggled for adoration — all the way from teachers to the men who wanted to fuck her. But the family was crazy traditional. They wanted Claire married to a respectable name and all the rest of it."

"She *told* you all this?"

I was trying to picture Claire opening up like that, but couldn't.

"No, I've got all of this through Tommy, mostly. Claire is fine, there's no problem with her. But she's a bit different from the rest of us, you know? She goes way back with him, and she'll always be his number one. I'm sure she knows quite a lot that we don't."

Kate was certainly right on that point. I knew of at least *one* big, dark secret with which only Claire had been entrusted. It made complete sense that Claire had been assigned to take care of me during my first days in the building — nobody else was allowed to know I was down there.

"I guess you're right," I said disingenuously. "So, Claire obviously didn't see things the same way as her family?"

"You could say that," Kate chuckled. "All they achieved was creating a rebel. I know it's hard to believe now, when you see her doing as she's told all day. But she made a point of going against everything they said and stood for. I believe she fooled around with drugs quite a lot at one point. She slept with women, partly just because it wasn't the done thing, but then really got into it. Once she met Tommy, she realized she could take unconventional sex to yet another level. As for doing his bidding the way she does, that was her choice and part of her rebellion. And...here we are!"

"It sounds a lot like those poor princesses in the Middle East. They always end up doing all the stuff that gives their fathers nightmares."

"That's a good analogy," she nodded sagely. "It's exactly the way it is with Claire, as far as I understand. And I wouldn't be at all surprised if we end up with a princess from some conservative country in our midst someday."

I could well believe it. But I repeatedly reminded myself that I wasn't going to be sticking around to see it happen.

CHAPTER 26

*T*he very next day, Claire arrived at my room with a little white envelope. Inside was a small plastic rectangle and the code I would need to use it. The fruits of the trust I'd built. My one-way ticket to freedom.

My heart raced. I couldn't believe this was *actually* happening. That credit card in my hand meant I could have no more delays or excuses. And that, in turn, was terrifying.

"So I can use this for shopping — tomorrow, for example?" I asked, still incredulous.

"Yes, please do," said Claire, walking over to my closet. "Tommy is bringing some visitors in the evening. You haven't experienced this up here yet, have you? All of us will be in the display for a period of time, probably while the gentlemen have dinner. We may be tied up in some way. No masks, of course. We should each have an excellent evening dress for this part — and it is best for you to choose something you really like. That way, it will shine on you."

I gulped. Was I really going to choose to miss this?

Yes, Laura, you ARE! This is where you stop playing along to his script. Go any deeper down this rabbit hole and...

"That sounds like a nice assignment. And should I buy underwear too?"

"This is always a good idea. Essentially, you can buy anything you like. Fifth Avenue is always good, of course."

"So there's no...limit on the card or anything like that?"

She made a contemptuous little sound.

"Tommy takes care of all the costs."

Okay, no limit then.

Good to know.

I lay awake pretty much the whole night, trying to piece together the mechanics of my escape. It was hard to focus, because it didn't seem right that I had fooled both Tommy and Claire into trusting me to go out alone at all. But he was clearly blinded by his own ego — I'd seen this for myself. And she basically followed his thoughts on all matters, didn't she? I had to assume we were all systems go. That I *wasn't* going to find the pair of them waiting for me when I made it down to the foyer this time.

So how was this going to work, then? I was still getting used to the idea that my day wasn't planned out according to a rigid timetable. That I could spend it indulging myself as I wished. That I could enjoy sitting in the library, or the bathtub, or even request a massage from one of the servants. I began to dream about such a treat, wondering if some fresh, willing soul had taken my place downstairs. A new girl, one that hadn't been 'left behind' and wouldn't give me weird, guilty feelings.

Maybe I could leave time for one last extravagance before I slipped out of my gilded cage?

No! I would set out after breakfast, before the day's temptations ran away with me.

I forced my mind back to the practicalities of the escape mission. Crucial to its success was the fact that I would have a credit card as well as clothes on my back. I wasn't going to awaken any suspicions by asking for my phone, however — which meant I couldn't get hold of anybody in a hurry. I wished I had memorized a couple of key numbers.

I couldn't seriously consider heading back to my town-house either. It was way too obvious. Plus, I wouldn't feel safe there at all. There was a good chance, in fact, that those two thugs Tommy had hired had also delivered him a set of my keys. So I wouldn't be going there for any length of time unless I had company — and ideally a fierce dog at my heel. In the short term, I had to get as far away as I could *without* leaving any tracks. Or I had to get to somebody who could protect me.

The police, Laura — remember them?

Ugh. It was patently the first move to make. Why did I still keep pushing the idea away? Was I *embarrassed* about what had happened to me? Was I worried they were going to blame me for going along with it for so long, while so clearly enjoying my encounters with Tommy? I'd read how common this fear was with victims of abuse. Was I letting myself fall into the same trap?

I reminded myself that I was stronger than that. I had resolved to go to the cops, and go to the cops I would.

But I *was* leaning towards delaying my visit to the police station. For one thing, I wanted to figure out the whole thing with Andre for myself. Because if he was part of the kidnapping deal, then he was getting reported as well! I had to speak to him myself before any detectives did. I suppose I could have just let them do their job — but I reveled in the idea of confronting the guy with whom I'd spent so many hours in meeting rooms. I wanted to see his reaction for myself. I would know the truth right away.

On top of that, I didn't feel ready for a bunch of questioning and unpleasant recollections just yet. Yes, I could probably have Tommy arrested the same day. And, practically speaking, it made sense to do so before he realized I was actually missing and skipped the country or something. But my instinct to get away from the whole thing was overpowering. I needed some space — even if it was only for a couple of days. I had to figure out what I was going to say to my parents, my kids and my employer…if I still had a job at all, that was. There was a whole bunch of processing to be done.

That left getting as far away as possible as the option I liked best. I toyed with Georgetown, where Luke was at college. I'd have some measure of protection there — but on the other hand, Tommy *knew* my son was there. It would probably be the second most obvious place to look for me. And it would mean doing a lot of explaining to Luke, probably with a bunch of frat boys listening in. I wasn't jumping into that scenario whilst running scared.

Canada?

Yes, Canada!

Shit, no! I didn't have my passport! Actually, I had no ID of any description. Nor my driving license. That ruled out renting a car.

I might have clothes on when I went out in the morning — but it was dawning on me that I would still be naked in some ways.

So my options were down to taxis and long-distance

buses. And if I wanted to be smart about this, I would draw a bunch of cash on the credit card. Otherwise, all my transactions could be traced by my abductor and his sidekick.

In one way, I was more worried about Claire than Tommy. Now that I knew something of her background, I was more inclined than ever to think of her as the kind of woman with the potential to turn psycho if something upset her balance. What if Tommy got arrested but she didn't? Would she go to bloody lengths to avenge my treachery? It didn't seem all that far-fetched.

Nobody was waiting for me in the foyer. The door to the street opened when I pressed the green plastic button. And it slammed shut behind me with terrifying finality.

God, I was *doing* this!

And I had exactly one shot at getting it right.

I clutched the credit card in the pocket of my jeans. The day was overcast and muggy. New York City was going about its business the way it always did. It knew nothing of the drama I was playing out. Just like *that* night.

Aware that I might still be under surveillance from the building, I tried to look casual and unhurried as I climbed the stairs to reach the pavement. Then, turning in the right direction for Fifth Avenue, I placed one foot in front of the other.

One step at a time, I was putting distance between myself and Tommy.

I walked a few blocks in a bizarre kind of trance, until I was sure I was completely out of sight of the building. That nobody — not even with a telescope from the top floor — would be able to see what I was doing.

It was time to act, but my head was still spinning. I could see a sign for a police station at the next crossroads. I knew the Kerstein office was probably no more than twenty minutes walk away — all I had to do was present myself in the foyer and Alan would take care of everything! *Those* were the smart options. Not traveling solo to a place where I knew nobody and I could be hunted down like a hog in the woods.

Yet some magnetic force dragged me towards the tougher road.

I spotted an ATM. Glancing over my shoulder, half-expecting to see Claire chasing me up the sidewalk with a switch-blade, I stepped up to the money machine. How much? This had to be both my first and last cash withdrawal. The very fact I was taking cash on a credit card might well raise the alarm — and there was a good chance somebody would get a notification of what I was about to do.

I settled on three thousand bucks. Enough to get me somewhere far away, a hotel room, internet access and food. I could rebuild my life from there.

Adrenaline surged through my body as the machine made its whirring noises and confirmed the transaction. I took the bills, folded them into my pocket and reclaimed the card. Now it was time to act *fast*.

I hailed a cab and instructed the driver to take me to the bus terminal at George Washington Bridge. I hadn't been on that kind of bus in years, but recalled that my kids had gotten in and out of the city from that station. And I knew it was at the furthest end of Manhattan Island

— in the opposite direction to Tommy's lair. The last thing I wanted was to end up doubling back past *that* building.

My taxi driver seemed to revel in the sense of urgency I had communicated, and got me across town as quickly as he could. There were still way too many red lights for my liking, but at least he sped away from them pronto and never let himself get stuck behind anything slow.

He slammed on the brakes as we pulled up in front of the terminal. I threw him plenty of cash, leaped out of the car and ran into the station at full speed. I was terrified that Tommy had somehow followed me here. I wanted to be rolling out of the city as soon as possible.

I checked out the screens for the next bus scheduled to leave. Anywhere, anywhere! I could go to Cleveland in ten minutes. Three states away! Sounded good to me. I rushed to the counter, where I was greeted by a bored-looking woman sealed off behind a glass screen. Her voice crackled through a microphone.

"Can I help you?"

"Yes, please, I need a ticket to Cleveland — the bus leaving in ten minutes, please — I can't miss it!"

"You know you could buy it using the app? There's a surcharge for…"

"I don't care," I yelped, panicking about missing my departure and being left hanging around in the waiting room. "I don't have a phone! Just let me pay!"

She raised her eyebrows, punched a couple of keys on her computer and indicated the credit card terminal on my side of the window.

"No, cash! I need to pay cash!"

"You don't have a card?"

She looked incredulous. I shook my head. I simply couldn't leave a transaction trail.

"Hmm, it's been a while. Everyone pays electronically nowadays. I'll have to open up the cash drawer at the back."

I wanted to scream as she heaved herself off her chair and disappeared through a door behind her. Technology... real convenient until the moment you haven't got it. I eyed the clock on the monitor across the room.

She came back with a money box and took the cash I'd already slipped under the window.

"Keep the change! I just need the ticket!"

"Can't do that, ma'am. Regulations, sorry." And she began laboriously counting out my change. I must have looked over my shoulder twenty times as she did so.

I made the bus with three minutes to spare. After galloping up the steps and showing my old-fashioned paper ticket to the driver, I made my way to the very back, where a few seats seemed to be vacant.

The handful of people who were paying any attention at all gave me strange looks. After all, I was still breathing heavily. And I didn't have any luggage, not even a handbag. But I was just glad there *were* other people on the bus. It would be hard for my kidnappers to try and reclaim me from here.

The journey away from New York City began exactly on time.

I'd done it. I'd *actually* done it.

We traveled all day. Just as every turn of the wheels made me feel a little safer, the thought that Tommy would now be looking for me, fuming, scared the living daylights out of me. This was a man who had figured out a lot about me before I even knew he existed. A man capable of planning a spontaneous kidnapping in a matter of hours. In what for him was a foreign country. I couldn't drop my guard when we reached Cleveland.

I spent the bus ride staring out of the window and dreading some awful twist. We made a couple of scheduled stops, but I didn't dare venture away from the bus driver as he enjoyed his smoke breaks just outside the cab. Not that his slight build inspired a lot of confidence…but I felt reasonably safe as long as there were other people around.

By the time of our penultimate break in Youngstown, I was busting for the toilet. But holding it in was better than getting isolated from the herd in the bowels of some godforsaken truck stop. It was still daylight, but an empty restroom wasn't a smart place to venture.

What had I *done*? At this very moment, the others would be preening themselves for another unforgettable voyage into a privileged, sensual world. I could have opted for the lustful games, rather than concocting terror scenarios in some parking lot next to the Interstate.

But wait, no…tonight's frolics would be off, surely? I'd been gone long enough now that the hunt would be on. They'd be on a red alert! Or were Tommy and Claire so complacent that they thought I was still out on the mother of all shopping sprees? I couldn't quite bring myself to believe that. Especially if they'd seen that cash had been withdrawn on the credit card.

And it was *my* fault that Kimiko, Kate and Claire weren't going to get their fun tonight. They might even be helping Tommy pack his bags and get to the airport. I was the horrible snitch who'd ruined everything for them! Women who had *volunteered* for the life they had in that building!

I wrestled and wrestled with this guilt and shame. I couldn't shake these oppressive feelings, though I knew they were ludicrous and irrational. They were fueled by my fear. And that fear would not go away until I was behind a heavily locked door.

As we pulled into Cleveland in gathering dusk, I scanned the terminal concourse for any sign of raging Celtic eyes. Finding nothing, I told myself to get off the bus before that situation changed. Disembarking without any luggage made me feel like I'd forgotten something. Naked, almost. Yet again.

But that was the boiled-down, no-frills reality of the moment. It was just my body and soul on this escape mission. Plus the hard currency in my pocket.

I scurried into the nearest taxi.

"I don't know Cleveland," I explained in a breathless hurry. "But I need you to take me to a busy hotel in the city. One big enough to have a vacant room. As fast as you can, please."

The cab driver nodded. "I'll do my best, ma'am. We should be there in ten minutes."

"Okay," I replied, checking for the umpteenth time that the wad of cash was still nestling next to my hip.

I tapped my fingers on my thigh as we made our way towards the center of town. I was still looking over my shoulder every now and then. No sign of any pursuit.

The driver must have wondered about me, but didn't try to ask questions. And for that I was grateful.

We pulled up in front of a suitably anonymous chain hotel. I settled the taxi fare and tried to pull myself together before I got out and walked up to reception. I knew I couldn't arrive there looking too frazzled and crazy. Despite the cash payment, I might not get a room if I projected freaky vibes to the staff. And then I would end up wandering the streets in search of another place to stay. Streets I didn't want to be on.

I slowed myself down enough to thank the driver properly. Then I took a deep breath and exited the taxi. I couldn't help glancing sideways in each direction: nothing untoward. Then I walked into the lobby as calmly as I could. I crossed the cool marble floor and rounded an over-size pot plant as I made my way to the check-in desk.

Luckily, there wasn't a line.

"How can I help you, ma'am?" said the wiry receptionist, a guy who couldn't have been long out of high school. My son's age, or thereabouts.

"Hi there," I began, deliberately keeping my speech slow. "Do you have a room for a couple of nights?"

"We do have some rooms available! How many nights do you want to stay, exactly?" he asked, already beginning to punch his keyboard.

That was a great question. How long did I need in order to figure out my next move and be ready to face the world again? My cash was limited, and I still had to eat as well. One thing I knew for sure was that tomorrow morning was way too soon to have check-out pressure to deal with.

"Make it three nights for now," I replied. "I'll pay upfront with cash, if that's okay?"

I held my breath, suddenly recalling how so many hotels liked to demand credit cards for minibar security. But the kid didn't bat an eyelid.

"Of course, that's no problem, ma'am. Just a second... I've found you a room. That would be $600."

"Sure, fine."

I reached for my money and counted out the right amount.

A few moments later, the young man was holding a keycard out to me.

"Your room is on the nineteenth floor. Just take the elevator on the—"

I stopped hearing him.

The nineteenth floor?

Adrenaline surged.

Settle down, Laura. It's a coincidence, that's all.

I dumbly held the receptionist's gaze as he placed the card in my hand.

"Everything okay, ma'am?"

"Sorry, yes. It's just, I'm...I know this is weird, but I'm a little superstitious about that number. Nineteen, I mean. Do you by any chance have something on another floor? Lower down, maybe?"

He chuckled.

"I'm sure I can find you something. Not a problem, give me a moment."

Sweet kid. I smiled back at him as he re-jigged my booking.

"Thank you. Sorry about that. Say, do they still have telephones in hotel rooms these days? I've lost my cellphone, you see..."

"I'm not sure about other hotels, but we do have phones in the rooms here. No cellphone, huh? That must be awkward! If it helps, we also have a small business center over there with a couple of computers you can use."

He was nodding in the direction of a modest glass-fronted room opposite the reception desk. You could see everything that went on in there, all the way through to the street beyond. It looked like a great place to piece my life together without being isolated and vulnerable.

"Oh, thank you! That sounds useful!"

"Great. And I've found you a room on the third floor, will that do?"

"Perfect."

I was beginning to feel edgy again, keen to get behind that locked door. I wished I had luggage, just so I would have an excuse for someone to escort me upstairs. Bad things happened in elevators.

Just do it, Laura. He's not here!

By the time I had my new key in my hand and turned away from reception, my heart was pounding again. I prayed someone else might also be calling the elevator to go up, but there were no potential travel companions waiting for a ride.

The trip to room 317 felt like the longest journey of my life. I touched the card on the door pad with shaking hands, eyeing the empty hallway left and right. It took a few tries for the key to work and the door to click open. I tumbled breathlessly into the room and slammed the thing behind me. Then I sealed the bolt and hooked the chain. I was triple-locked inside.

I wasn't in any state to take in much about the room apart from the fact that the door was secured. I was more worried that a bad guy might be waiting for me, concealed. I checked the little bathroom. I opened the closet. I looked under the bed. But I was alone, of course.

So I could breathe again. I could sit down on the bed and gather myself.

I had got what I wanted. I was safely locked inside a hotel room. One that was far, *far* away from New York City. Three states away from Tommy's harem. But I'd been absolutely right on one thing: this was going to take some time to process.

I knew I couldn't hide here forever. That I was going to have to pick up that phone and reconnect with people who were on my side. That I needed to speak to the cops sooner rather than later. But the escape itself was complete. My plan had worked. I'd fooled them all.

And as that reality sank in, a smile broke out across my face.

End of Book 2

ABOUT JAMES GREY

He may write his erotica under a nom-de-plume, but James Grey has been widely published by magazines and newspapers around the world for the best part of two decades. He still spends much of his working life writing about topics other than hardcore sex. This includes travel books under a different author name.

Grey began writing erotica in the run-up to Christmas 2013, inspired by a recent visit to a sauna in Germany and prompted by a subsequent period of ennui at his aunt's house in France. His self-published author ego was then born on a grim, hung-over New Year's Day in England, when he uploaded *Hot Wet Touches* to the Kindle Store.

He has gone on to become a regular category best-seller on Amazon, and is one of only a small handful of male authors writing erotica. Connect with him online, and you might even find a picture of the well-travelled Grey at a book signing event.

Grey is in his late thirties and lives in a European capital city. And yes, he likes to keep you guessing. But if you want to know something, why not simply ask him? ;)

www.jamesgreyauthor.com

CONNECTING WITH JAMES GREY

I suggest your first port of call be my official website at jamesgreyauthor.com. It's the best place to learn all about me and my work — and it's the *only* place to order those coveted signed paperbacks!

To connect with my community of fans and I, Facebook's ideal. So make a request to join the James Grey Fan Group. That's where I bounce cover ideas, run reader polls, take requests and announce my news first!

I love fan mail! Just like I love constructive criticism, meeting prospective beta readers or even hearing your fantasies. You can write to me via my website contact form or email jamesgreyerotic@gmail.com.

Finally, I strongly encourage you to join my mailing list. Not just so I can let you know when new books are out or offer you free bonus content. But also because I am at the mercy of the digital bookstores, and *they don't tell me who you are*. They could even decide to ban me overnight without warning (it happens to us smut merchants!), destroying my livelihood and all the years of working to build up a fan base. If I have your email, at least I can find you again and let you know my latest hiding place! For this scenario as much as anything else, won't you consider signing up via my website?

ALSO BY JAMES GREY

The Emma Series:

Escort in Training (Book 1)

Escort Unleashed (Book 2)

Her Calling (Book 3)

Novellas:

Hot Wet Touches (eBook only)

Hot Wet Touches Amsterdam (eBook only)

The Sex Club Diaries

Short Story Collections:

Breaking Free

Ravenous Desires

Choose Your Own Adventure Erotica:

Her Desire Awakened (eBook only)

The Laura Series:

Out of Office

Access all titles and formats via jamesgreyauthor.com

ACKNOWLEDGMENTS

Oh my, where do I even begin?

I guess I'll start with you, dear reader. Thank you for buying this book – you've helped me to eat! And thanks for every like, share, review and wild raving about my signed copies. Remember, your seal of approval counts for everything in the book world.

Lori, thank you for your patience. And thanks too for all the stunning bookmarks, the grumpy 2am takeovers, those beautiful Excel spreadsheets (!) and the crisis management. I won't forget you being with me in the most troubled of times, and your sticking on my side. You too, Sharon...you deserve wonderful things, and thanks so much for inspiring me.

Debs, you have been a star for your teasers, your help with sexy cover pictures and your role as Senior Tax Affairs Officer. The IRS still makes me want to seek out a tall building every time I hear its name, but you've helped me handle it all a little better than I might have done.

Kelly, you've been a true friend and I can't thank you enough. Well done for nagging me to get to a signing – Dublin was surely the start of something! You are far too generous and kind to me, you've been an absolute blessing and you are...umm...usually right.

Thanks to all you bloggers who keep on letting the world know I exist. The online book world was a bewildering, bombarding, higgledy-piggledy place to me at first, and I've probably not communicated as I should have done. But now that I've finally started to put names to faces and figure out who *you* all are, I'm looking forward to truly knowing you.

Thanks to my parents for encouraging me to read when the other kids my age were content with chucking sand at each other. The same goes for everyone who has ever affirmed that I should write, from my first English teachers at school to my university lecturers. I have doubts about this business every single day, and you've all helped to silence them in your own way.

I must thank the dozens of magazine and newspaper editors who have published the writing I've done in other fields. You've paid me to write, and that's sent an important message about what I should be doing in life. I should also thank the editors (many of them the same people!) who couldn't answer a pitch email or take a phone call. Your silences are what led me to writing directly for my readers via self-publishing. I hope that it will prove to be the best move I have ever made.

Thanks to those who have beta-read my stories, and thanks also to Ida at Amygdala Design for some wonderful work on my covers. To my fellow authors who have shared your wisdom and experiences with me, thank you so much and let's keep doing it!

I should also thank the man upstairs for creating woman. Without the fairer sex, my life and my writing would be stricken. It seems I can never grow tired of womankind, and I cherish each encounter I have with you. You spellbind me, and I'm so glad I can put that feeling down in words for a living each day. Good job, Mr God!

More of you will come along and shower me with undeserved support, I'm sure. It just keeps on happening. And every time it does, it's a reminder that my writing makes a difference to people. Thanks in advance for those reminders. They make me carry on with this crazy, wonderful life.

Printed in Great Britain
by Amazon